THE LUCY VARIATIONS

Sara Zarr

Little, Brown and Company

New York Boston

Little, Brown and Company

Hachette Book Group
237 Park Avenue, New York, NY 10017
Visit our website at lb-teens.com

Little, Brown and Company is a division of Hachette Book Group, Inc.
The Little, Brown name and logo are trademarks of Hachette Book Group, Inc.

The publisher is not responsible for websites (or their content) that are not owned by the publisher.

First Paperback Edition: May 2014
First published in hardcover in May 2013 by Little, Brown and Company

Library of Congress Cataloging-in-Publication Data

Zarr, Sara.
The Lucy variations / by Sara Zarr.—1st ed.
p. cm.
Summary: "Sixteen year old San Franciscan Lucy Beck-Moreau once had a promising future as a concert pianist. Her chance at a career has passed, and she decides to help her ten-year-old piano prodigy brother, Gus, map out his own future, even as she explores why she enjoyed piano in the first place."—Provided by publisher.
ISBN 978-0-316-20501-6 (hc)—ISBN 978-0-316-20500-9 (pb)
[1. Pianists—Fiction. 2. Ability—Fiction. 3. Family life—California—Fiction. 4. Brothers and sisters—Fiction. 5. Self-actualization (Psychology)—Fiction. 6. San Francisco (Calif.)—Fiction.] I. Title.
PZ7.Z26715Luc 2013 [Fic]—dc23 2012029852

10 9 8 7 6 5 4 3 2 1

RRD-C

Printed in the United States of America

for Gordon,
the skillful accompanist to
all my variations

I.

Tempo Rubato

(IN ROBBED TIME)

1.

Try harder, Lucy.

Lucy stared down at Madame Temnikova's face.

Which seemed incredibly gray.

Try.

Harder.

Lucy.

She put her hands over Temnikova's sternum again, and again hesitated.

Stage fright: an opportunity to prove herself or a chance to fail. Which was nothing new for her. It just hadn't been a life-or-death issue until now.

This isn't a performance. Do *something.*

But an actual dying person in the living room wasn't the same as a Red Cross dummy in the school gym. Lucy tried not to think about Temnikova's skin under her hands. Or the way, from the looks of things, that skin now encased only a body, no longer a soul.

Except the moment wasn't definite. More like Temnikova was not there and then there and then not there. Mostly not.

Gus, Lucy's ten-year-old brother, started to ask the question she didn't want to answer. "Is she..."

Dead?

"Call nine-one-one, Gus," she told him for the second time. He'd been motionless, mesmerized. Lucy kept her voice unwavering, though she felt like screaming. She didn't want to freak him out. Channeling her mother's dispassion and authority, she said, "Go do it right now."

Gus hurried across the room to the phone, and Lucy looked at the ceiling, trying to remember the steps in the Cardiac Chain of Survival—what went where and for how long. Where were her mother and grandfather, anyway? They were usually and annoyingly *there*, running the house and everything, every*one*, in it like a Fortune 500 company.

The metronome on top of the piano ticked steadily; Lucy fought off the urge to throw a pillow at it. Instead she used it to time the chest compressions.

Still...

That sound.

Tick tick tick tick.

A slow adagio. A death march.

She didn't know how Gus could stand it. Spending day after day after day after lonely day in this room, with this old woman.

Everything good (tick) *is passing you by* (tick) *as you sit here* (tick) *and practice your life away* (tick).

Except she did know, because she'd done it herself for more than eleven years. Not with Temnikova, but in this room. This house. These parents. This family history.

"My sister is doing that," Gus said into the phone. Then to Lucy, "They want you to try mouth-to-mouth."

When Lucy and Reyna signed up for the CPR workshop at school last spring, they'd assumed their future patients would be sexy, male, and under forty, an idea which now seemed obviously idiotic. Lucy swept her hair back over one shoulder and braced herself.

Their lips met. Lucy's breath filled Temnikova's lungs. They inflated and deflated, inflated and deflated. Nothing. She went back to the chest compressions.

Gus was speaking, but his voice seemed far away. The order of Lucy's actions felt wrong; the backs of her thighs cramped. She looked up at Gus, finally, and tried to read his face. Maybe her inadequacy was engraving permanent trauma onto his psyche. Twenty years from now, in therapy, he'd confide to some bearded middle-aged man that his problems all began when his sister let his piano teacher die right in front of him. Maybe she should have sent him out of the room.

Too late now.

"Tell them I think...I'm pretty sure she's dead."

Gus held the phone out to Lucy. "You tell them." She stood and took it, wincing at the needles that shot through her sleeping left foot while Gus walked to the piano, stopped the metronome, and slid its metal pendulum into place.

The house seemed to exhale. Lucy gave the bad news to "them." After going over the details they needed, she hung up, and Gus asked, "Do we just leave her body here?"

Temnikova had dropped to the Persian rug, behind the piano bench, where she'd been standing and listening to Gus. Right in the middle of a Chopin nocturne.

"Yeah. They'll be here soon. Let's go...somewhere else."

"I don't want her to be alone," he said, and sat in Grandpa Beck's armchair, a few feet away from Temnikova's head. She'd been coloring her short hair an unnatural dark red as long as Lucy's family had known her.

Lucy went to Gus and rested her hip against the chair. She should try her mom's cell, or her grandfather's, and her dad's office. Only she didn't want to. And the situation was no longer urgent, clearly.

"Sorry, Gus."

Fail.

♪

One of the EMTs said it looked like a stroke, not a heart attack, and there was "probably" nothing Lucy could have done. He typed into his phone or radio or whatever it was while he talked.

Probably. It wasn't exactly a word of comfort.

While the other EMTs loaded Temnikova's body onto a gurney they'd parked in the foyer, the "probably" guy clipped his radio back onto his belt and checked off things on a form. Lucy gave her name and parents' names and the house phone number. He paused halfway down the page and rested his finger over one of the check boxes. "You're over eighteen, right?"

"Sixteen."

"Really." He—small and wiry, maybe two inches shorter than Lucy—gave her a once-over. Their eyes didn't quite meet. "You look older."

She never knew what to say to that. Was it supposed to be a compliment? Maybe she didn't want to look older. Maybe she didn't even want to be sixteen. Twelve. Twelve had been a good age: going to the symphony with Grandma Beck in excessively fancy dresses, unembarrassed to hold her hand. Being light enough that her dad could carry her from the car to the front door on late nights. Shopping with her mother and not winding up in a fight every time.

"So I've been told," she said. He smiled. There should be some kind of rule against smiling in his job. She said, "Just another day for you, I guess."

"I wouldn't put it that way." He handed her a card. "I'll need to have one of your parents call this number as soon as they can. You said she's not a relative?"

His look turned into a stare that lingered somewhere between Lucy's neck and waist. She stood straighter, and he returned his attention to the clipboard. "She's my brother's piano teacher."

Lucy gestured to Gus, who'd been sitting on the stairs, his chin in his hands. He didn't appear traumatized. Bored, possibly. Or, knowing him, simply thinking. Maybe thinking about how if he'd been allowed to go to his school sleepover at the Academy of Sciences, like he wanted, this wouldn't even be happening. But, as usual, their parents and Temnikova had said no, reluctant to take any time away from his scheduled practice.

The EMT blew a breath through his thin lips. "That's rough. It happening right here, during a lesson."

Where else would it happen? Temnikova practically lived there, in the piano room. Gus wasn't your average ten-year-old, fumbling through "Clair de lune" and "London Bridge" while everyone who was forced to listen held back the eye rolls. He had a career. A following. Like Lucy used to have. And Zoya Temnikova had been working with him since he turned four, when Lucy's grandfather flew her to the States from Volgograd, set her up in an apartment down the street, and helped her become a legalized citizen.

Her dying at the piano made perfect sense.

Still, it was sad. She'd given her life to their family, and now it was over.

After the EMTs rolled the body out, Gus got up off the stairs and stood next to Lucy in the starkly hushed foyer. If he was upset about Temnikova, he didn't show it. When Lucy asked, "You okay, Gustav?" all he had to say about the death of the woman with whom he'd spent so much of his time over the last six years was:

"Mom's going to be pissed."

2.

"She wasn't even that old." Lucy's mother, tall and straight-backed at the kitchen island, slapped a flank steak onto the cutting board.

"She was ancient," Lucy said, skulking in the serving pantry between the kitchen and the dining room. Her father had parked himself on a stool at the island, Gus next to him. The two of them created a handy buffer zone between Lucy and her mom. She'd already gotten in trouble for not calling either of her parents or Grandpa Beck—or even Martin, their housekeeper, who'd been off—until the EMTs left. Her defense, which her mother did not appreciate, was, "It's not like any of you could have brought her back to life."

Now her father said, "Lucy's right. She was at that age when you can go anytime."

"She had a dinosaur neck," Gus added.

"Gus," Lucy said. "A little respect?"

"Sorry."

Lucy's dad took a swallow of his Old Fashioned while her mother whacked the steak with a mallet and Lucy felt the in-and-out of her own breath. Since Temnikova's exit, she'd become weirdly aware of her lungs, her heart, everything in her body that worked to keep her alive.

"Well, it's terrible timing," her mother said. She put a grill pan down on the stove top. While it heated she strode toward Lucy, who took a nervous step back, until she realized the actual object of her mother's displeasure was the calendar that hung just inside the pantry. "Seven weeks." She gave Lucy a hard look, pointing at the calendar. "Not even seven. Closer to six and a half."

The winter showcase at the symphony hall.

CPR isn't as easy as it looks on TV, Mom. "Gus'll be ready. He's ready *now*."

"Of course he's ready *now*." Her mother went back to the island and put the steak into the pan. Sizzle and smoke. "But he won't be ready in six weeks without anyone on him. How am I going to find someone at this time of year? With the holidays coming up."

"It's okay, Mom," Gus said. "I'll practice the same amount."

"It's a showcase, Kat." Lucy's dad turned his glass in his hand. "Not a competition. He'll do fine."

He must have forgotten that *fine* wasn't in their family's vocabulary. If you were a Beck-Moreau, and you got up on stage for *any* reason—showcase, competition, recital, or just to roll a piano stool into place—you'd better surpass *fine* by about a million miles.

Granted, that was more a Beck issue than a Moreau one.

"The Swanner isn't long after, and that *is* a competition. I'll send out e-mails tonight," her mother said. "After Grandpa gets home and I have a chance to talk to him about it. We'll find out who's available on such short notice. No one good, I'm sure."

Lucy ventured two steps into the kitchen, placing her body in front of the calendar. "Maybe Gus could take a little break. Some people do, you know. Some people believe it actually helps. And then he could—"

Her mother cut her off. "Lucy, I'm sorry, but you're not exactly the first person I'm going to turn to for advice about this."

"Kat..." Lucy waited for her dad to say more than that. Perhaps even mount a minor defense on Lucy's behalf. But no. Of course not.

"Do you want me to set the table, Mom?" Gus asked.

"I'll help," Lucy said, and followed him into their large formal dining room. It took immense self-control to not ruffle his hair. She loved his curls; he didn't like anyone touching them.

"Set for four," their mother called after them. "Grandpa's meeting friends tonight."

Given how Grandma's death had gone down, it was no big surprise that Grandpa Beck hadn't canceled his plans and come running home upon hearing the news about Temnikova. No surprise, but still cold.

They laid out clean place mats and napkins, dinner plates, salad plates, dinner forks, salad forks, knives, spoons. No dessert stuff on weekdays. Wineglasses for their parents. Water goblets for everyone. Even without Grandpa Beck, even under the circumstances, they would conform to tradition. Generally, Lucy didn't mind. It would be nice, though, once in a while, to be the kind of family that on a crap day like this would order a pizza and eat it in the kitchen. Maybe even *talk* about the fact that it was *kinda sad and awful* that someone who mattered to them had died *in their house* that afternoon.

"Nice work, Gustav," Lucy said, double-checking the table. She rubbed a butter knife clean of water spots. Martin would never let an unclean knife leave the kitchen.

Gus rested his hands on the back of one of the dining chairs and nodded. Lucy went to stand beside him. She wasn't much of a crier, but, God. What a day. Temnikova was gone. Just...gone. Like Grandma. Except Grandma was *Grandma*. So it was different. But Lucy hadn't been here for that, and now that she'd seen this death up close, she couldn't help but think about the one she'd missed.

She put her arm around Gus and leaned way down to rest her head on his shoulder. "Someday you'll be taller, and this won't be so awkward."

"Oh, is *that* why it's awkward?"

"Funny." She straightened up, the urge to cry gone. "I'm sorry I couldn't save her."

"You said that already. It's okay."

"Aren't you a little bit sad?" she asked.

"I don't know," Gus said. "Are you?"

"It makes me think of Grandma."

Gus nodded, and Lucy set her hand on his head for a few seconds until he squirmed out from under it and took his seat. He put his napkin on his lap, so mannered and adult. He'd never had a messy phase. He'd never been sent away from the table. He never got crazy. Their parents took it as something to be proud of. Lucy thought maybe it wasn't how a ten-year-old boy's life should look, and she wished he *would* get crazy once in a while. A sugar bender. A tantrum. Inappropriate jokes.

But in their house, childhood, like grief, was an episode merely tolerated. An inconvenience and an obstacle to the real work of life: proving to the world and to yourself that you weren't just taking up space.

No pressure.

She sat across from Gus and flapped her napkin out dramatically, to make him smile.

Maybe it was good he was such a perfect kid. It left her free to screw up for both of them.

A cocktail party at a hotel, eight months ago. Lucy, nervous and in a new dress; one she and her mother had picked out together and agreed on, back when they used to agree on at least some things. It was slightly more adult than the rest of Lucy's wardrobe. She was about to turn sixteen, and her mother didn't mind Lucy showing leg as long as the neckline stayed appropriate and the heel low. The dress—silver jersey with ruching that gathered at the left side of her waist—stopped midthigh. Lucy was supposed to be wearing tights.

But her mother wasn't there to check. She'd stayed home to take care of Grandma Beck, whose bad cold had suddenly become pneumonia. So Lucy's dad had come instead to Prague, for the festival. Grandpa Beck, too, of course, because he believed he had to be at everything. Later, Lucy didn't understand how he could have left his sick wife behind the way he did.

She was talking to two of the other pianists playing the festival but, unlike her, not competing: a guy from Tokyo and a girl from a European city Lucy didn't quite catch over the noise of the room, whose name was Liesel or Louisa or something. They were both older than she was by about ten years, both good enough English speakers to talk about the pieces they were playing, where else they'd traveled recently, and where they were going next.

"I think I'm doing Tanglewood this summer," Lucy told them.

It sounded impressive. Not that she *wanted* to go to Tanglewood. As she hadn't wanted to do so many of the things that filled her time: the concerts and festivals and recording sessions and competitions that took her around the world and caused her to miss such massive chunks of school that she wasn't officially enrolled anymore. Instead she worked with various tutors from USF. Marnie and cute Bennett and sometimes Allison.

She hadn't even wanted to come to the Prague, which only took fifteen pianists in her age group from around the world. Out of thousands of applicants, she'd made it. There'd been a party. Grandma Beck wouldn't let anyone else pick the flowers or the food. Lucy's dad bought her a white-gold necklace with an *L* pendant to congratulate her, and Gus got all caught up in imagining himself at the same festival one day. Grace Chang, her teacher, took Lucy out for a special dinner to strategize a repertoire.

The thing was, Lucy hadn't even applied.

Her mother had filled out the form and sent in the CD.

"I didn't want you to be disappointed if you didn't get in," her mom had said.

Right, Lucy had thought. *More like you didn't want to give me the chance to say no.*

That was when Lucy still believed that rocking the boat was the worst thing a person could do, and it didn't even cross her mind to try to back out.

The guy from Tokyo leaned forward as if he had misheard her. "Tanglewood?"

"Yeah."

"How old are you?"

"Fifteen."

He exchanged a glance with Liesel/Louisa, who said, "Wow."

Lucy hadn't meant to brag. It could be hard to find the line between sharing credentials in an effort to fit in and showing off. "It's just part of this new youth-spotlight thing they're going to try...."

"Excuse me," Liesel/Louisa said, looking across the room as if she saw someone she had to go talk to.

Tokyo stayed. "Have you ever been to Japan?" He had long, shaggy hair, like a lot of the guy musicians had, to show the world they may be music nerds but they were rebel music nerds.

"Once. When I was, like, eight."

He started to reply when Grandpa Beck appeared at Lucy's elbow.

"Lucy, let me introduce you to someone." He took her arm and pulled her away from the conversation. She scanned the room for her dad and didn't see him. "Your father is up in our room. And don't get too friendly with the competition."

"They're not the competition."

"Everyone is the competition."

She shivered in the arctic climate of the hotel ballroom while her grandfather ferried her around and made her talk to everyone he thought important: an up-and-coming conductor, an international booking agent, a Grammy-winning producer of classical albums. Lucy smiled and nodded a lot, hearing about half of what was said.

They left the party. In the elevator to their suite, Grandpa Beck turned to her. "You did well in there, Lucy. I'm proud of you." His eyes were soft, and he touched her shoulder with real affection. "This is an important festival, and there's a buzz about you. They all know who you are."

She did like that part. Being somebody. Even if it meant certain people were jealous or thought she was too young to get the kind of attention she did.

Being a concert pianist didn't win her any special respect from the kids she'd been at school with. Even her best friend, Reyna, didn't know and wouldn't care that she could nail a Rachmaninoff allegro. But in places like this, she knew she mattered.

"How's Grandma?" she asked as they exited the elevator and walked over the hotel's ornate carpet.

"Just fine."

"Let's call her. I want to say hi." And she wanted to hear Gus's voice, and ask her mom's advice about how to wear her hair for the main part of the competition.

He pulled back the sleeve of his suit jacket to check his watch. "It's complicated with the time difference. We don't want to interrupt her rest."

Before leaving for Prague, Lucy'd gone into her grandmother's room to say good-bye, but she'd been asleep. Lucy had stared for a few minutes at her face: powdered and tweezed but also naturally beautiful. The face of a woman who was kind without being a pushover. Someone who'd managed to live with Grandpa Beck for more than fifty years without killing him.

"I don't want to go," Lucy had whispered, hoping Grandma would open her eyes and say she didn't have to.

Her mother had heard. "You're just nervous," she'd said softly, joining her on the edge of Grandma's bed.

Lucy had turned to her. Maybe there, in that quiet space, the afternoon light filtering through the gauzy curtains, dust motes in the beams and only the sound of Grandma's breathing, her mother would listen. "I'm not nervous. I feel like I should stay here."

"You have to go, honey. It's the *Prague*."

Lucy had looked back at her grandmother. "Isn't this a family emergency?"

"Grandma's going to be fine. And you won't do her any good by not going."

♪

Lying awake in the Prague hotel room, Lucy had the sense that something wasn't right.

Her parents hadn't given her cell international access. She got out of bed and went into the suite's living room, in search of her father's phone. He was asleep on the pull-out sofa bed; Grandpa Beck's room had two kings, but he wasn't sharing. She found the phone and crept back to her room, got under the covers, and called her mom.

"Marc, it must be the middle of the night there," her mother said as an answer.

"It's me."

"Lucy?"

"I want to talk to Grandma."

A pause. "You can't right now, honey. I'm sorry."

"She's sleeping?"

"We're actually at the hospital," her mother said. "She's okay," she added quickly, "but she's resisting the antibiotics a little bit.

And just needs some help breathing. She's *fine*, Lucy. It's all routine for someone her age."

"Does Grandpa know?"

"Yes."

Why hadn't he said something? "Is Gus with you?" she asked her mother.

"No, there's no reason for him to be. Because everything is all right. You just concentrate on your job over there."

"She's really okay?" *Is there a tube in her throat? Does it hurt?*

"Yes."

"Tell Gus I say hi. And tell Grandma I love her."

"I will. Get some sleep."

Lucy hung up and realized she'd forgotten to ask her mom about how she should wear her hair.

3.

Lucy heard Gus coming up the stairs that connected her room in the attic to the third floor, where his was, and knew she'd overslept. Again. Her mother thought she did it on purpose, as if she sat around twenty-four hours a day thinking up Ways to Piss Off Mom. The truth was simple: She stayed up too late. All the time.

She scrambled out of bed, and by the time Gus came in had on school khakis and sneakers plus the sweatshirt she'd slept in. "Give me two minutes." She dug through a pile in her walk-in closet, in search of a sweater. Or maybe not a sweater. Maybe a polo. "What's it like out?"

Gus went to one of the little windows under the eaves and squeakily twisted open the blind. "It looks . . . beige."

Sweater. Lucy finished dressing in the closet, grabbed her book bag and a hair clip, and followed Gus downstairs. She kept him between her and her mother, who stood waiting in the foyer, in the exact spot recently occupied by Temnikova's body on a gurney. Lucy almost said something about it: *They covered her face. The wheels got caught on the entry table. I had to move it a few inches to the left, see?*

But her mother already had her hand on the doorknob; no time to acknowledge death.

"I'm not even going to say it, Lucy."

"You could leave without me, you know."

"Sure. Then you could skip school entirely."

Her mother walked out, and Lucy said to Gus, "When we get in the car, ask if we can stop for coffee."

"*You* ask her."

It was one thing to live on an average of four hours of sleep a night; quite another to do it without caffeine. She'd have to make a dash for CC's after her mom dropped her off.

Outside the house a gust of wind blew up the hill, carrying the smell of some bacony breakfast cooking nearby—maybe at one of the restaurants on Union Street. Last year she and Allison would sometimes have their tutoring sessions at Rose's or Ella's; Rose's for the smoked-salmon breakfast pizza, Ella's for the chicken hash.

Lucy's stomach growled. Chalk one up in the "pro" column for being a semifamous pianist: leisurely breakfasts. After a few years off of a normal school schedule, and only recently back on, she didn't get why first period had to be so *early*.

Gus sat in the front seat, and Lucy brushed her hair and put it back in the clip.

At the intersection at the bottom of the hill, she allowed herself one red light's worth of guilt. Being late so often actually *was* kind of rude, she knew that. But she had to be careful with guilt. Once she went off that edge, the downward slide might never stop.

It would start with feeling bad for being the kind of person who made people wait and for not showing her mom more basic courtesy. That would lead to guilt over not being grateful for the life she had and for not making good use of her privilege.

19

Grandpa Beck had a lot to say about Making Good Use of Privilege; it was the family religion. Then there was what happened in Prague after all that time and money spent. Or invested. Thrown away? However you wanted to put it.

Time and money her parents would never get back. That Lucy would never get back.

Time, that was the main thing. Years of it.

Aka: her childhood. Gone.

But what was the point of going there? Nothing could be done about it. Except maybe for Gus, who now bore the sole responsibility for achieving something really special in the family name. All that pressure, a weight they used to share, was his alone, thanks to her. Which brought her back to...

Guilt.

So she tried to stop herself at mild remorse over hitting the snooze button a few too many times.

When they pulled up to Gus's school, the other kids were already going inside.

"Hurry," their mother said. "I'm sorry Lucy couldn't be on time."

Lucy leaned her head on the seat back and sighed.

♪

Speare Academy was generally known to be the second-best private high school in San Francisco, where you went if you came from a family that could afford it, and if you couldn't get into Parker Day, which only had like eighty spots.

Other than having to be somewhere so early in the morning, Lucy liked it. She'd gone there for the last quarter of sophomore year, which involved a lot of time in the library, doing independent study to catch up with her classmates, the majority of whom she still didn't really know. She had her best friend, Reyna, and sometimes Carson Lin, and that was fine by her; being part of huge groups was never her thing.

This year what she most loved about Speare was Mr. Charles.

Today he wore the shirt-and-tie combination she especially liked. The shirt: your basic Brooks Brothers pinstripe, blue. The tie: silver, with tiny purple shapes that she'd once stared at long enough to believe were otters. He also had some good stubble going on, blond and darker blond.

They stood together at the front of the classroom, the rest of the class already in critique groups. In a whisper she told him the story of Temnikova dying in her arms, how it had upset Gus, the family in shock. And that's why she was late.

But her coffee cup from CC's told the real truth.

The pleasant flow of caffeine working through her system, the sharpening of her mind that came with it, the comfort of the warm cup in her hand—it all left her suddenly as she realized Mr. Charles was over it. This being-late thing.

At the start of term, he'd been patient. He understood that the school routine was relatively new to her, and that she was used to functioning independently, more like an adult. Plus she'd been teacher's pet since the first week of school, when he'd taught some obscure Dylan Thomas poem no one got, and Lucy had made a comment she could not now remember and he'd walked over to her desk to hand her his personal copy of the Thomas book. "In thanks for saving this hour from complete pointlessness," he'd said.

After that she started hanging around his room an extra minute or two after class and, once in a while, at lunch. Working with Bennett and Allison and Marnie had made her see teachers less like extra parents and more like older, smarter friends, and that's how she treated Mr. Charles.

It had become a crush. And she could be the *tiniest* bit obsessive about him. He didn't seem to mind; the gift of the Thomas book proved he thought she was special.

She also knew that she'd been taking advantage of that.

"I'm sorry for your family's loss," he said. "And I know you're still adjusting to the schedule. But Lucy, this ... no more, okay?"

"I'm sorry." She ran her thumb around the sharp under-edge of the coffee lid. "I'm working on it."

"Really?" He sounded skeptical, and gestured with his head for her to follow him out into the hall and its ever-present smell of floor wax.

Lucy caught a glimpse of herself in the glass door of the classroom across the hall. Coffee cup, Italian leather messenger bag, sunglasses she didn't need in this weather atop her head. *Entitled brat.* Words her grandfather had used to describe her, just one day after the moment in the elevator when he'd expressed his pride.

"I'm sorry," she said again.

"What's the deal?" he asked. "I mean it. Teachers are trained to worry that this kind of stuff is a symptom of drug use or major problems at home. But I know you better than that. You're not doing drugs. You're not drinking. Your problems at home are normal, even if they don't always feel like it. I know you like school, and I know you like my class especially."

"I do."

"So be on time."

"I will." She couldn't stand how disappointed he was. She wanted their usual friendly talk. "What are those things on your tie, anyway?"

"What?" He glanced down, picked up the end of his tie, then dropped it. "I had to put my dog to sleep last weekend, Lucy. She was fourteen. My dad got her for me as a high school graduation present. She lived with me in Boston, all through college. She rode across the country in the passenger seat of my car. And I'm on time." He didn't sound angry. More like he was about to cry. "Okay?"

Miserable, Lucy nodded, finding a sliver of comfort in the fact that he'd confided in her about the dog. She could only repeat, "I'm sorry. About your dog, and..." She stared at her shoes. Custom saddle oxfords her mom had bought for her sixteenth birthday. She didn't know how much they'd cost, but one time a computer file with the teachers' salaries got leaked among students, and she had a feeling Mr. Charles wouldn't be able to afford these shoes. She could at least be on time.

Fail.

"We're still friends," Mr. Charles said. "But I know you can do better."

Still friends. The words restored her a little. But she hated that she had to add him to the list of people she'd let down.

♪

She met Reyna at their usual spot for lunch—a small, round café table in the second-floor lounge, far from the cafeteria. If

Reyna made other friends during the time Lucy had private tutors, they weren't close friends, because she seemed to have dumped them all upon Lucy's return. It was always either only the two of them at their table, or them plus Carson if he was tired of his guy friends. Today they had their privacy.

"Here's the latest divorce news flash," Reyna said. "One of my dad's girlfriends or whatever was—wait for it—"

Lucy slid down in her chair. "I'm scared to know."

Reyna's parents were in the midst of an epically brutal divorce involving adultery and hiding money and people basically at their worst. Also a house in Pacific Heights, a cottage in Stinson Beach, and Reyna's little sister, Abigail. To add to the awkwardness, Reyna's dad was Lucy's orthodontist.

"You should be scared. Soon-Yi Pak's mom."

"Oh. God." Soon-Yi was a sophomore and a tennis star, sweet but kind of boring off the court. "How did they meet?"

"How do you think? Have you seen Soon-Yi's teeth? Here." Reyna passed Lucy half the turkey wrap they were sharing.

"Speaking of teeth," Lucy said, "I have an appointment with your dad next Saturday. I'll come over after." Dr. Bauman's office was in the lower level of Reyna's house, which added yet another complication to the divorce.

"You're still seeing him?" Reyna made a face and pushed her half of the wrap away.

"Only a few more times. Then I'm officially finished with the retainer."

Then Lucy told her about Temnikova. She made it into a story, because if she thought too hard about the idea of death, as in not being alive, as in being *done*, she might lose it. So she lingered on the CPR details Reyna would appreciate. "Mouth. To. Mouth."

Reyna shuddered. "Ew. I can't believe you came to school today. That seems like a totally believable reason for skipping."

"Because staying home is so much fun?"

"Yeah, maybe not. You guys need to move out of your grandfather's house."

"Never going to happen," Lucy said. "And anyway, it's half my mom's, too." She finished her food and ran her tongue over her teeth, checking for lettuce. She pictured the back of her mother's head in the car that morning. Blond chignon. No stray hairs allowed. Competent and in charge; someone who would have executed CPR perfectly. Temnikova wouldn't have dared die. "I think my mom blames me for not being able to resurrect Temnikova."

"Your mom has issues."

"Understatement," Lucy said. They'd never been the "best friends" kind of mother and daughter, but the last year, especially, had been...tense.

"Well, it's better than living with a cheater and embezzler."

"At least your dad smiles more than once a week."

"He's an orthodontist." Reyna squashed what was left of her lunch into a ball. "That's not a smile. That's advertising."

♪

After school Lucy fast-walked back to CC's and got coffee for herself and a piece of chocolate-chip pumpkin bread for Mr. Charles. She wanted to talk to him one more time, to be double sure he wasn't mad. In the CC's bathroom, she redid her hair clip and tried to see herself through Mr. Charles's eyes. He liked her. She knew he did. But how did he *see* her? Older than sixteen, the way the EMT had? The way practically everyone in the music world had? Which...not that it mattered. As long as he didn't lump her in with all the other students.

She wrinkled her nose at her reflection, and against the overpowering lemonesque smell of the bathroom's plug-in air freshener.

So what.

Crushing on a teacher. Sort of pathetic.

When she returned to his room, he wasn't even there. The lights were out. She tried the door; it was still unlocked. What an eerie, dead thing an empty classroom was. Lucy quickly found a Post-it on Mr. Charles's desk and jotted:

> Good morning. I bet you this pumpkin bread I'm on time today. -Lucy

She stuck the note to the bread and put it in his in-box.

4.

At first Lucy didn't hear her mother's knock. She had her laptop hooked up to the good speakers, blasting a little Holst—decent homework-doing music. In the middle of a decrescendo, the knocking came through loud and clear.

She turned down the music and opened the door. Somehow her mother looked as perfect and beautiful as she had in the car that morning, nearly fourteen hours ago.

The playlist jumped to Mussorgsky, and it sounded ominous as her mother came into the room. "I want to talk about yesterday," her mother said. "Can you tell me exactly what happened?"

"I told you." Lucy sat at her desk and stopped the music, to type a few words into her English paper.

"Tell me again. Maybe I missed something."

Her mother went over to the bed and perched on the edge of it, forcing Lucy to turn in her chair, away from the laptop.

What was there to miss? Temnikova died.

Still, Lucy rerecited the facts, from Gus calling out to the moment the paramedics showed up. When she got to the part about giving CPR, her mother kept interrupting with questions:

"How long before Gus actually dialed nine-one-one?"

"Was she breathing at that point?"

"Did she say anything?"

"Like what?" Lucy asked.

"Anything, Lucy. Anything at all."

She would have loved to be able to tell her mother something she wanted to hear for a change. That Temnikova had meaningful dying words about Gus or had thanked the Beck-Moreaus for changing her life.

"No, Mom. She died. It was fast."

"It seems like if you'd called nine-one-one a few minutes sooner..."

"Mom. They said there was nothing anyone could have done." *Probably.*

"Why didn't you call me right away?"

"I don't know," Lucy said.

"Did you even *think* about it?"

Like you thought about calling me about Grandma? Like that? "She was dead. And whether you found out right away or later, she'd still be dead."

Her mother nodded and dropped her hand on top of the pile of Lucy's blankets. "I wish you'd make your bed. The whole room looks neater when the bed is made."

"So I've been told." She turned back to her homework.

"Grandpa wants to start the process of hiring a new teacher as soon as possible. To keep Gus on track for the showcase and the Swanner. I'm tempted to call Grace Chang, but I know Grandpa would have a fit."

Lucy stopped typing. "You can't call Grace." It would be like inviting an ex-boyfriend over to maybe date someone else in the family.

Grace had been her Temnikova. Only not sour and scary.

She was a mentor, teacher, guide, and sort of like a cool aunt. A cool aunt Lucy'd abandoned.

"Call someone at the Academy," she said.

Lucy and her mother locked eyes. They both knew that would never happen. Grandpa Beck had an ancient feud with the Symphony Academy having to do with the performing career Lucy's mother was supposed to have had when she was Gus's age and never did. Grandpa blamed the Academy, her mother's teachers there, the system, anti-Beck bias, the seventies, and of course her mother—everything and everyone but himself.

"We'll find somebody." Her mother stood. On her way out, she stopped to touch Lucy's head. "You should dry your hair before you get in bed."

"I like it natural."

"It would look so much better with—"

"I like it natural." Lucy jerked her head away and rolled her chair back a foot or so.

Her mother's arm dropped. "Don't stay up too late."

"I have a lot to do," Lucy mumbled.

Her mother opened her mouth, closed it. Then folded her arms and paused in front of the picture that hung by Lucy's door: Lucy, age thirteen, getting her fifth-place prize at the Loretta Himmelman International. Excellent placement.

The whole week, actually, had been a dream. They'd gone to Utah for the competition, and for once it was only the four of them—Lucy, Gus, their parents. They'd stayed at this huge hotel in Salt Lake and had room-service breakfast every morning: crepes filled with bananas and Nutella; eggs Benedict; homemade granola.

Lucy'd made instant friends with another girl in the competition, Madchen. She'd come all the way from Bavaria, and her English wasn't great, but the two of them had run around the hotel together between events. One night they'd had a sleepover in Madchen's room, and Madchen's mother let them take the bed while she slept on a roll-away and talked them to sleep. Her voice had been hypnotic, precise, musical, speaking low as Lucy and Madchen drifted away, the hotel pillows smelling faintly of bleach.

It was probably the last time she felt happy at one of those things. Maybe her happiness had come from the family being together without Grandpa's anxiety over every little detail, and the way he'd never let anyone forget the competitive aspect. Or maybe it was that Lucy loved the program she'd prepared, especially the Brahms. The Rhapsody in B Minor. Her mother had wanted her to do something showier, and Grandpa nearly fired Grace Chang over it, but Lucy and Grace wanted to prove she could be expressive as well as technical.

Madchen and her mother had come to hear Lucy play and smiled through it even though Madchen's piece that morning hadn't gone well.

Maybe it was all of those things.

Her mother stopped staring at the picture, and before leaving said, "Try the silk pillowcase I bought you. It helps with the frizz."

5.

By the weekend Lucy's mother and grandfather had accepted that Temnikova was dead and it was no one's fault. They turned their attention to plotting what, or who, would be next for Gus and did it mostly behind closed doors.

Lucy was anxious to know what was going on but didn't ask. She knew her grandfather would think she had no right to be involved or even have an opinion. Not anymore. Of course she did have one, and always would, especially when it came to Gus. She wanted someone good for him. Not just musically. Someone he could look up to, the way he used to look up to her.

But her family had no reason to listen to her, so she avoided it all as much as she could by holing up in her room to work on her next paper for Mr. Charles.

They were studying short stories. Each student had to choose a writer, read at least five of his or her stories, and write a paper on that body of work. It would account for a big chunk of their fall-semester grade, and Lucy wanted to impress Mr. Charles. After a little Googling in the wee hours, she'd discovered he'd gotten a special award at Harvard for a critical paper he'd done on a writer named Alice Munro. So Lucy picked her.

Sunday afternoon she was taking notes on a Munro story

when Gus came up to visit, a book in his hand, asking if he could read in her room.

"As long as you're quiet," Lucy said.

He lay on his stomach on the floor, a pillow from Lucy's bed tucked under his arms. She sat nearby, also on the floor, typing a few sentences now and then.

In every assignment she did for Mr. Charles, she tried to find that perfect balance of sounding smart without coming off like a know-it-all. She didn't want to be like Bryan Oxenford, who sprinkled his papers with esoteric words arranged in overly complicated sentences that wound up making no sense when he read aloud in class.

"Can I ask something?" Gus said.

"You just did."

"Do you think Temnikova went to heaven?"

"Sure," she said absently. "Why not."

"So you think there *is* a heaven?"

"I don't know."

"Then why'd you say Temnikova went there?"

"I didn't."

"What about Grandma?"

Lucy swirled her finger on the track pad. They didn't often discuss Grandma, and she didn't feel capable of it at the moment. "I don't know, Gus. She never talked about that stuff."

"So? Not talking about it doesn't mean it doesn't exist."

"I *know*," Lucy said. "Now let me work."

After a few minutes of quiet, Gus said, "Can I say something else?"

"No."

"I think maybe they got somebody," he said. He didn't look up from his book. His finger rested on the upper corner of the right-hand page, ready to turn it but on pause.

Lucy immediately knew what he meant. "You've been meeting people?" she asked, surprised.

"No."

"They're not going to hire someone you haven't met." She deleted a sentence on her screen and considered how to reword it in a non-Oxenford way.

"I heard them talking." Gus rolled over and sat up, his book still open. "They were in Mom's office. Dad was in there, too."

Lucy moved her laptop aside. Surely even her grandfather wouldn't pull something like this. Gus should have some say in who he worked with; he wasn't five anymore. "What did you hear, exactly?"

"I kind of heard the whole thing. I sort of put my ear to the door."

"You kind of sort of spied?"

"His name is Will something," Gus said. "Grandpa heard about him from one of his symphony friends."

"Did you get a last name?"

"I forget. But I remember Brightman Quintet."

Lucy pulled her computer back onto her lap and commenced Googling. Gus had to have misheard, about the hiring, anyway. Maybe he'd gotten the name right but the context wrong. Briteman Quintet, she found, not Brightman. She followed a link and scanned it quickly. "Will R. Devi?"

"Yeah." He set down his book and crawled over next to her, and they read through a screen of links about Will R. Devi. Pianist, violist, teacher. Judge of a few well-known competitions.

Host of some local public television show about young musicians that had been canceled a couple of years back.

"You weren't on that," Lucy said to Gus. "If he was anybody, you would have been on that show." Or she would have.

They found more stuff about this Will person: articles and blog entries and whatnot. Then, their mother announced herself outside Lucy's door. "Lucy? Is Gus with you?"

"Yes," she said. Her mother came in. She wore a gray wool pencil skirt and tights, riding boots, a red sweater, and matching red lipstick. Her hair was down but brushed back. "Why so fancy?" Lucy asked. Sunday typically meant jeans or upscale yoga outfits.

"We're having company for dinner. I'd like you two to dress."

A formal dinner, on a Sunday night, with virtually no notice? Lucy looked at Gus, who asked, "Who's coming?" As if they couldn't guess.

"Their names are Will and Aruna Devi." Here, her mother looked down and picked a piece of nonexistent lint off the arm of her sweater. "And be on good behavior, Gus. You start working with Will on Tuesday."

Lucy glanced at Gus, hoping he'd say something like: *You decided? Without me?* But she knew those were her thoughts. Gus was still sweet and agreeable and mostly unquestioning. He said, "Okay," and got up to follow their mom downstairs.

After they left, Lucy stared at the door. Temnikova's death hadn't changed anything. Decisions were made the usual way: Grandpa Beck steamrolling over everyone, aided by her mother, her dad standing off to the side letting the whole thing happen.

Play this piece, Lucy.

Wear this dress.

Come here. This person wants to meet you.

Make eye contact with one of the judges before you sit down at the piano.

Hold your head up. You know who you are.

She knew who *he* wanted her to be. Not the same thing.

She put Alice Munro on hold and searched for pictures of Will Devi online. He looked pretty young. Good-looking enough to have his own local TV show but maybe not enough to go national. His face had an odd asymmetry to it, with one eye that didn't open as wide as the other and a nose that sort of veered off to the left. He exuded a determined warmth that helped offset the imperfections.

It didn't matter. He could be the nicest person in the world. It still wasn't right to force him on Gus. The way they'd forced Prague and the other stuff on her, robbing her of her life, little by little, until quitting felt like the only choice that was hers to make.

♪

An hour before the Devis were to arrive, Lucy finally peeled off her pajamas to get in the shower. She had her own giant bathroom—"the spa," Reyna called it—with a comically enormous tub and walk-in shower with dual heads and a marble ledge to sit on. She propped her right leg up on the ledge to shave, then her left. She felt her big-sister resolve kicking in and was eager to meet Will. If she didn't like him, she'd definitely say something to her mom even if it got her yelled at or, more likely, frozen out.

She dried and moisturized and pumped keratin serum into her

hair, which she gathered into a subdued ponytail. Some powder, some tinted lip balm. There were perfume samples in her bathroom drawer but nothing she liked. In the closet she vacillated between two outfits. The first: a blue-and-cream polka-dot dress that was sort of fifties-looking; her go-to dress, comfortable and flattering. The other: a simple black sheath.

The polka dots seemed overly cheerful, given her mood, so she went with the sheath. A jade-green cardigan would pep it up a little.

She checked the wardrobe mirror. Boring but appropriate.

The older sister, not the star.

She was getting used to it.

At the last minute, she put on the *L* pendant her dad had given her, then thought, *Time to face the music*, and laughed at her own stupid joke.

6.

Voices came from the parlor. Grandpa Beck would be serving cocktails right about now. Lucy could picture him, wearing his signature bow tie, his full, white hair brushed back and sprayed with the old-fashioned stuff he got at the barbershop he went to every week. He'd smell chemical from that and also like Chanel Pour Monsieur and gin martinis.

She slipped into the kitchen first, in search of Martin. Seeing him always helped her feel grounded. Normally he was off on Sundays, but no way would her mother suddenly become a gourmet cook who could handle a dinner party. Instead of Martin, Lucy found two guys and a frazzled-looking woman in green aprons hustling around the kitchen island. "Oh," she said just as Martin came up from the cellar holding a couple of bottles of wine.

He set the wine on the counter and came over to Lucy. "Hi, doll. Do you need something? It's a little crowded in here right now."

"Caterers?" she whispered. "Really?"

"That was my call," Martin said. "Apparently they're vegans. I didn't know what to make! They don't even eat *cheese*, Lucy."

"I can't believe Grandpa knowingly hired a vegan." He

thought vegans were sitting in judgment of everyone else. Vegans didn't bathe, he thought. Vegans didn't pay taxes.

"The old man is full of surprises." Martin lifted Lucy's chin with two fingers and studied her face. "You look beautiful. Chic. You'd better get out there and join the fun."

♪

They were all in a semicircle, their backs to the doorway. Looking at Wilhelm Furtwängler's conductor's baton. Of course. It was the first thing Grandpa Beck showed new guests. He had a whole elaborate story about it, involving a spontaneous flight to Berlin for the auction and the trouble he had getting the huge amount of cash he needed from the foreign bank. Based on where he was in the story now, pretty soon he'd say, *I outbid a very good friend of mine, and he hasn't talked to me since!* Followed by hearty laughter, like that was hilarious.

Also he was somehow able to say "Furtwängler" with a straight face, every time.

Lucy stared at their backs, feeling like a party crasher.

Gus had on his school blazer and khakis, his curls damp from the shower. Her dad was in his charcoal fitted suit. Will's wife, Aruna, wore her hair in a glossy black braid that trailed almost to her waist. Her dress was floatier and softer than anything in Lucy's mother's wardrobe, semiboho. Will's hand rested just below the tip of his wife's braid, and Lucy tracked her eyes up his sweatered arm, to his neck, to the back of his head. He seemed so relaxed. That would end soon enough; he had no idea what he was in for, working here, with the Beck-Moreaus.

Then he glanced over his shoulder that way you do, absently, when you think there might be something to see if you only look. His eyes, behind wire-rimmed glasses, met Lucy's. She lifted her hand in a way meaning both *Hello* and also *Interrupt Grandpa Beck at your peril.*

He didn't pick up on the second meaning.

He turned all the way around, dropping his hand, and said— right as Grandpa Beck was going to announce exactly how much he'd paid for the baton—"Lucy."

Everyone else turned, too, all but Will and Gus holding martini glasses. Lucy's dad's face lit up, as if he hadn't seen her in ages, and he came to her and kissed her cheek. "Hey, lovely."

"Lucy," her grandfather said, in a volume that would have made more sense in a much bigger room—an auditorium, for instance—"I want you to meet Will R. Devi."

She extended her hand; Will shook it.

He said her name again. Her full name. "Lucy Beck-Moreau." Slowly. It meant something to him. "It's a thrill."

If she hadn't been so busy thinking about what to wear, she might have taken a moment to consider the obvious: Will Devi would know all about her. The party-crasher feeling disappeared, replaced with a crackle of excitement. Like how it used to be, her presence mattering.

It didn't feel bad.

"Thank you. Nice to meet you, too."

"I'm Aruna," his wife said. Her hand was warmer and smoother than Will's. She had golden skin, perfectly shaped lips, perfectly shaped everything.

Lucy's mother excused herself to go check on the caterers, and Grandpa Beck blurted out, "Anyway, seventeen thousand dollars didn't seem like too much to pay. This was twenty years ago, mind you. A lot of money at the time for that sort of thing."

Will laughed. "It still is."

Grandpa's expression froze momentarily. Lucy caught her dad's eye and suppressed a smile. No one had responded that way before, which meant Grandpa was off his script. Lucy mentally prompted him: *You consider yourself a curator of sorts.*

"Well, I consider myself a curator of sorts. We wouldn't want these things lost to history." Then he stepped to the liquor tray. "Who's ready for another?"

Aruna went to him with her martini glass held out, and Lucy's dad followed. Will, though, abandoned the other adults and said, "Hey, Gus, why don't you come over and talk to Lucy and me?"

He did, and Lucy could see from his body language and open expression that he already liked Will better than he'd ever liked Temnikova. "Will told Mom I should play more video games."

"He did not." Lucy glanced at Will. "Did he?"

"Yes, he did," Will said. His smile, like everything else on his face, was crooked. "It's actually good for the hands and for the brain, to take those kind of breaks."

"And after you told her that, you still have the job?"

"It would seem."

One of the caterers came in to circulate a tray of hors d'oeuvres. "Vegan artichoke tarts," he announced. Will took one, Lucy took two, and Gus shook his head.

"So, Lucy." Will turned his full attention to her. "I'm dying to ask. Do you still play?"

She hesitated. Not because she didn't know the answer, but because she hadn't expected the question and should have. "No."

"For fun, I mean," he said, as if she hadn't understood. "For yourself."

"No."

He still seemed confused, raising his brows at her. She shrugged and put an entire artichoke tart in her mouth. "This is good," she said, after swallowing, before Will could ask anything else about piano. "Considering it has no butter or cheese or anything." She held the other tart up to Gus's mouth. "Here, try it."

He mashed his lips together.

Will gave Gus a nudge. "Go ahead. It won't poison you."

"I don't—" Lucy shoved the tart into his open mouth. He bugged out his eyes, making Lucy and Will laugh. "It *is* good," Gus said, when he could speak.

"See?" Will said. "You should listen to your sister." He winked at her. She wished she'd worn the polka dots after all.

♪

"A toast." Grandpa Beck clinked his butter knife against his wineglass, smug, happy, and a little red-faced. After the martinis, they'd finished off two bottles of wine throughout the meal, and the caterers had just brought out another. Lucy was pretty sure that she, Will, and Gus were the only sober ones at the table.

"To Will," her grandfather said. "And to Gustav..."

Lucy held up her water goblet and grinned at Gus. She still thought her parents should have let him meet Will before they made a decision, but it seemed likely to work out great. He deserved to be as happy as he looked right now, always.

"...To their hard work and the many successes to come."

"Hear, hear," Lucy's mother said. Her dad had barely gotten in a word the whole night but now managed to say, "Cheers," without being interrupted.

They all touched glasses and drank, then Will said, "May I make another?"

"Please." Grandpa Beck held up the bottle of wine. "Anyone need a topper?"

Aruna reached her glass across the table with a smile. She truly was stunning; Lucy'd noticed her dad and grandfather and even Gus sneaking glances all night. Everything she said came off witty and charming and smart, and her voice had a low, soothing quality. She touched Will's hand a lot.

It reminded Lucy of Grandma Beck and how she always touched whoever she was talking to. Lightly, and with a calmness. Not clutching or intense. Lucy missed that.

Will raised his glass of water, and everyone got quiet, waiting for him to speak. Lucy tried to anticipate the kind of thing he'd say. Something funny? Sappy?

He caught her eyes and seemed to lose focus for a second.

"Go ahead, Devi," Grandpa Beck said. "This is a 'drink now' vintage."

Will laughed and nodded at him. "It's really a privilege to be working with this family. I've admired...well, everyone knows what a talented gene pool you've got. You've already made such a great contribution with your art. And so, here's to that. And to art. To music. To the joy of creation, and the wonder of beauty in all its forms."

A collective pause stilled them. He was so…sincere. Could he, could anyone, really mean that? She watched him, wondering.

The moment snapped in two when Grandpa Beck stood up—his way of ordering everyone from the table—and said, "To the piano. I can't think of a finer moment to hear what's in store for us."

♪

The piano.

There were better pianos out there, but this one had a story all its own. The baton was an anecdote; this was a tale. Of war and tragedy and overseas travel. Lucy tuned out while Grandpa Beck recited it to Will and Aruna. She already had the key facts etched into her soul:

Fully restored Hagspiel baby grand.

Made in Dresden in 1890, by Gustav Hagspiel—one of the two people Gus was named after. Him and Mahler, the composer.

Bought by Grandpa Beck's uncle Kristoff in 1912.

Kristoff was killed in World War I, in the Battle of the Marne. No one in the family knew what to do with the piano; Kristoff had been the only one who played. They almost sold it before their move to America, when Lucy's great-grandmother could see where Hitler was taking the country. They decided to ship it, as a way to honor and remember Kristoff, who should have been with them.

It came on an ocean liner, separated from the family by six months, and arrived without a scratch.

Grandpa Beck, as the only child, inherited it the same year Lucy's mother was born, and determined that she would play.

"And did you?" Aruna asked Lucy's mother.

"For a time," she answered.

All eyes in the room were on the piano. Maybe Aruna and Will were imagining its wartime journey in a below-decks crate. Lucy thought about her mom and the picture on her mom's nightstand of Lucy, as a baby, sitting in her lap at the keys of this thing that had been a presence, a force in her life as long as she could remember.

She mostly avoided this room now. The smell of old sheet music, and the particular view from the piano bench, brought on a combination of nostalgia for her former self and memories of the despair before she quit, those years between the Himmelman and Prague. This room had been the site of her personal high, high, highs and low, low, lows, not to mention Temnikova's death. And Great-Uncle Kristoff's Hagspiel was there for all of it.

Will said, "I'd love to try it out."

Grandpa Beck gestured to the bench. "That's what we're here for."

Will and Gus sat at the piano. Aruna had settled onto the small love seat, and Lucy joined her. Grandpa Beck took the wingback, of course, which meant Lucy's parents had to stand. Martin had followed behind them with a tray full of glasses and a bottle of brandy tucked under his arm.

Aruna leaned into Lucy and put her lips close enough to her ear that Lucy felt her breath. "When it's time for us to go, just give me the elbow, and I'll get Will out of here. Once he's at the piano, he loses track of things like time and space and social niceties."

"Don't worry, my mom never loses track of social niceties," Lucy muttered.

"What are we going to play?" Will asked Gus.

Gus looked blank. Usually he was told, not asked.

Will hit a few notes. "Oh, this is nice. I feel the history." He launched into some Gershwin, one of Lucy's grandmother's favorite modern composers.

How did he know? But then, Gershwin was only one of the most well-known composers of the twentieth century; Will choosing him was coincidence. Lucy stole a glance at Grandpa Beck to see if he was thinking about Grandma, too, but his face showed nothing.

So she watched Will.

His left leg moved up and down with the gentle tapping of his heel. His fingers, confident, glided across the keys. They had less arch to them than Grace Chang's but more flexibility than Temnikova's and produced rich dynamics. He was good. Better than good.

"Gus," he said, while playing, "do you know this?"

"Sort of. Not really." Gus had scooted over to the far right edge of the bench.

"Play what you were working on with Madame Temnikova for the showcase," Grandpa Beck said.

Will grimaced, then smiled, at Gus. Only Lucy and Aruna could see. "Nah. Work starts Tuesday. Let's just have fun."

Lucy waited for her grandpa to make a pronouncement about

what Gus should be playing and when. He stayed silent, though, and so did everyone else. Will had cast a spell on them.

"Okay, Gus," he said. "How about we improvise a little?"

He abandoned Gershwin and started to play a bass line that was not classical or jazz. More blues, or rock.

Gus kept his hands on his thighs. "I don't..."

"Yes you do." Will didn't stop. "Go ahead."

Lucy's breath became shallow. She felt as nervous as if it were her sitting there instead of Gus, asked to be spontaneous in front of Grandpa, the king of calculation. And yet, the whole situation excited her. When was the last time she felt anything but some combination of boredom and suffocation here in the house? Will had energy. It filled the room.

"Come on, Gustav," he said, "jump in."

"Go ahead, kiddo," her father said, tapping his toe and looking dangerously close to dancing. *"Ça passe ou ça casse!"*

Roughly: sink or swim. The French came out when he was tipsy.

Lucy's leg twitched. She didn't want this moment to wither away. She wanted it to bloom. And she wanted to hear her little brother blow their minds, like she knew he could. "Have some fun, Gus," she urged.

He turned to her, and she grinned. *Show them,* she thought.

He did. At first his notes didn't exactly go with what Will played, but then he picked it up. Lucy exhaled and leaned back against the love-seat cushion. If Will was the person he seemed to be, then things could be different for Gus. Maybe the choke hold could come off and—

"Lucy," Will said, loud and sudden, startling her out of her thoughts. "Now you!" He gestured with his head for her to get up.

Me?

She wedged her hands under her thighs. Gus stopped playing and scooted off the bench to make room, his eyes alight. He actually thought she was going to do it.

"No, thank you," she said, keeping her voice steady.

Will's bass line continued.

Aruna nudged her. What right did Aruna have to *nudge* her? They'd just met. Lucy shook her head. "No." *No, no, and hell no.*

She'd *just said* to Will in the parlor that she didn't play anymore. Not for "fun." Not for "herself." And most definitely not in front of *them*.

She got up, staying turned away from her grandfather. She imagined him saying, *Didn't you hear that our Lucy is a quitter?*

On her way out of the room, her father reached to gently hold her arm. "Stay, Luce." She freed herself. Why couldn't he be sweet to her like this without the help of excess wine?

Will stopped playing. Lucy's mother said quietly, "Our guests."

Lucy took a deep breath and turned to face the room. "I'm sorry. I don't feel well. Good night." It sounded so fake. She didn't wait for them to reply.

In the hall she bumped into Martin, who'd been standing in the shadows and listening to the whole thing, she guessed. She brushed by him and climbed the two and a half flights of stairs to her room. And, too far away for them to hear, slammed her door.

7.

"What made you choose Alice Munro?" Mr. Charles asked. They were having their one-on-one meeting about the semester project, Lucy in the chair next to him at his desk while the rest of the class met in their critique groups.

"Um." *Because you like her?* "She seems direct. The people in the stories seem...real."

Mr. Charles brightened. "I studied her in grad school, you know."

"Oh. Really?"

"So I can point you to some good resources if you hit a wall. Otherwise I'll stay out of it." It wasn't his best hair day. He'd either just gotten it cut or needed to. Lucy wanted to smooth down a piece of ashy blond that tweaked out to the side, over his ear. "Have you decided how you'll choose which five stories to write about?" he asked. "Because you could do a broad selection spanning decades, or you could hone in on a particular collection or time period."

Lucy studied his wrists, which were crossed and resting on his knee. She imagined him with a pen in one hand, reading her paper after she turned it in. She imagined him as a college student, hunched over a dorm desk, his dog at his feet. Then she pictured herself doing the same. Maybe English could be her new thing. What would it take for that to count with her mom? A PhD then tenure at an Ivy League school, probably. That should take only, what, twenty years?

"Well, I've started writing some stuff," she said. "But I don't totally have it narrowed down to five. What do you think?"

He answered, but Lucy didn't have her usual intense ability to concentrate on him. She kept reliving the night before, that hopeful expression on Will's face when he tried to get her to play. No one had mentioned it that morning, except Gus, who'd only said, "Will is neat," over their hurried cereal.

Lucy'd made an *mm* noise through her food and avoided his eyes.

"...the scope of a career," Mr. Charles was saying. "Taking, maybe, her first published story and comparing it to her most recent. That's one way. Up to you."

"I'll think about it."

He swiveled in his chair, away from her. "Whichever way you go, I'm sure you'll do a good job."

"You are?" Lucy asked, snapping her attention back to him.

"Of course," he said. "You're not worried, are you?"

"It's my first really in-depth paper since coming back to school. In a normal class, I mean, without a tutor."

"Lucy." His eyes scrunched in this way he had of smiling without actually smiling. "You're very bright. And your insights in class are always on point and thoughtful. I can't wait to see what you do with Munro, and if you need help, I'm here for you."

Her chest warmed, and she put Will and piano out of her mind. It could be a depressing thing to believe, at sixteen, that your best years were behind you. The promise Mr. Charles saw in her gave her a little hope.

"Thanks, Mr. Charles."

"And thank *you* for the pumpkin bread on Friday. Sorry I ate it before giving you a chance to win your bet."

She grinned at him. "I knew you would."

♪

By the next afternoon, her mood had continued to improve.

Mr. Charles loaned her a thick collection of Munro stories, and when she flipped through it in class she saw his penciled notes and underlines and a couple of Post-its with comments specifically for her.

During PE she won a tennis match against Soon-Yi Pak. Soon-Yi totally smashed her in the overall game, but still. During the match she caught a glimpse of her own flexing quad as she waited for a serve, and felt powerful. A guy whose name she didn't know said, "Nice game," when he passed her in the hall.

Reyna didn't bring up the divorce even once at lunch, and Carson ate with them, which was always fun.

And when she walked through the back door of her house, into the kitchen, the room was full of sunlight and Martin was pulling a pan of brownies out of the oven.

"You're the perfect mother," Lucy told Martin, and gave him a kiss on the cheek.

"I try." He set the brownies down and sniffed the pan, then poked at them warily with a spatula. "These are vegan. Special request from Gus."

"Is he turning? Grandpa's gonna love that."

"I don't think so. He just wants something to offer Will. To sort of celebrate his first lesson. You know your brother. Sweet."

Lucy's good vibe about the day dipped a little. She'd forgotten Will would be there; she didn't want to run into him and have some awkward interaction about what happened Sunday night.

She poked a brownie. "They look pretty normal."

"We'll see."

♪

The music-room door had been left open a crack, and Lucy worried how she'd get by without being spotted. Then she noticed there was no sound or movement or any indication of live bodies inside. Maybe Will and Gus were in Grandpa Beck's study, looking for a CD or album from his vast collection.

She got to the bottom of the stairs and heard Gus's voice from above. "Lucy!" She looked up. He leaned over the second-floor railing, flushed. "Me and Will are playing Wii tennis. He's really good."

Tennis? He hadn't been joking about video games. She put one foot on a step. "Better get back to it. You don't want to get on his bad side on the first day." She jogged up the stairs, Gus disappearing from her sight line for a second. When she got to the second-floor landing, Will had joined Gus at the rail.

"How about a match, Lucy? I see from the scoreboard you have a winning streak going."

The expression on his face was nearly the same as when he'd asked her to play piano. It unnerved her, still. Any invitation from him might be dangerous. "It doesn't take much to beat Gus." She added, "Sorry, Gustav."

"It's okay. I know. But Will says I'll get better."

"I'm sure Grandpa will be thrilled to hear that. You can do a Wii demonstration at the winter showcase." She shouldn't have said that. She should have been happy the noose around her little brother's life was loosening. "I'm kidding," she added, trying to erase the creeping envy. Gus and Will would play video games, eat brownies, maybe bang out a few bars of "Chopsticks." Nice for them.

"I break every forty-five minutes," Will said. "It helps the brain. Science says so."

"Okay, anyway, I have homework." She headed up the next flight of stairs.

Gus called after her, "You always say that now."

"Well, I always do now."

"Lucy, wait." Will's voice was right behind her; he'd followed her up the stairs.

She turned and shifted her bag, swept hair out of her eyes.

He leaned over the rail and said to Gus, "You can head down now; be there in a minute." Then to Lucy, "The other night. I'm sorry I put you on the spot. Aruna said—"

"Don't worry about it."

"I guess I assumed you still played at least a little."

"I don't. I told you." She went up three more steps.

"Never?"

He was still on her heels. She spun and found him directly on the stair beneath her, which put them eye to eye. "Are you going to follow me all the way to my room?"

She felt like she could cry. The stupid smell of brownies, Gus looking happy, Will's toast on Sunday night. *The wonder of beauty.* Gus and Will at the piano, creating joy.

All conspiring to remind her that she'd once loved all of this. With her whole heart.

Writing a boring English paper would never be a substitute.

Will put his hand on the railing. "Sorry. I only wanted to apologize."

"I said don't worry about it."

He lifted his hand and held it in the air between them, his fingers shaping something, a word, maybe—something he wanted to say but couldn't. She watched his hand, watched his mouth, waiting to see what would come out. While she waited she noticed: One ear appeared to be placed slightly lower on that side of his face. Crooked nose, crooked ears, the smaller eye.

"What?" she finally asked.

"You *never* play. You. Lucy Beck-Moreau. Never play."

Her vision went watery. She shook her head. "Never."

"That makes me sad."

What could she say to that? It was a compliment and a judgment, and it made her sad, too. The tears were about to come, so she turned her back on him and got all the way up to the bottom of the attic stairs before he said more:

"Do you want to? Ever?"

She could laugh. She could tell him to leave her alone and be mad that he'd asked. Or stand there on the step and explain the complicated emotional mechanism by which the idea of playing again had become all wrapped up with giving in to her grandfather and missing her grandmother and betraying herself.

But.

What do you want, Lucy? What do you want?

She wiped off her face but didn't look back at him. "I don't know."

Maybe. Maybe.

The morning of her first performance in Prague, Lucy had woken up with a headache and a stiff neck and something weird in her lower back. Stress. Wincing, she got on the hotel-room floor and did the stretching and yoga moves Grace Chang taught her and deep breathing to get calm.

She was ready. She'd been working on the piece for more than three months; time enough to learn it, memorize it, and make it her own. But she rarely *felt* ready when the moment came.

The stretching helped, but she had trouble stilling her mind. She'd been in plenty of high-pressure situations before, and normally she could summon the combination of fierce determination and deep serenity that made her a winner. Even in the last year or so, when she wasn't so much feeling the love, at go-time she could pull herself together and execute.

She tried meditating; that sometimes worked.

Think one word.

The word she kept landing on: *win.*

Which didn't exactly help.

This particular competition seemed to mean even more to Grandpa Beck than usual. Maybe because Lucy's mom had applied for it a bunch of times back when she'd tried to have the kind of career Lucy did. Maybe because he was getting older and would probably have to cut back on his travel before the next Prague came around. It wasn't held every year.

She was getting less relaxed, not more.

Come on, Lucy, a word. A neutral word.

Table, banana, muffin...

Banana muffin.

She was hungry. She got up off the floor, rolled her neck again, did a few toe touches, and went out into the main part of the suite. Both her dad and grandfather were awake; Grandpa dressed and standing by the window, looking out onto the city. Her dad sat on the sofa where he'd slept, still in his white hotel robe. "Did you order breakfast?" she asked him.

"Not yet."

She picked up the folder of hotel services and dropped herself down next to him to look at the menu. "Can I? Grandpa," she said over her shoulder, "what do you want?"

He didn't turn. To the window he said, "Nothing for me."

Lucy raised her eyebrows at her dad. Grandpa Beck ate oatmeal and fruit every morning like it was a religious duty. But her dad didn't look back at her. Lucy noticed his cell in his hand. "What's wrong?" she asked.

"There isn't anything wrong," Grandpa Beck answered. He finally came away from the window and stood in front of them. "I changed my mind. Order me some bacon and eggs, Lucy. Over *easy*. Make *sure* that is clear."

"Stefan..." Lucy's dad started.

"What's going on? Is it Grandma?"

"Everything is fine," her grandfather said.

"I want to talk to her."

"She's still resting."

Lucy said to her father, "Just long enough to hear her voice."

"Lucy." He rubbed the back of his neck. "She can't. She—"

"Talking requires too much breath," Grandpa interjected. "We need to put her out of our minds for the day, Lucy. Focus on your performance. Get through this round. Tomorrow, we'll see."

"We'll see what?" *Put Grandma out of our minds?* "She'll be okay, right?" Lucy asked.

Sternly, Grandpa Beck said, "Of course."

Lucy's father got up off the sofa. "I'm taking my shower. Only coffee and toast for me, Lucy."

♪

She could win this, she realized, listening to the three competitors who went before her.

Well, maybe not the whole thing, but this round of it.

And she didn't care.

After breakfast she'd gotten her dad to admit that Grandma Beck wasn't doing quite as well as they'd said, that everything wasn't "fine." He claimed not to know the details, though, and repeated Grandpa's advice to focus on her performance. Lucy did her best to put it all out of her mind and, after her shower, got her hair into a complicated updo and went to the concert hall early to warm up on one of the backstage pianos.

Her neck finally loosened, and her headache was mostly gone.

She sat with the other competitors in the front row, stage right. She'd be first up after the intermission.

When it came she stayed in her seat and used the time to think through her piece. Even though she didn't care about winning, she definitely didn't want to embarrass herself in front of all these people and possibly the Czech prime minister, who she heard often attended.

She was Lucy Beck-Moreau. She'd do this.

"Lucy."

Upon hearing her father's voice, she snapped out of her pre-playing trance, assuming he'd come down front to wish her luck. "Hey," she said.

He crouched in front of her. "I have to tell you something. Because . . . I just have to. Grandpa thought we should wait until after, but it's not right. I think you'd hate me."

"It's Grandma."

"It got . . . there's something called sepsis. The pneumonia is bacterial. It's bad." He put one hand on each of her knees. "It mostly happened while we were in-flight here. She's been on a ventilator, and that's why we couldn't call her. She's in the ICU."

Lucy listened, trying to catch up. "Is she going to be okay?"

"Her kidneys have already shut down. Her liver is on its way out. And her heart."

People had started to come back in to take their seats. Laughter. Conversation.

"She's going to die," Lucy said, because he wouldn't. Her father leaned forward, as if to hug her. She pushed him away. "No."

"We were going to tell you today, *poulette*. Right after."

"Why did you change your mind? Why did you change your mind right *now*?" Her shock was turning to panic, and she spoke in a shrieky whisper. "I'm supposed to go up there! Why didn't you tell me last night? Or this morning? What am I supposed to do?"

"You don't have to play."

Now you tell me, Lucy thought. *After all these years. Now you tell me I don't have to.*

Then Grandpa Beck was standing there, his eyes blazing. "Of course she has to play. Lucy, your grandmother would want you to."

The girl who'd played, and not that well, right before intermission sat two chairs away and pretended not to be listening and looking. Others were starting to notice, too: the Beck-Moreaus clustered in an obviously unhappy conversation.

"Stefan," her father said, "let's—"

"Dad, it's too late. I can't just . . . I have to go up."

"Good girl," her grandfather said.

Good girl. She heard the words, but the houselights went down, and so she didn't have to see his face. He'd known that morning, when he said everything was fine. And he'd known the night before, when he said everything was fine.

One of the festival workers came out of the wings to remind the audience to silence their phones and that they weren't allowed to take pictures or video. He said it in Czech, English, French, and German.

He introduced Lucy.

Applause.

She stood. The dark blue dress her mother had helped her pick out felt stiff and too young, and she wished she'd worn something else.

Her body, now, operated on momentum.

Climb the stage stairs. Go to the piano. Sit on the bench; adjust the pedals. Because you're on the program.

Momentum.

Decisions made for her, performances planned a year in advance.

I don't want to go, she'd told her grandmother.

You have to, her mother had said.

She'd been doing what she'd been expected to do all along—working hard, performing well, topping herself, living up.

The audience quieted, getting out the last few coughs, holding their programs still.

Lucy rested her hands in her lap and took deep breaths. All she had to do was play like she always did. Just get through it; then whether she made the next round or not she could gracefully bow out of the rest of the festival, citing a family emergency, and they would be on their way home. People would feel sorry for her and admire her dedication.

Lucy usually kept her eyes straight ahead when playing in public, but this time she turned and stretched until she spotted her grandfather, who always sat where he could see her hands. He nodded once. What kind of heart of stone did it take to sit there and not weep?

And what was she doing at this piano, in front of this audience?

Momentum.

Great-Uncle Kristoff bought a piano and died in the war.

And now she didn't get to say good-bye to her grandmother.

She looked down at her hands on the keys, and they weren't hers anymore. What she did at the piano didn't belong to her. It hadn't for a long time. It didn't make her feel connected to herself or her family or the audience or the universe. It used to. When had that stopped? Before this trip. Too long ago to remember.

She lifted her arms. She could play and avoid a scene, then deal with this in private twenty minutes from now. Not make waves.

Or.

She could make a wave. A big one.

The audience stirred, impatient.

And Lucy stood, scooting the piano bench back. She faced her grandfather and father for a moment so they could see her calm, her certainty. This wasn't panic. Not stage fright. Or even shock about her grandma. Nothing but her own decision, her own will, carrying her into the dark wings of the stage. A cluster of festival workers stepped aside as she passed. One said, "Ms. Beck-Moreau? Are you all right?"

"Yes."

She walked until she found a door and, with no idea where it led, opened it.

It took her straight out into an alleyway, the sky bright, the air with a foreign tang. She walked down the alley and out onto the streets of Prague and kept going, getting looks from people who must have wondered what she was doing in that dress, with her hair up and sprayed stiff, like an escapee from prom.

After a few blocks, she cried. For her grandmother and for herself.

Then she saw her surroundings. The city was a miracle of stone and arches, spires and water. Lucy took in the beauty and thought about all of the places around the world she'd been without really seeing them. There was never any time. What else had she been missing? Besides cities, besides school, besides her grandmother's death? What else? What?

She didn't have any money on her and didn't know where she was going. Eventually she got completely lost, and her feet killed from walking all day in flimsy flats, and she found a cab to take her back to the hotel. The concierge covered the fare; he knew who she was.

After her father alternately hugged her in relief and yelled at her for scaring him, she'd had to face her grandfather. Whose expression was impassive when he said, "I take this as your final decision, Lucy. Do not come to me tomorrow and say that you've changed your mind."

And that was the end of that.

Momentum: stopped.

7a.

Will had gone back downstairs to Gus, and Lucy lay on her bed in the dark until she was sure he'd left the house. She listened to her breath, felt the way her fingers interlaced and rested on her stomach.

Do you want to play again? Ever?

His question scared her.

Just like his "Now you" on Sunday night had scared her and made her run.

Because underneath the surprise of being called out in front of everyone, underneath her determination to never let her grandfather think she had any regrets about Prague, underneath the agitation of being cajoled...

She'd wanted to do it.

For the first time in eight months, she wanted to sit down at the piano, and play.

8.

Lucy was nearly late again on Wednesday; she swooshed into class just as the bell rang, the last to arrive. When Mr. Charles saw her, he smiled and said, "Close shave. Next pumpkin bread on me."

Mary Auerbach, from her seat in front, paused in the unloading of her bag to look at them for a couple of seconds, then at Lucy, with her trademark *I know every single thing that's going on in this school, but what's this?* expression. Which Lucy ignored. She settled into her desk in the middle of the room and tried to focus.

English. School. Reyna. Being Mr. Charles's pet.

A week ago those things had been enough. With piano behind her, she was under the radar at home, and that's how she liked it. Better to be the object of disappointment than have to constantly pretend to care about something she didn't.

Unless she still did.

"Lucy?" Mr. Charles stood near her desk. "You look like you want to say something."

"I do?"

A couple of people laughed.

"About what?" she asked.

He held up his copy of *Othello*.

"Oh. No. Sorry."

"I'm going to call on you again in about five minutes, okay?"

"Okay."

She stared at her book, the words on the page turning into musical notes in her imagination.

♪

By lunchtime Lucy mostly felt normal again. She'd spent second period explaining to herself why whatever she was feeling didn't matter. It wasn't like she'd ever be able to sit down at the Hagspiel again, as if she belonged there as much as Gus did. No way would her grandfather sit by and watch that happen.

And she didn't even want that. She was just experiencing a little nostalgia was all. She should be enjoying her freedom, not daydreaming about being back in the cage.

Carson found Lucy and Reyna at their second-floor table. "I need to be with sane people," he said, dropping his bag on the floor.

"And you picked us?" Lucy asked.

"My boys will *not* stop talking about Halo, and also Soon-Yi Pak is stalking me."

"Wait," Reyna said. "Weren't *you* stalking *her?*"

"Yes. Yes, I was. Then I actually sat at her table and found out she can't eat cheese or wheat or tomatoes or peanuts or pork or sugar and this whole list of other stuff. I do not have time for that."

Lucy pulled out her own lunch, which in fact included a peanut butter sandwich on wheat bread and an orange. "Everyone's got flaws."

"Wrong. I decided Jules Shanahan is perfect, but she never eats lunch on campus, and we have zero classes together."

"Which is why she seems perfect to you," Lucy said. "You're scared of real, up-close girls."

Carson gestured to Reyna and Lucy. "Hello, do I look scared of you guys?"

"We don't count."

"Anyway, be happy you're alone," Reyna said. "Love is hell and will end in a fight." She gave them the update on her parents' divorce: Her mother's lawyer was on a two-week vacation in Italy, so everything was on hold. "I just want it to be over," she said.

Lucy half listened and half focused on trying to peel her orange all in one strip while Reyna went on about how her dad suddenly wanted them to all go to temple together, getting way too into the family-therapy stuff and "expressing his feelings" to Reyna and her sister. "He's constantly asking us how we're doing. He doesn't get that it's too late."

"Men," Carson said disdainfully.

"It's not a joke."

"I know. Sorry. Lay your divorce woes on me, and I will joke no more."

"That's it for today," Reyna said.

Carson looked to Lucy. "So what's going on with you?"

She held up her orange peel. "This. Bow to me."

"Nice."

"Lucy didn't tell you about Temnikova dying?" Reyna asked.

"Who?"

"My brother's piano teacher."

"Lucy gave her mouth-to-mouth."

"Lucky lady," Carson said. "Except for the dying part."

"They already replaced her," Lucy said.

66

Reyna raised her eyebrows. "Whoa. Whiplash."

"The guy they got is like…" Lucy shrugged. "Young."

"Cute?"

Lucy got out her phone and looked up Will's head shot online. She passed it to Reyna, who said, "He's not *that* young. Or cute."

She handed the phone to Carson. "I have no opinion," he said.

"Cute is as cute does," Lucy said, taking back her phone. Her standards of attraction were…different from her peers, as far as she could tell. She didn't find any of the so-called hot guys at school very interesting, and she was pretty sure she was the only person at Speare who understood Mr. Charles's appeal. For her it was a combination of kindness and smartness and good humor. And the eyes. Something in the eyes. It all came together to make his face more than the sum of its parts. It was kind of the same way with Will. She didn't know him that well yet, but she could tell he had one of those personalities that might make up for whatever was missing.

"Anyway, it's supposed to be nice this weekend," Reyna said. "We should do something."

Carson scrolled through his phone with his thumb. "When you say 'we,' am I actually invited, too, or are you talking about you and Lucy like usual? I mean, should I be paying attention right now or tuning you out and pretending my feelings aren't hurt?"

"The first one."

They made a plan to get Carson after Lucy's orthodontist appointment and drive down to Half Moon Bay, in Reyna's car, while she still had it. It was another potential casualty of the divorce, since the lease was in Dr. Bauman's name.

It would be good to get out of the house and be reminded there was more to life than what went on there.

♪

When she got home after school, she went in the back door, sweaty from her walk up the hill. Martin sat on a stool at the kitchen island, his notebook and a cup of tea in front of him. He'd worked for their family forever; Grandma Beck had hired him when Lucy was a baby, after Martin had just turned forty.

"There she is," he said, looking up briefly. "I'm making a grocery list. Anything you need?"

Lucy set her bag in the serving pantry and inventoried the snack situation. "Can you get pistachios? And some hot chocolate? The spicy kind."

He jotted a note with his fountain pen. Martin never used a roller-ball or gel pen, and most definitely not an old-school ballpoint. One shelf on the spice rack was totally dedicated to storing his little bottles of ink—mostly shades of blue and purple. Once, when Lucy was a kid, she'd taken a bottle of ink up to her room to play with, dipping her fingers in it and making abstract art in one of her schoolbooks. The ink didn't wash off her hands for a couple of days, but Martin never got her in trouble with her parents about it, which made her love him.

"I'll hide the nuts from your mom," he said. "She thinks they're fattening."

"Did she say something about my weight?" Lucy studied herself in the upper oven door. Same as always. Not gaunt, not chubby.

"No, sweetie. About *her* weight." Martin set down his pen

and ran his hand over the gray stubble that dotted his shaved head. "So what do you think of the new teacher?"

Lucy turned away from her reflection. "I don't know. I mean, Gus loves him. That makes me happy."

"*Mm.*"

"What do you think?"

Martin folded his arms on the kitchen island. "Zoya Temnikova was an extraordinary woman. You probably don't realize this, but she and I got to know each other in the way only two employees of the household can."

"Martin. No one thinks of you as an 'employee of the household.'"

He smiled. "Okay. The point is I admired her. I'm sad she's gone. And I'll miss the bottle of Stoli she gave me every Christmas." He straightened up and tore his grocery list off of his notepad. "That said, I think Will is exactly what Gus needs. And I'll tell you this: Your grandmother would have absolutely adored him."

"How do you know?" Lucy asked. She suspected he was right. "You've only met him like twice."

"I just do. The two of them are—would be—kindred spirits."

9.

For the rest of the week, Lucy made a point of not being home when Will was there. She didn't want to hear any follow-up questions, invitations to play, any more comments about how tragic it was that she'd quit. Each day she went to CC's after school and picked up coffee for her and Mr. Charles, then did homework in his room while he graded papers. She felt safe with him; no surprises.

When Saturday morning arrived, she balked at the idea of seeing Dr. Bauman, Reyna's dad. It would be her first visit to the office since the more sordid details of the divorce had come out. How were you supposed to look people in the face when they knew that *you* knew something they—and you—wished you didn't know?

"I could probably just stop wearing it." Lucy sat at the kitchen island bolting down cereal, her mom across from her, working on her laptop. Gus and her dad were off doing some father-son thing that Lucy suspected involved doughnuts they'd never confess to.

"Wearing what?"

"My retainer."

Her mother looked up. "You can't stop *now*. That would be like quitting the marathon at the twenty-fifth mile." Their eyes met for a second as they both thought the obvious: It wouldn't be the first time.

Lucy let it pass. "Maybe I could go to someone else."

"I know. It's unpleasant." Her mother's eyes drifted up to Lucy's hair, which declared with every flyaway that she hadn't been using the silk pillowcase.

"I used to look forward to seeing him," Lucy said. She'd always, always liked Dr. Bauman. Of all the dads she knew, he was the cutest and nicest. He had the black hair and intense blue eyes Reyna had inherited, and he was funny and charming. Hot moms flocked to him for a reason.

Lucy wanted her to admit that it was more than unpleasant. That something had been lost. Instead, her mom went back to typing and said, "You don't have to think of him as a role model. Just go and get it over with."

"But it's so..." *Sad.* "Never mind." She should know better than to look to her mom for consolation, about basically anything.

The walk to Reyna's house felt long. Even though it was only seven or eight blocks, the last couple were hills. When she arrived, she stood in front of the office entrance and thought again about ditching the appointment and going straight up to Reyna's room. But that would only get her in trouble, and she'd have to come back later.

The new receptionist was a guy. A handy way to thwart any more inappropriateness while the divorce remained unsettled. "Hi," Lucy said. "I have a ten o'clock appointment."

"Make yourself comfortable. Dr. Bauman will be right with you."

She sat in one of the wingback chairs that were impossible to make oneself comfortable in, texting Reyna, until Dr. Bauman came out of the inner office, smiling. "Lucy, you get more beautiful every time I see you."

He'd been saying it to her forever, even during her über-awkward years when it had been an obvious lie. Before it always felt like friendly dad-talk. Now she couldn't help but cringe away from his hug the best she could without being rude. "Thanks," she said.

"Take a seat, honey." He steered her by the shoulders into his office.

What proceeded was the same kind of checkup he always did, but the way he put his fingers on her lips and the smell of his latex gloves, the way his leg brushed against hers slightly when he had to reach for her chart, the little *mmm-hmm* noises he made while inspecting her mouth... suddenly everything formerly innocent seemed tainted by what she knew. The former receptionist. Soon-Yi Pak's mom. There were others.

The second he took his hand off her face, she turned away from him, a reflex. Not subtle. She pretended to study the poster of straight teeth, a dozen tiled pictures of lips drawn back from red gums.

Dr. Bauman rolled his chair to his desk, snapped off his gloves, and made some notes in her file. "Any headaches or any other kind of pain? Especially when you wake up in the morning?"

"No."

"Everything else going okay?"

"Yes."

"How's Gus?"

"Fine." She ran her hands over the seam at the knee of her jeans.

She thought he'd say something about her teeth, the kind of adjustment he would make to the retainer, increasing or decreasing the time she wore it.

"Hey. You threw up in my Jag when you were nine. I helped you put on a funeral for your guinea pig. We came to your concerts." He sounded hurt and tired. "This is me, Lucy."

She made herself look at him, and nodded.

"Things are always more complicated than you think," he continued. "You'll find out when you're older."

She hoped not.

"All right. Give me five minutes here, and then we're done till next time." He smiled a sad version of his old, winning smile. "I assume you're going up to see Rey. Tell her I said hi."

♪

Reyna had divided the contents of her closet into several piles. She pointed to one of the smaller ones. "That's stuff for you to try on. Mostly tops, obviously, since your legs are miles longer than mine. There are a couple of skirts, though, that might not be indecent."

"Thanks."

Lucy sat on the edge of the bed awhile, debating whether or not to pass on Dr. Bauman's greeting. Reyna's mood seemed a little...volatile. She whipped a sparkly cocktail dress off of a hanger and held it up. "My dad bought me this for the museum fund-raiser. Kinda slutty, don't you think?"

"It looks like the kind of thing people wear to that."

She threw the dress on a nearby pile. "Discard."

Lucy reached down to pick it up. It was so pretty, a kind of ruby red that looked absolutely gorgeous with Reyna's Snow White coloring. "Maybe you should save this. Put in a 'deal with later' pile?"

Reyna stood still for a second to stare at the dress, then shook her head and went back into the closet, jerking hangers across the rod. "I'm sorry, but I just hate him right now. And everything that reminds me of him." She glanced over her shoulder at Lucy. "Clothes. Try them on, please. It will cheer me up."

Some of Reyna's favorite tops were in the pile; for example, the Burberry polo with the checked sleeves she'd just gotten a month ago. Lucy put it on to make her happy; a tight squeeze across the chest. Then she noticed Reyna standing on tiptoe, grasping for some boxes of shoes on an upper closet shelf. Lucy went in. "Here." She reached the boxes easily and handed them to Reyna, whose face crumpled as she clutched them to her.

Lucy took the boxes back, set them on the floor, and put her arms around Reyna, who said, "Oh my God, Lucy. It's so awful. You don't know."

"I'm sorry." Reyna's stomach trembled a little against hers, as if she were holding back a bigger sob.

"We were, like, a happy family. I thought we were."

"I know. Me too."

Reyna let go, and Lucy got the box of tissues off the nightstand. Reyna took one and blew her nose. "And the worst is explaining it to Abby without *explaining* it. Me and Mom trying to be careful what we say. We can't be all, 'Daddy is a lying, cheating sack of crap,' you know?"

"Right."

"I hate men. I seriously do." Reyna threw the tissue on the floor and took another, and while blowing her nose a second time finally got a good look at Lucy in the polo. She laugh-sobbed. "You can't wear that. When did your boobs get so awesome? It's obscene."

"I'll keep it for you. And the dress, okay? And whatever else. I'll keep them with my stuff at home in case someday you realize you actually want them."

Reyna nodded and hugged Lucy again briefly. "You're a good friend. The best."

"You too." Lucy stripped off the polo and put her own shirt back on. "Let's get out of here. We can fix this mess later."

♪

They picked up Carson and wound down Highway 1 in Reyna's Mini, Lucy up front and Carson folded into the tiny backseat. To their right the Pacific sparkled deep blue, and the midday light cut depth and shadow into the crags of the bluff. Mesmerizingly. Gorgeously.

Lucy thought:

Beautiful beautiful beautiful.

It had been too long since she had that thought, that feeling. Of joy and things being right or at least okay, because even if your own life wasn't perfect, there was this *world*. And you were *living* in it, somehow, away from parents and classes and practice rooms.

"The wonder of beauty, in all its forms," she said aloud, to feel the shape of Will's words from the toast coming out of her own mouth.

"What?" Reyna shouted, over Usher, over the wind blowing in through the windows, which were down a couple of inches, over the noisy car.

"Nothing."

There had to be a way to know wonder again, without it needing to be connected to piano. More time in nature, maybe, like this? Helping others? She could sign up for a well-digging trip to the Sudan or something.

"No, I just can't hear you!"

Carson lurched forward to yank the jack to Reyna's phone out of the dashboard. "*Anyway,*" he said, tapping Lucy's shoulder. "What were you saying?"

"It's nice out. That's all." She turned awkwardly in the bucket seat to see if he had his phone in his hand, like always. He did. "Which you'd notice if you'd put that thing away for five minutes."

"Ha-ha, well, guess what, I *did* notice and was updating my followers on how brilliant the view is right now."

He waved the phone at her; she grabbed it. "Your *followers*? Well, now I'm telling your followers that you're going away to experience life for a couple of hours."

"Lucy! Give it!"

"You sound like my little sister, Carson Lin," Reyna said, laughing.

Lucy dodged Carson's hands coming at her over both shoulders, leaning forward until she shut down the phone and stuffed it into the bottom of her bag. "There."

Carson slumped back. "Wow. I don't even know what to say about this. I feel violated."

"It's called an intervention," Reyna said. "You'll live. Now somebody plug my Usher back in."

"My turn to pick the music." Lucy connected the stereo cord to her phone and thumbed through screens until she found Vivaldi and hit Play.

As soon as the opening notes filled the car, Reyna groaned. "Didn't you get enough of this for the first fifteen years of your life?"

"Maybe instead of assuming you hate it, you could listen."

"It's not bad," Carson conceded.

"*Shh.*"

The allegro of the "Winter" concerto began. Lucy loved this piece. Obsessively.

She turned it up and rolled down her window all the way, the wind whipping cold, almost painful. The violins made their steady advance toward the moment about a minute and a half into the piece when they exploded into the main theme. That was Lucy's favorite part: the microsecond between anticipation and full-born joy.

Joy.

Joy on steroids.

Lucy closed her eyes and reached her arm out of the car to feel the air. And reached and reached and let out a yell. Tentative at first, then louder. Vaguely aware of Carson and Reyna laughing, she beat her hand on the car door and opened her eyes again, the wind stinging tears into them, the ocean relentlessly dazzling.

The world was full of beauty.

She wanted to grab hold of it and take it all down into her

bones. Yet always it seemed beyond her grasp. Sometimes only by a little, like now. The thinnest membrane.

Usually, though, by miles.

You couldn't expect to be that kind of happy all the time. She knew that.

But sometimes, you could. Sometimes, you should be allowed a tiny bit of joy that would stay with you for more than five minutes. That wasn't too much to ask. To have a moment like this, and be able to hold on to it.

To cross that membrane, and feel alive.

10.

Her legs: lead. She tried to run anyway, and it seemed like the hundredth time around the track, at least. Her body was huge and clumsy, and Mr. Charles appeared to be the coach, only he never looked up from his clipboard. Was she invisible? And, she realized, she had to pee. *Now.* She found a public bathroom, but the toilets in every stall were flooded or nasty, and none of the stall doors closed all the way. She would have to lean forward and hold the door while squatting in filth.

Someone was trying to get in, pushing at the door, pushing, saying her name, *Lucy, Lucy, get out of there, Lucy . . .*

"Lucy?"

She opened her eyes. Her father stood over the bed, jacket on.

"Shit," she muttered, wincing at the pressure in her bladder. "What time is it?"

"Time to go."

"What *day* is it?"

"Monday, chicken. Up, up, up. *Allez.*"

She flung off the covers and raced to the bathroom.

♪

"Mom got tired of waiting, so she and Gus left." They were in her dad's little Audi, Lucy's book bag crowding her legs, random papers spilling out of it. "I think you're going to have a conversation with her when you get home today."

"I'm sure I am."

She was desperate to stop for coffee and figured her dad would probably go for it, but she could absolutely not turn up late to English again with a coffee cup in her hand.

"Everything okay?" He nudged her knee with his forearm.

He had a knack for asking that kind of question in moments with zero time for what would come after "no," so she always found herself saying, as she did now, "Yeah."

They were sort of strangers lately. He rarely seemed to be around, even though he didn't have what you'd call a job other than being Gus's manager and also being on the board of a few of Grandpa Beck's trusts. Anyway, how could she explain? She barely understood it herself. *What if I want to play again?* She imagined asking it. Of all the people in her house, her dad would be the easiest to say it to.

"Anxiety dream," she said. They were a block from Speare.

"Ah. Test today?"

She shook her head. "Just life, I guess."

"Life," her dad repeated, stopping in front of the entrance. "That'll do it." He leaned over and gave her a kiss on the cheek, his face rough. She caught a whiff of coffee on his breath; her senses perked up. Maybe she could squeeze in a CC's run after English. "Apologize to your mom later, okay? About being late."

"Dad . . ."

"Just do it."

♪

She walked into English, and Mr. Charles, who stood at the front of the room with his back to the door, didn't even turn around. "Is that Lucy?" he asked the class. The tone of his voice stopped her from going any farther than the doorway.

The class gave him a collective affirmation. Mary Auerbach had a look on her face that was possibly a smirk.

He raised his hand and, still without turning, waved it. "Bye-bye."

Wait. What? Was he serious? He should look at her, at least. He should turn around and see her and . . .

He couldn't just kick her out of class.

"I'm . . . sorry, I . . ."

Mr. Charles lifted his hand again. "Nope."

Mary snickered.

Bitch. Lucy turned on her heels and pushed through the door, out into the hall, humiliated and furious. She knew it was her own fault for being late, but did he have to do that in front of the whole class? Especially to her. Who else brought him coffee and pumpkin bread and understood his lectures the way he wanted them to? No one, that's who.

She walked down the hall, wiping away a few embarrassed tears. She should probably go into the library or something and work on her paper or other homework. Except her stomach growled, and she needed caffeine, and most of all she wanted to get out of the building.

Maybe Reyna would be willing to cut second period and go

get breakfast. But in the middle of texting her, Lucy realized she didn't want to talk to anyone.

She left school, alone.

♪

Lucy thought she'd be safe sneaking in through the kitchen around ten thirty—her mom so rarely did anything in that part of the house unless Martin was off. But both she and Martin were there, in the middle of a conversation that stopped abruptly when she walked in. "Don't try to tell me you're sick," she said. "Dad said you were fine."

"I'm . . . I was. I don't feel very good now." Truth. She'd stopped at a diner between school and home for coffee, eggs, bacon, but her stomach still ached every time she thought of Mr. Charles's *Nope*.

Her mother narrowed her eyes. Lucy readied herself to fabricate some additional symptoms. But then her mother came over to her and stood close, and tucked Lucy's hair behind her left ear. "Well, my aunt Birgit passed away this morning. We just got the call."

"Oh." Grandma Beck's much older sister, who'd never left Germany. Lucy'd met her only once, years ago, while there on tour. "What happened?"

"She was ninety-seven is what happened." Her mother's eyes met hers, and Lucy saw tears there, or at least some grief, and didn't know why it should surprise her, but it did.

"Sorry," she said, and hugged her mother. Which felt unnatural. She held on an extra few seconds, anyway.

Her mother stepped back and took a short, loud breath

through her nose. "Grandpa and I are going to go to Dresden for the memorial. It's been a long time since he went back home. And we'll spread Grandma's ashes."

Lucy caught Martin's eye; he looked down. The ashes had been a question for months now. When Grandma had first died, there'd been talk of getting a niche at the columbarium or spreading them at sea. Then Grandpa didn't want to discuss it and kept them in his room, and Lucy figured that was where they'd stay. "Why not here?" Lucy asked. She didn't like the idea of her grandmother's remains being that far away.

"It's where she was born. Where she and Grandpa met. She always wanted to go back after the reunification."

I don't think this is how she pictured it. "Is Grandpa home?"

"He's probably in his study. Why?" Her mother sounded suspicious.

"Why do you think? I want to talk to him."

"He's tired, Lucy."

"I'm not going to ask him to go jogging." She wanted to see about the ashes; maybe there was a way to be a part of the ceremony even if she couldn't be there. Given how she hadn't had the chance to say good-bye, he owed it to her.

"All right, smarty. Then you're getting in bed, since you're sick enough to come home from school."

♪

Her grandfather's study used to be a bewitching place for Lucy. Mysterious. The walls were lined with records, reel-to-reels, CDs, cassette tapes. Mostly records—vinyl, with foldout covers and long liner notes. They had a smell. Mold, dust, a little bit of

Pour Monsieur. He'd taught her how to use his turntable. He wasn't stingy or controlling that way; he'd wanted her to know his collection as well as he did. Once upon a time.

He wasn't actually there at the moment. Maybe napping. Which was fine, because now that she'd reached the threshold of his space, she'd lost her nerve about Grandma. She went in, anyway, nudging the door open with her foot.

It was dark. He kept the blinds closed to protect the recordings from sun and heat. She went to his desk and clicked on the banker's lamp; a pool of light warmed the room. The items on his desk never changed: a blotter, a stack of index cards, his pen set and stand, the framed picture of Grandma. Lucy sat in his chair and touched everything and neatened his stack of index cards.

They were for his catalog.

Every single recording in the room had an index card that went with it, and written on that card was his critique, what Lucy thought of as his "I know better than anyone" notes.

Sometimes his careful cursive covered the whole card. Sometimes there were just a few words, about the piece or the recording or the conductor or the soloist:

A disappointment.

First movement compelling but as a whole fails.

Colorful and energetic in the scherzo, with an appropriately sorrowful adagio. Lovely acoustics for a live recording. I would have liked to have been there.

Mediocrity wins again! Why does this man still have a career?

She got up and scanned the shelves until she found the recording she was looking for, exactly where it should be, with the Early Romantics: Schubert and Schumann, Berlioz, Verdi. It was an LP of a lesser-known composer from that era, something Lucy'd discovered years ago during a time of insatiable longing to know everything her grandfather did. When she had cared about her music more than anything.

It had its index card, too, of course. She slid the record out and put it on the turntable to play, easing the noise-canceling headphones on, and stood there reading the album's index card, almost from memory:

Acceptable recording of a beautiful piece. The execution of the free cadenza is astute, and lives up to what a free cadenza should be. Jubilant. Vivid. It brings to mind Hannah. Whenever I listen, I find myself remembering our barefoot walks through the leaves in those first few autumns of our marriage, and how she would let her long hair fall down her back. I always wanted to reach out to touch it, and now I cannot remember if I did.

How time betrays us.

Lucy had often wondered why he left something so personal in a place he knew she'd find it. There were other personal notes and memories scattered throughout this collection, but none like this. The conclusion she'd come to was that this was how he expressed himself. Maybe the only way.

If she didn't know he'd notice, she'd steal the card.

The music described on it now flowed into her ears, and her heart. She imagined her grandfather and grandmother, Hannah, walking barefoot through leaves. The cool crunch of it. Her grandmother's dark hair, which Lucy had only known as bobbed and gray, cascading down her back and her grandfather extending a hand to touch it, and then changing his mind.

And she wondered what his last line had meant, and if he'd ever told her grandmother how this music made him feel.

That's what music did. It made you feel. If you were Grandpa Beck, it *allowed* you to feel. Listening to it and reading his words and imagining how his memories felt to him let Lucy see him as more than the stony heart who'd sat in an audience while his wife died.

Music, her grandfather always told her, was language. A special language, a gift from the Muses, something all people are born understanding but few people can thoroughly translate.

She could, he'd told her.

Listening and playing were two different things; each involved its own kind of translation. She listened now, and translated.

The leaves. Their naked feet. Her grandmother's freed hair. Her grandfather's almost-touch.

Yes, the world was beautiful.

But music made that beauty personal.

Nothing else could do that. Nothing.

11.

That afternoon she snuck downstairs during Gus's time with Will and lurked in the hall outside the piano room. She recognized the relentless, steady rhythms of Bach. Not her favorite. A ricercar she'd once done in competition herself.

Then the playing stopped, and Will said, "Okay, think about the phrasing. Emphasize the strangeness of that diminished seventh, right?"

More playing. Different. Better.

"Great," Will had said. "Did you hear that?"

"Yeah." Gus sounded excited, like he'd made a discovery. He played the section again.

Lucy leaned against the wall and went through the piece in her head along with Gus, sense memory in her fingers, a snapshot of the music in her inner vision.

"If you relate these two measures to these two measures," Will said, stopping Gus again, "what have you got?"

"Um..."

"Hang on a sec, Gus. Keep working that phrase."

The door to the music room opened, and Will leaned out. He looked nice, in jeans and a navy-blue long-sleeved T-shirt. "Oh," he said. "It's you. I had this feeling someone was out here. Thought it might be your mom or grandpa. You know, spying."

Lucy stood up straight. "Sorry." She peeked through the door; she could see a sliver of Gus from the back, working through the music with full concentration.

"It's fine. I'm happy to see you. You sort of disappeared after we talked last week."

"Been busy."

"Did you . . . want to come in?"

She shook her head but didn't move. He pulled the door most of the way closed behind him. "Are you okay?"

"I came home early from school today. But I mean, yeah. I'm not sick."

There was a certain way that he studied her, like he had on the stairs, like he had the night they met, that made her feel like he was always willing to hear more of whatever she wanted to say.

"I was in my grandpa's study earlier," she continued. "Listening to this piece, and . . ." She touched her hair, touched her face. Glanced over her shoulder to make sure no one was coming. Listened to Gus diligently practicing. "You know what you asked me? About if I ever want to play?"

He nodded.

"Do you think I actually could?"

"Like would you be capable?" he asked, with a puzzled smile. "Of course. Eight months isn't short, but it isn't that long, either. Not for someone with your talent."

"No. As in . . . *could* I . . ." It was too hard to explain. "Never mind."

She started to turn.

"You mean would you be allowed," Will said, keeping his voice low. "After the way you quit."

Their eyes met. She waited for an answer.

He smiled a little. "No one is going to arrest you."

Lucy put her hand on the wall, running it over the textured plaster. "I know," she said, unsure of what she'd thought he could tell her. "Sorry. You're busy."

"It's okay. I mean I am, but, look, whatever you decide, will you do me a favor? If you need to talk about this stuff, if you want advice or an opinion or just an ear, think of me as a friend?"

She let her arm fall to her side. "Really?"

He nodded. "Really."

"Okay."

"Good," he said. "I'd better go back in. Meanwhile you could try imagining what it would be like to play again, for yourself. No mom or grandpa. No competing. Forget all that stuff. Imagine: you." He pointed. "Only you. And the music."

♪

That night, Lucy did imagine it.

She didn't sleep, trying to picture things the way Will had said. Only her and the music. That took a lot of effort, but she got there, mentally, and it felt . . .

Well, it felt painful. Because it seemed impossible.

Where she stumbled was the part where her grandfather would find out.

I take this as your final decision, Lucy.

It hadn't been a question; she'd never had a chance to say whether it was or wasn't.

Never had the chance to be sure.

Intermezzo

When she'd arrived home from Prague, she had an opportunity to see her grandmother's body before the cremation. The whole idea seemed gruesome. It wouldn't change anything. Her father went, her grandfather, her mother, Martin. Lucy decided to stay home with Gus, who hadn't wanted to go, either.

"I saw her at the hospital," he told Lucy, while they were down in the TV room, reclined in their favorite spots on the sectional, the TV on but muted. "Right after."

"What was the last thing she said to you?" Lucy asked.

"I don't remember."

She sat up. "What do you mean you don't remember?"

"Don't yell at me. I don't remember. She wasn't talking that much. She was kind of spaced-out."

Lucy leaned back again. "Okay."

They stared at the silent TV. Then Gus said, "You really just walked off the stage?"

"Yep."

"Did you feel . . ." He swirled his finger around near his temple. "Crazy? Like you didn't know what you were doing?"

"No. I knew."

"What did you—"

"Gus, I don't want to talk about it." She stood and unmuted the television, then left to go up to her room.

She found herself stopping in to look at the Hagspiel. She went right to the bench. The honey walnut of the piano begged to be touched, but she refused it.

Carefully, so as not to make actual contact with the wood, she removed the various scores she'd been working on before leaving for Prague, separating them from Gus's work and making a pile that she placed in the cabinet where they kept their music. She never wanted to see notes on a page again.

She scanned the room for any possessions she might have left behind, and collected them: the special pillow she used for long practice sessions, the nail file on the side table next to the love seat, a stack of CDs.

When sure she'd removed all evidence of herself, she walked out and closed the door behind her.

12.

In the car Tuesday morning—on time—she said, "I heard you working on the Bach yesterday, Gus. Sounded good."

"I started it with Temnikova. Like a month ago."

"You're learning fast."

Their mother's eyes flicked to Lucy's in the rearview mirror for the briefest second. Then, glancing at Gus, she said, "Is *that* what you're doing for the showcase? I wonder if you should do something you've known longer. I'll talk to Will about it." They were at a stoplight; she thumbed a reminder into her phone.

After they dropped off Gus at his school, she asked Lucy, "Do you think the Bach is a good idea? It's so complicated. Remember how you..."

"Yeah, I remember." She'd done that same piece at a competition once and had gotten a little confused in the middle. The motif repeated in so many ways, it was easy to get lost.

"I worry it's a bit...dry. And technically ambitious? It's a showcase, a fund-raiser. Not a competition. People want to be entertained."

Lucy stared out the window. *Only you. And the music.* Easy for Will to say. "We wouldn't want to let down the all-important 'people.'"

With an exasperated sigh, her mother said, "You know what I mean, Lucy."

"Yes, you're right. No point in playing at all if you can't be perfect every single time, I always say."

Whatever last words her mother had, she didn't say them. She stayed silent all the way to Speare, where Lucy got out and slammed the car door, hoping Mr. Charles didn't totally hate her for the day before.

♪

She was early. Mary Auerbach and Mr. Charles were the only ones in the classroom, at his desk, laughing about something as Lucy walked in. She kept her eyes ahead and went straight to her seat to unload her bag. They kept chatting. Lucy took the Munro book Mr. Charles had loaned her up to them, interrupting. "Thanks for this. I know it's your own special copy. Do you want it back? Or..."

Mary rolled her eyes and went to her seat. A few other students trickled in.

"Well, eventually. But you keep it as long as you need to, Lucy."

"I'm sorry I was late again," she muttered, holding the book to her chest. "After I promised I'd try harder."

"Thank you for saying so."

She waited for more. A *still friends* or an *I know you can do better.*

He raised his eyebrows, as if wondering why she was standing there.

"I had a quick question about my paper." She put her

93

fingertips on his desk and looked at the in-box where she'd left the note and the pumpkin bread eons ago.

"If it's quick." The bell would ring in a minute; the classroom filled.

"It's..." She studied the two or three chest hairs that showed above his shirt collar. And realized she didn't care about her paper anymore, or about impressing him. How could she have ever thought she'd find the same thing in writing an English paper that she'd had with music? "I forgot what I was going to say."

"When you remember ask me again after class?"

"Yeah, okay," she said, suspecting she wouldn't.

♪

At lunch she told Reyna she wanted to hang out after school.

"Let's walk some hills," Reyna said. "I've been stress eating for a month."

They decided to brave the Lyon Street stairs. There were something like three hundred steps, and an amazing view when you made it to the top. Also lots of tourists, because it was that kind of day, the kind postcards were made of, small fluffy clouds floating in a crisp blue sky over multimillion-dollar houses. They did the stairs twice, then Reyna declared they'd earned a trip to Stella to split a piece of cake.

"I don't think it works that way," Lucy said.

"It doesn't. But I want cake."

They found an outdoor table. "My grandma used to bring me here all the time. She almost always got a cream puff."

"You still miss her a lot?" Reyna asked.

"Yeah." She wanted to say more but was pretty sure that if she did, she'd start crying.

Reyna made a sympathetic face, then held a huge forkful of cake up to Lucy's mouth. "Eat this. It will ease the pain."

Lucy opened wide, and Reyna shoved the cake in. "Classy," Lucy said, laughing when she could speak again.

"So how come you wanted to hang out with me instead of with Mr. Charles like usual?"

"Because I miss you, obviously." She picked up her own fork and ate more cake. "Also I think I'm getting over him." She'd always joked with Reyna about her weird crushes, like on the violinist Joshua Bell, whom she stalked once at a music festival in Portland, or her tutor Bennett, even though he was definitely gay.

"Aw. The magic is gone?" Reyna asked.

Lucy shrugged. "A little bit." The sudden absence of her crush felt like more of a loss than she wanted to let on. She didn't understand how that worked, the on/off switch in her subconscious or whatever. Maybe the way he'd acted yesterday pretty much killed it.

"Here's an idea: someone under thirty, someone from school."

"Eh. No offers." Also she couldn't think of one guy at school who interested her. Her last boyfriend and her first kiss had been in eighth grade. Not from school but another pianist— Christian Lundberg, a big Swedish kid with pale eyes and a soft mouth. They both did this charity event in Berkeley, a twenty-four-hour piano play-off with the proceeds going to who knew what, something her mom was into. She and Christian hung out during the breaks, and at around two in the morning, goofy from no sleep and too much sugar, they wandered outside and he asked if she'd be his girlfriend. Just like that. "Will you be my girlfriend?"

Lucy had agreed with an "okay."

They held hands that night, exchanged phone numbers. And had the kind of relationship two busy overachievers tend to have in eighth grade—that is, mostly texting and a few phone calls and then one actual date to a movie. That's where he kissed her. Not during the previews or over the credits, but right in the middle of the story, which Lucy had been enjoying. So she was annoyed, and also the kiss wasn't that great.

"Speare boys are scared of you," Reyna said.

She'd heard that from her before. "Explain to me again why I'd want to go out with anyone who's scared of me?"

Reyna set down her fork. "Okay, maybe not scared. It's more an attitude or something. When you came back last year you were 'that girl in the library who's always drinking coffee' and you never talked to anyone but teachers and me and Carson. And we always eat alone, and you never do any extracurriculars."

"My whole *life* was an extracurricular. I'm tired."

"I know, but before you quit piano, you used to complain about how you wanted to do quote-unquote normal stuff like student council or the Model UN or the tennis team or even *parties*. You do none of that. Which is why you don't know people, and they don't know you, and boys are scared or think you're stuck-up."

"I took that Red Cross class with you," Lucy said. "That was school-sponsored."

"Look how that worked out."

"I guess I'm still adjusting. To my freedom and everything."

Reyna pointed her finger in a fake-menacing way. "Adjust faster. Senior year is coming." Then she signaled with her eyes, and Lucy turned to see what she was looking at. An older woman had approached their table—distinguished, slender, her white hair pulled back into a bun, pink lipstick. She seemed familiar, but Lucy couldn't place her.

"Excuse me," she said, resting a hand on Lucy's shoulder. "I heard your brother on the radio last month. He was just wonderful. Would you tell him?"

Lucy smiled. "Yes, I will. Thank you."

"He should keep at it."

"He is."

"And I hope you girls will consider volunteering for the Opening Gala next year," she told them, before going into the bakery. That's why she looked familiar—the Symphony Gala, which Grandpa Beck wrote a huge check to every year. She ran the thing.

"'He should keep at it,'" Reyna whispered, imitating the woman. "'And not quit, like *some* people.'"

"She might as well have just said it, right?"

Reyna nodded, and stared at Lucy a few seconds before taking the last bite of cake.

"What?" Lucy said.

"Nothing."

"Don't do that, Rey. What?"

"Do you ever...Like, does seeing Gus do all this cool stuff ever make you wish you hadn't quit? That it was still you?" Reyna leaned forward. "I mean, I know you're the perfect big sister and everything. But sometimes, only *sometimes*, do you get jealous?"

"Of the attention? No. Well, maybe a little." She scraped

frosting off the plate with her fork. "But more that he still loves to play." And got to work with a teacher like Will. Grace Chang had been nice, and good, but Will was...

Reyna tilted her head. "Do you think you ever could? Again?"

"I don't know." It was the truth, if not the whole truth.

"Well, I would miss the attention." She stood up and stretched her arms over her head. "But also I'd miss you if you went back to it. It's awesome having you at Speare. Don't leave me again."

"I won't," Lucy promised.

13.

The memorial for Great-Aunt Birgit would be the Monday after Thanksgiving. Lucy's mom and grandpa were going to leave the Wednesday before to help with the arrangements and some issues with the estate and visit distant relatives; her dad would stay with Lucy and Gus.

"I'll talk to Martin about making sure you have all the usual things." Lucy's mother had her phone and laptop out on the table during dinner—a simple Saturday meal of a large salad topped with leftover chicken, an assortment of cheeses, and toasted baguette. Grandpa Beck's reading glasses were perched on the end of his nose as he flipped through the small leather daybook he'd been using and refilling for as long as Lucy could remember.

By "the usual things" Lucy guessed her mom meant apple-and-sausage stuffing, corn soufflé, chocolate pecan pie. But it would be the first Thanksgiving without Grandma. *And* the first one in years without Temnikova, who'd always been their guest at holidays. Now, also, the first without her mom or grandpa.

She pushed some salad around on her plate and looked at her dad. "Can I invite Reyna and Abby?"

Her mother answered before her father could. "Won't they be with their family?"

"I think, with the divorce, it's kind of awkward." She asked her dad again: "So can I?"

"You can invite them, sure, of course." He poured himself more wine and tore off a piece from the baguette. "Invite anyone you want."

"Will and Aruna?" Gus asked.

"Good idea," Lucy said. She'd sat outside the music room during their practice most days that week, on the floor, her back to the wall. Imagining, thinking, listening, her presence unbeknownst to Gus and only sometimes beknownst to Will. On Thursday afternoon, before he left, he'd found her in the kitchen, eating from a bag of tortilla chips.

"Hey there," he'd said.

She'd held out the bag to him. "Hi."

"Thanks." He'd taken a few chips, and they stood there crunching. "This reminds me," he'd said, and then paused. Lucy stopped eating and waited for him to say one of his profound, insightful things. He held up a chip. "I make amazing guacamole."

They'd laughed. "It can't beat Martin's," she'd said.

"So how are you doing?"

She'd shrugged, rolling down the top of the chip bag. "Confused, I guess."

Then he'd torn off a little square from the magnetic notepad Martin kept on the fridge, scribbled something on it, and handed it to her. It was his phone number. "If you ever want to talk. Because, you know, friends call friends."

She'd smiled at the note. "Do friends text friends?"

"They do. As long as friends aren't driving."

"I'm *confused*," she'd joked, "not suicidal."

She hadn't called or texted yet. Not that she hadn't thought about it, but she wasn't sure what she'd say.

Now Grandpa Beck took off his glasses and used them to mark his place in his daybook. "Before we go inviting the whole of creation, let's talk about what we think of Mr. Devi so far."

"He told us to call him Will."

"Yes, fine. Do you think, Gus, that we made the right choice?"

His voice had that slow, low pitch it got before he was about to announce his disapproval. On the other hand, the fact that he asked Gus's opinion was a good sign, and Lucy could tell from the way he turned his best ear toward Gus that he actually cared about the answer.

Gus was emphatic with his "yes."

"He's certainly got an excellent reputation," their dad said. "Peter Blakely called him 'the Miracle Worker' in an article I dug up online." He winked at Gus. "Not that you need a miracle, Gustav."

"Peter Blakely is a blowhard," Grandpa Beck said. "And a sycophant."

"What's that?" Gus asked.

"Someone who makes a career of riding the tails of other people's glory."

"He's a respected journalist," Lucy's father told Gus. "Whom your grandfather happens to hate."

Lucy didn't think there was anyone in the business Grandpa Beck actually *liked*. His enemies, real and imagined, were everywhere.

Then her mother gestured to her. "Lucy heard him working with Gus the other day and thought it was going well."

Her grandfather and father both turned to Lucy.

"You did?" Grandpa Beck asked. "Please share." He folded his hands in front of him and stared, expectant. It was a challenge. Whatever she'd say, he could shoot down solely because she'd quit. Not just that she'd quit, but that she was a Quitter.

She chose not to back down. "He has a kind of fuller, I don't know, musicality. Temnikova didn't really have that, you know. She was great with technique, she—"

"The best," her grandfather said, his gaze unemotional, steady.

"Yeah, maybe, but kind of...cold." She searched for what she meant. "The technique seemed detached from everything else. More what to do than *why* to do it, when—"

"And you know better how this all should go?"

"Dad," Lucy's mother said. "Let her finish."

"It's just amusing to me that Lucy's the expert now," Grandpa Beck said.

She met his eyes. He wasn't unemotional anymore. His face had reddened. She'd thought, for a while, that his anger over everything had passed, and his main feelings for her were disappointment and disinterest. Wrong. His rage was as fresh as it had been that day in Prague when she returned to the hotel.

You entitled little brat. You ungrateful, careless...You think what you did honors your grandmother's life? It disgraces her, Lucy.

"I heard him practicing with her every day," she said. "I've gone to every performance I could. I know as much as you do." She drew herself up, feeling the wood of the dining chair against her back. She tried to remember the quote, the Vladimir Horowitz one that Grace Chang had once written out for her that her grandfather knew and liked. It was at the tip of her memory.

He laughed. "Oh, yes, I'm sure. How do you explain your brother's success, if Temnikova was such a failure as a teacher?"

"I didn't say that."

"Really, Stefan," Lucy's father said. "Enough."

"He's better than everyone else his age. That doesn't mean he's as good as he *can* be." Then she remembered how the quote went: "Brain, heart, and means. 'Without heart, you're a machine.' Will has *heart*. I know it hasn't been long, but you can tell that five seconds after you meet him. And that's what I hear when he's working with Gus."

Gus said, "Yeah."

Lucy wouldn't look away from her grandfather's stare—a silent continuation of that conversation in Prague.

"I have to say," her mother spoke in the tone she used when she wanted the subject changed—loud, cheery, "now that it's getting out that we took Will on, I've yet to hear one negative word about him. And you know what a bunch of gossips these people are."

Yes, we know, Lucy thought.

"We'll see." Grandpa Beck rose from the table. He had to steady himself on the back of his chair for a second, but they all knew better than to express concern or offer help.

"Good night, Grandpa," Gus said.

Lucy watched him walk out.

Brain, heart, means. Her grandfather had two of those. When Grandma Beck died, he lost the third. And Lucy worried that she had, too.

14.

On Monday Lucy still buzzed from the high of standing up to her grandfather.

All of Sunday he'd acted like nothing had happened, that nothing was different. But she felt the shift. For so long she'd kept her mouth shut, believing his unspoken message: Quitting had forfeited any claim she had on music.

This isn't allowed to matter to you anymore.

And she saw, now, that was bullshit.

It did matter to her. Music. It had never stopped mattering.

Imagine there is no Grandpa, Will had said.

Impossible. To deal with piano, she'd have to deal with Grandpa. She'd stood up to him once, and she could probably do it again. But how many more times would it take?

She would need help, from someone who understood.

From the backseat of her mother's car, on the way to school, she sent her first text to Will.

Friend to friend. Ready to talk.

♪

She checked between every class for a reply. The more time that passed without one, the more she questioned herself.

Really? You're just going to start playing again as if it's not that big a deal to your family?

And questioned her questions: *Stop thinking about them. Only you. And music. Or maybe it's the attention you miss, like Reyna wondered.*

At lunch Reyna was telling Carson about coming to Lucy's for Thanksgiving when Lucy finally got a text. She grabbed for her phone and smiled to see it was Will's reply:

I'll be at the house tomorrow. Can you wait till then?

Lucy texted a quick **yes** and put down her phone.

"Pretty quick on the draw, there, cowgirl," Carson said.

"Yeah," Reyna said, "who was that? All your friends are right here."

She looked at them, considering if and what to share. "Will."

In unison they asked, "Who?"

"My brother's new teacher."

"The cute-not-cute guy?" Carson asked.

"Who you might meet on Thursday," she told Reyna. "Gus is inviting him. And his wife."

"Soooo," Carson said, rubbing his chin, "silly question—why are you guys texting?"

Lucy shrugged. "Just setting up a time to talk."

"About what?" Reyna asked.

"I..." He was going to listen to her. That's all she was certain of so far. After that, who knew what she'd decide about piano? She wasn't ready to attempt an explanation of what she wasn't sure of. "A surprise for Gus."

Reyna dropped it, but when they drove to CC's after school for coffee to go, she brought it up again. "So the cute, young piano teacher is texting you. Tell me more about that."

She made it sound...creepy. "You said yourself he's not that cute or young."

"Young by *your* standards. So he's married?"

"Reyna, I'm not—"

"Crap. There's no parking. You run in; I'll drive around the block a few times."

Lucy got their coffee and stood on the street waiting for Reyna to come back. It was colder out than she'd expected. Thanksgiving this week. Christmas after that. Then the long stretch of January and February. She wondered what her life would look like by then.

Reyna's car pulled up, and as soon as Lucy got in, Reyna said, "I'm just saying remember that teacher at Parker Day who got fired for texting with students?"

"He's sent me *one* text."

"...And you should see the records of my dad's texts that my mom's lawyer got."

"Okay, stop. Seriously. One, he's not my teacher. Two: gross. Three...can we talk about something else?"

"Yes. If you promise me you'll be careful."

"Reyna!"

"I mean with your heart, okay?" She glanced at Lucy. "I know you. Now talk about whatever you want."

Lucy tried to think of a new subject. She wished she hadn't mentioned Will, not yet. She wound up telling Reyna that even though she was looking forward to her mom and grandpa being gone for the holiday, she also wished she could be there for her grandmother's memorial in Germany, and the spreading of the ashes.

"*Hm*," Reyna said, handing her coffee to Lucy while she made a left turn. "Do you think your grandpa would, like, notice if there were a few ashes missing? Like, I don't know, half a cup?"

Lucy, catching up, turned to Reyna. "I don't know...do you think?"

"*I* wouldn't notice, if I were him." She took her coffee back. "Or you could just ask him. Maybe he'd give you some."

"No. He'd be offended and appalled and make me feel like a sociopath for even thinking it." It might hurt him, too, to think about dividing up Grandma's body that way, even though it had already been reduced to so little. "Plus it would require actually talking about Grandma's death. It's not our family's favorite subject."

"Right. You have to steal them." When they got to the house, she asked, "You're totally sure about Thanksgiving? It's okay for us to come?"

"Totally sure."

"Love you, Luce. I don't know how I'd be getting through this divorce stuff without you." They hugged, and Reyna asked, "What are we going to do with them? The ashes?"

"We?" Lucy laughed.

"Obviously. It was my idea!"

"I'm not sure. Maybe spread them at Seal Rock or something?" Every year for Lucy's birthday, her grandma had taken her to the Cliff House for dinner, and afterward they'd stand at the cement wall and watch and listen to the waves. "But maybe I want to keep some. I don't know."

"Then don't skimp when you have your moment. Get a nice big scoop."

♪

Martin stood over the dishwasher, unloading and polishing and putting away dishes. "Hey, doll," he said.

Lucy put her bag on the island. "Are there any of those brownies left?" Martin gestured to a plastic container on top of the fridge. She took it down, removed two brownies, and put it back. "What do you drink with vegan brownies instead of milk?"

"I shudder to think."

She poured herself milk and sat at the island. "Can I tell you a secret?" He would understand about her grandmother's ashes. He'd loved her at least as much as Lucy had.

"Not if it's going to get me in trouble later." Martin closed the dishwasher, then wiped out the sink and ran the disposal.

When the grinding stopped, Lucy said, "Never mind. I'll tell you after it's too late to stop me."

"I appreciate that. Anything you need before I take off?"

She shook her head and watched him roll down his sleeves, put his watch back on, and take off his black apron and hang it on the pantry hook. They said good-bye and Lucy sat still, feeling herself there, in her kitchen, the sweetness of the brownie on her tongue, the cold milk glass in her hand.

These little things, even, were a kind of beauty.

She held them close.

15.

It was difficult to wait until Tuesday afternoon to talk to Will. She nearly texted him Monday night to see if he could talk then but stopped herself, picturing Carson's and Reyna's faces if they could see her.

When she got home, she bolted into the house and went straight to the piano room, where Will and Gus were working. She paused just outside, listening.

"...hear that odd repeated note?" Will asked. "It's a striking thing about the theme, right?"

"Sometimes I can't hear it," Gus confessed.

She shouldn't barge in.

"That's because you're getting too caught up in the measure-to-measure stuff. Let yourself mess up a little on that and listen for the big picture. You want a map of the piece in your head, but don't think about it step-by-step. Here."

Unable to wait any longer, she burst into the room. "Sorry to interrupt."

Gus stopped playing. Will, leaning on the piano, smiled. "You can interrupt anytime." He wore black jeans and sneakers, a chocolate-brown hooded sweater. He had really good style. Casual but classy.

Gus slid off the bench and came over to her, making fake punches in her general vicinity. "Wii boxing. Let's go."

She put her hand on his forehead while he threw fists at the air, giggling. She caught Will's eye and they both laughed. "I want to talk to Will for a minute."

Gus let his arms drop to his sides. "Why?"

"Just because."

"You can go box or take a quick run," Will said to Gus. "It's almost time for a break, anyway."

He left them, reluctant. And Lucy felt shy, suddenly, not sure where to stand. She chose a spot behind her grandfather's armchair; Will sat on the piano bench, his hands holding the edge of it on either side of his legs.

"Hey, I heard you stuck up for me with your grandpa the other night," he said. "I appreciate that. I like this job, you know. And I do sort of feel like I'm on probation here."

"Gus told you about that?"

He nodded.

"If you haven't figured this out yet," Lucy said, "my grandfather is a little obsessed with results."

"Yeah, I got that. Your mom, too."

"That's not really her. She's just..." Just what? Trying to make up for letting her dad down all those years ago? Afraid of him? Staying on his good side for the sake of all the money that would come when he died? No, her mom wasn't greedy, and she had her own inheritance from Grandma, anyway. "She just doesn't know how else to be, I think."

Will nodded.

"I was sort of sticking up for myself, too," she said. "With my grandpa."

"Ah, good for you!" His pocket chimed; he took out his phone. "Sorry. Hang on." He thumb-typed into it, then put it away. "Proceed."

"So," she said, "what we were talking about..." She paused. "You know?"

"Yes. The thing about which we were talking. On the stairs. In the hallway. That thing. I'm following." He rested his hands on his knees and sat forward a bit, and Lucy wondered momentarily why she trusted him. He was on Grandpa Beck's payroll. He'd barely been around for a couple of weeks. And as far as this house, he sort of belonged to Gus.

"This is confidential, okay? I mean, maybe I shouldn't." She clenched the back of the chair. "Yeah, I think, no. It's kind of..."

"Did you rob a bank?"

She laughed. "No."

"Well, as long as it's not something that, by *law*, I have to report, go ahead. I'll treat it as classified."

"I think...I think I *know* that the answer is yes."

He smiled. Her hands relaxed, but a tide of emotion rose in her chest. "This is hard for me," she continued. "Because it's like you said. I'm not allowed. I'm not...he wouldn't want me to. And in a weird way, I feel like he's right. Or like playing is giving in to him or something and I know that's crazy because I also feel like *not* playing is giving in and—"

"Lucy." He held up one hand. "Forget about him."

"I can't." The emotion turned into a few tears, which she brushed away.

He nodded. "All right." He got up and brought a box of tissues from the end table over to her, standing on the other side of the armchair. "It must be hard," he said.

She blew her nose. "When I quit I didn't mean to quit. I mean, I meant to. I did mean to. But I didn't know I was quitting *forever*."

"Of course not. No decision is forever."

"But he said it was."

"Oh."

"You don't even know the whole story, I bet. Only what the blogs and everything said."

"You walked offstage in Prague and never came back." He offered her another tissue; she took it. "I assume there's more to it."

She laugh-cried and wiped her nose again. "Uh, yeah."

Will took a few steps back and perched on the piano bench. "Why did you? I was pretty curious, myself. I followed the story for a while, hoping you'd explain, but it seemed like you didn't want to."

She tried to picture it. Him, eight months or less before they'd met, reading about her online, on purpose, looking for answers while she had no clue he even existed.

"What did people say?" she asked. "Back then? I made a point not to find out."

"Let's see, the popular guesses were nervous breakdown, stage fright, just hitting that wall where you'd had enough. Everyone in the business knows the pressure."

"Is that all?" Like Lucy's mom had said, people loved to gossip. And they loved to see those who'd been a big deal fall on their faces. "Come on. There had to be worse stuff than that. That I was on drugs? Pregnant? In the loony bin?"

He folded his arms and shook his head. "Nope. Hey, it's the Internet. It's humans being at their best, all the time. Nothing but love for Lucy Beck-Moreau." He smiled crookedly; she smiled back and said, "Ha."

"Do you want to now?" he asked. "Tell your side of it?"

"How many hours do you have?"

He pretended to examine his watch. "Well..."

Lucy came around and sat in the armchair. "The main thing I wanted to tell you is I want to play, but also I don't know how it's going to work. All I know is I miss it. Parts of it."

"Yeah."

"Maybe I'll play just for me. I don't want to be perfect, and I don't want—"

"You don't have to be perfect."

"Tell that to my grandfather."

"Why are we talking about him again?"

"Oops." Lucy took a deep breath. "I was thinking...maybe you could help me. Not like you help Gus. Not as a teacher. I don't need that. I need...sorry. I only thought of this all yesterday, and I guess it's kind of half-baked."

"Sounds pretty simple to me."

"It does?"

"When I said to think of me as a friend, I wasn't just talking because I love the sound of my own voice. You need a friend who gets it. You want support."

She watched his face. Trustworthy. Sincere.

They heard Gus's footsteps in the hall. Will glanced at the door. "Listen, the confidentiality has to go both ways. I could get in trouble with your family, you know, if they find out I'm helping you, or whatever you want to call it."

She nodded quickly before Gus burst into the room, flushed. "I ran around the block."

"Good job," Lucy said, standing up.

"What were you guys doing?"

"Lucy robbed a bank," Will said. "Needed legal advice."

"What?" Gus asked, with an uncertain smile.

"Just kidding, Gustav," Lucy said. "I'll go back into my homework cave."

♪

Later, when her grandfather was downstairs reading and her mom and dad had taken Gus out to shop for a new suit for the showcase, Lucy dug through the kitchen drawers until she found a medium-size glass container with a snap-on lid.

She stole up to her grandfather's bedroom. The urn sat on the dresser, on Grandma's lace scarf, still spread there to protect the wood. Lucy peeked inside. She'd forgotten that the ashes were inside a plastic bag in the urn, secured with a little piece of adhesive tape. She worked it open slowly and got it undone without ripping the bag.

Ashes didn't seem like the right word. It looked like ground-up seashells, white and chalky. Lucy touched the top layer. All of what had been her grandmother's body burned down to this.

The bag had more heft to it than she expected. Lucy carefully poured out as much as she could without leaving too noticeable a dent in what was left. A little spilled out onto the scarf, but she cleaned it all up, resealed the bag, put the top onto the urn, and made it to her room.

Lying on the bed with the container resting on her stomach, she texted Reyna.

Ashes retrieved. No problem.

A moment later, the reply:

that's my sneaky grl

She opened her contacts and looked at Will's number there. After waffling a few moments, she decided to text him, just a brief **Thanks for listening.**

He replied right away.

Anytime, Lucy.

16.

Wednesday before break was a half day, and there was a sub in English. When Lucy got home, her mother was in full packing frenzy, walking up and down the stairs with a checklist in her hand and the phone to her ear. She had on sensible but chic shoes for the trip, and a stretchy black knee-length skirt. Lucy went into the parlor, clear of the main line of action but close enough to help if her mother needed her to, and draped herself on the chaise before realizing Grandpa Beck was sitting in the chair across the room. As surprised as she was, he said, "Lucy. Did you just get home?"

By instinct she sat up straight. "Yes. I..." She'd strolled home, done some window-shopping. Was that something an "entitled brat" would do when she knew her mom was here packing? "...was working on my paper. In the library."

He gave an approving nod. "I've wondered what you do with your free time these days."

He'd wondered? Since when? If he wondered so much, he could have asked.

They hadn't really talked since their confrontation on Saturday; the fight might not be finished, and Lucy readied herself. But he seemed to have forgotten, or at least did an impressive job pretending he had. "Is English your favorite subject now?"

God. How uncomfortable could two family members be together?

"Yes," she said, with a definite nod.

"You're good at it, then?" He sat forward a bit, suddenly interested, the book still open on his lap. Lucy could almost see, flashing through his imagination: Ivy League, MFA, New York City, Pulitzer, world domination.

"I'm okay."

"Lucy, there's no shame in saying that you excel at something." He took off his reading glasses and folded them into his chest pocket. "You did homework in the library the day before break. I don't imagine very many students would do that."

"They would. They do."

He seemed not to hear. "I know you work hard. You're up in your room every night, putting in the time. Your grades are good. Of course there's room for improvement, but—"

"I just enjoy books. Now that I have time to read."

Her mother came in, speaking into her phone in broken German. "Here, Dad." She handed Grandpa Beck the phone. "It's about the car service in Dresden. They can't understand me." He took the phone and left the room; Lucy stood and picked up her things to make her escape while she could.

"I thought everyone there spoke English," she said.

"So did I," her mother replied. "Lucy, wait. I want to talk to you before we go."

Lucy waited, unmoving.

"Sit back down, honey."

She lowered herself onto the chaise while her mother sat in the chair. This was a page from her worst nightmares—being trapped in a small room with her grandfather and mother in quick succession. "What?"

"I'm a little bit concerned that while we're gone, Gustav's practice will fall by the wayside."

"Mom, you know Gus. He's not lazy."

"No, no, he's not."

"It's going to be, what, five days?"

"Five days is a long time to lose so close to a big performance," she said. "You know that."

Lucy reminded herself what she'd said to Will about her mother: that she didn't know any other way to be. "I'm sure Will has it under control," she said. She wanted to get out. She began to rise from her seat; her mother motioned her down.

"We're giving Will a fair chance at this, because Gus likes him so much. But I'm not totally convinced by his methods yet. Gus seems to be practicing *less* than ever." She looked toward the hall, where Grandpa Beck was still on the phone. "The showcase is so soon," she whispered. "Then after that the Swanner, and his schedule is filling up." She chewed on her pinky nail. "I'm thinking about pulling him out of school next year, but that's a whole different conversation."

What did she want? Reassurance? "Gus will be ready," Lucy said.

"I hope so. I thought, since you seem, lately, to be expressing more interest in what Gus is doing." She stopped, as if that had been a complete sentence.

"You thought what?"

"That you could keep an eye on things here. Make sure Gus keeps to his schedule. Note if you think there's any way Will is falling short. If you think—"

"I'm not going to monitor Will, Mom. Or Gus." Lucy stood and shouldered her bag. She practically had to step over her mother's feet to get out.

Her mother took hold of her arm. "You're his big sister."

"Exactly. And Dad is his dad. Get *him* to be your spy." She pulled her arm free.

Her mother got up so fast, Lucy felt the air behind her move. "You never appreciated it, Lucy."

There it was. Right out loud.

They were in the hall now. Grandpa Beck had gotten off the phone and stood, grimly attentive. Lucy almost bit her tongue just to save them all the drama. It was old news. Nothing was going to change. No matter what she did on her own, with Will, or with anyone else, it wouldn't fix *this*.

But then, maybe because they were all about to be separated by a hemisphere, Lucy asked what she'd always wanted to ask her mother. "Did *you*?"

Because, of course, her mom had been in exactly the same position when she was in high school. Playing to make Grandpa Beck happy. Placing in competitions. Traveling, performing, *being* somebody. And, just like Lucy, she'd quit.

Grandpa wouldn't describe it that way. He'd always said that Lucy's mother simply didn't have the innate talent that Lucy and Gus did. That she'd reached her potential and made the smart decision to move on, because why do it if you weren't destined for greatness? Only, she hadn't moved on very far. She was still trying to be Grandpa Beck's perfect daughter.

She folded her arms now, making a shield. "*I* did my best."

"So did I," Lucy insisted.

Grandpa Beck stepped forward. They had her surrounded, with no access to the stairs unless she walked straight through one of them. "You could have kept going," he said, the old fire in his eyes. "You could have *won* it. The Prague. And everything after."

She stared at him as she had at dinner the other night. "And what's the point of winning if you don't have a life? If you're miserable? If you miss important things that happen to the people you love?"

"You weren't miserable," he said, ignoring the allusion to Grandma.

Lucy laughed. He really believed it. He really thought he knew better than she did how she *felt*. "I just hope you don't do this to Gus," she said. "He still loves to play. But maybe not forever."

Grandpa Beck drew his eyebrows together. "Has he said something to you?"

"No, but..." She gave up. He'd never change. He'd never see.

"Think about what I asked, Lucy," her mother said, and stepped aside.

"I don't have to think about it. I said no."

She headed up the stairs, her mother's voice following her: "I'll be calling you to discuss this from the airport!"

"Go ahead!"

She didn't have to answer her phone, and she didn't have to see either of them for nearly a whole week. And right now she didn't care if she ever saw them again.

II.

Free Cadenza

17.

Lucy and Gus ate at the kitchen island while Martin cleaned up. He'd made night-before-Thanksgiving spaghetti; the sauce came from a jar, the Parmesan from a can, and the garlic bread was store-bought.

"This is the best food ever," Gus said, licking around the sides of his ice-cream sandwich—dessert from a box.

"Gee, thanks," Martin joked. "Why did I spend two days slicing and dicing for tomorrow if you're happy with a bottle of Ragú?"

Their dad hadn't yet returned from taking Mom and Grandpa Beck to the airport. Before they left he had come up to her room. She'd been lying on the bed with her earbuds in, listening to Kasey Chambers: loud, urgent-voiced, a little pissed off. She hadn't heard her dad knock.

He'd stood next to her bed, gesturing at her to take out her earbuds. When she hadn't he'd reached down and yanked the cord.

"*What?*" she'd asked.

"Come say good-bye to your mom and grandpa."

"I don't want to."

"I don't care. Come do it."

She'd looked away. Maybe she'd forgiven him for what happened in Prague, but he was no innocent in this mess. "I'll call her later," she'd muttered to the wall. Unless he wanted to phys-ically drag her out of her room, he'd have to accept it.

"Fine," he'd said, and left.

She'd lain there and fumed for ten minutes or so, with a trace of guilt and worry. Maybe she'd gone too far. Then she'd thought about her conversation with Will and the promise of his help and friendship, and felt some hope. She had decisions to make about her life. *Her* life. And she wasn't alone anymore.

Now, in the kitchen, a wave of something like euphoria came over her. Five whole days without Grandpa Beck's disapproval and her mom's judgment and fear. Time to imagine. Time to scheme.

"Can I sleep in your room tonight?" Gus asked.

"*Hm*," she said, pretending to think. "No."

"Why not?"

"Maybe I have my own plans."

Martin, who'd been massaging something into the turkey, glanced at her. "Plans for an overnight guest in your room? Don't make me tell on you."

"Ha-ha." She didn't actually *have* plans, but she felt like she should, with all this unsupervised time on her horizon. "Maybe tomorrow night, Gus, okay?"

He pouted. "Maybe I won't want to tomorrow night."

"It's a risk I guess I'll have to take." She gave him a big, wet kiss on the cheek; he squirmed away, but she knew he liked it.

♪

"I was thinking we could do the ashes thing tonight." Lucy stared into the closet with the phone to her ear. She didn't want to sit in her room all night, reliving the fight with her mom. "My stressful parent is out of town, leaving behind my dad, who's currently MIA. Grandpa, also gone. Martin is spending the night, so he can start the turkey at dawn; therefore, I don't have to watch Gus. And it's a holiday."

"A perfect storm," Reyna said.

"Meet me in ten minutes? At the bench." Her eye caught the ruby-red cocktail dress hanging off to the side with Reyna's other clothes. "And wear something nice. Like, hot."

"You assume I'm available."

"Are you?"

"Well, yeah. I'll need more than ten minutes to get hot-looking, though. Twenty?"

"See you then."

The dress was a challenge to get into—the zipper was nearly impossible to reach once it hit the middle of her back, but she got it up. When she saw herself in the wardrobe mirror, she let out a laugh. It was so not her. Tight, short, sparkly, red. On the other hand, why not? It *could* be her. For tonight, anyway.

♪

The bench at the top of the park stairs across from her house was their old meeting place from childhood. At first because that was as far as Lucy's parents let her go from home without them; then it became tradition through middle school. She couldn't remember the last time they'd met there.

The sun had gone down; the light in Gus's room on the third floor was on. She thought about him there in his room, reading probably, or he could be thinking about the showcase or about everything they'd get to eat tomorrow. He could be drawing. She hoped it was that, or some other activity at least distantly related to "fun."

Reyna's silhouette came bobbing up the stairs, hair whipping, her arms wrapped around her body. "It's freezing!" she shouted to Lucy from halfway up. "Let's get in the car!"

"Come up here first."

Lucy had the container of ashes in her lap, her cold fingers resting on the edges. She thought about holding the gritty remains in her bare hands. Sending her grandmother into the wind.

"Is that them?" Reyna asked, when she'd reached the top, breathing hard.

"My share."

"Are you okay?" She sat on the bench next to Lucy and put an arm around her shoulder. "Are you sure you're ready to do this?"

"I think so. I mean I can't keep them under my bed indefinitely."

Reyna pulled open Lucy's coat. "Oh my God. What are you wearing?"

Lucy stood and opened it all the way. "Recognize it?"

"Yowza."

"Do you mind? I thought..." She shrugged, not sure how she'd meant to complete that sentence. The dress was uncomfortably tight. She felt like she had to wear it, though, and couldn't explain why.

"No, it's fine. It's..." Reyna laughed. "Your legs are insane. But now I don't know if I'm dressy enough." She stood, too, and twirled to show off her black pencil skirt and a tucked-in polka-dot blouse with a wide belt. Super-high heels. The overall effect was forties pinup girl.

"Gorgeous. I wonder if we'd get away with dressing like this at an actual funeral."

"I think your grandma would appreciate it."

"Let's take a picture," Lucy said. She got her phone out of her pocket and they squished their faces together and opened their eyes wide, so they wouldn't blink at the flash.

"Carson needs to see us like this," Reyna said, after they got in the car. They were driving, aimlessly for now, undecided on where to start. "Text him and see if he's home."

Lucy followed orders, exchanging a few texts with Carson. "He's home," she reported to Reyna, "and desperate to escape. His grandmother is lecturing him about his grades."

"Let's take him with us. Is that okay?"

"Definitely."

Carson lived near the Embarcadero. His dad had come from Taiwan in the late eighties with the savings of his entire extended family, bought a run-down warehouse-y building, and turned it into lofts that now sold for more than a million dollars each.

There was nowhere to park, so Reyna circled the neighborhood until Carson made it down to the street to meet them. Lucy had to get out to let him in. She'd wrestled off her coat in Reyna's overheated Mini, so Carson got the full red-cocktail-dress version of her and went speechless for a few seconds.

"Um, hi," he said, staring. He ducked his head into the car to ask Reyna, "Should I go up and change?"

"Just get in."

They explained the plan and the occasion to Carson. "Is this legal?" he asked. "Can you just put ashes anywhere, without permission?"

"*Hm*." Lucy hadn't considered this. "Ask the Internet."

He had his phone out before she even finished talking. "Oh, now that you *need* something from me, you're happy I'm the Mobile Googling Champion of the Greater Bay Area."

"Is that really a thing?" Reyna asked.

"No. But it should be. Okay, give me approximately seventeen seconds."

"Where are we going, Luce? Are we doing Seal Rock?"

"Yeah. Not yet, though. Let's do something not funeral-like first." The lights along the Bay front were pretty, festive. "I know! Pier 39! I haven't been there since I was, like, twelve."

Reyna groaned. "On a holiday? It'll be crawling with tourists."

"About the ashes: This one site says California has all these strict rules," Carson said. "But it also says they aren't really enforced, and I quote: 'Your own moral compass-slash-judgment can be equally right within the reasons of common sense.'"

Reyna nodded. "Like I always say."

"*Pssht*," Carson scoffed. "You've never said that."

"I should have."

"'The reasons of common sense'? Is that even English?" Lucy asked. "So the pier? We're good?"

"I can't walk in these shoes," Reyna warned.

"Easy solution," Carson said. "I'll carry you."

"We won't stay long," Lucy assured her. "My shoes are brutal, too."

"I'll carry both of you."

Fifteen minutes later they'd made it to the center of the action. Reyna was right—despite the cold, tourists and sailors and college kids crowded the pier, going in and out of shops and restaurants and stopping to watch street performers.

"What do you think my grandma would say if I decided to be a juggler?" Carson asked as they weaved through the mob. "Like, as my career."

"You could try my new strategy with grandparental guilt," Lucy said. "Ignoring it and refusing it."

Reyna laughed. "Since when?"

"Since now." Easy to say with Grandpa on a plane.

"It's the immigrant thing," Carson said. "How many generations before the kids don't have to make all the sacrifice worthwhile?"

"My grandfather didn't exactly sacrifice," she said. "His family always had money, from way back." He'd been a kid when his parents came over and had only the faintest trace of an accent no one would notice particularly. "He didn't have to work for it like your dad did. And the weight of the whole family on your dad's back—it's different."

"Don't forget not being white."

"Chinese is like the white of San Francisco, though," Reyna said.

Carson put his arm around Reyna. "I love you, but that's one of the dumbest things I've ever heard, my little white friend. Anyway, we're Taiwanese, remember?"

She wobbled on her heels under the weight of his arm. "This is all very interesting, but these bricks are hell. I'm going to break my ankle."

"Let's get candy," Lucy said, spotting a display of chocolate in a window that was already Christmas-themed. A family that had been sitting on a bench outside the shop got up. "Grab that," she told Reyna and Carson. She went in and thought about what she'd get: rock candy, small braided bars of white chocolate, and some pecan turtles. All her grandma's favorites. It was warm in the crowded shop; she unbuttoned her coat.

Two guys in navy whites were right in front of her in the long line. They turned and gave her that look, that same look the EMT had given her the day of Temnikova's death. She didn't mind it this time. "Hi," one said. He looked young and pinkish, his face fresh-scrubbed.

"Hi." Lucy smiled.

"How are you?"

"Fine. You?"

"Okay." He smiled, showing a small gap between his front teeth.

The line inched forward. His taller, darker friend said, "His name is Scott."

Scott turned pinker and extended his hand. Lucy shook it. "Lucy."

"Scott's girlfriend just broke up with him."

Lucy could tell that the friend teased Scott like this all the time, probably intentionally embarrassed him every chance he got. "That was stupid of her," Lucy said, to be nice, to make Scott feel better.

"Thanks," he said.

An old U2 song came on the store radio. Scott was close

enough that she could see the peach-fuzzy hair on his cheek. She felt the song in her veins, and then she was noticing everything: the heavy smell of sugar and cocoa all around them, the man in a 49ers knit cap and how he grinned at his young daughter, who had a green ribbon in her hair. The way the girl behind the counter, kind of heavy and pimply, joked with each customer, made them laugh. The wave of cold air that came into the warm shop every time anyone came in or went out.

Life was...good. And beautiful.

And Lucy felt beautiful in it.

"You'll find someone else," she told Scott. And without planning to, kissed his cheek.

"Uh, I think he just did," his friend said.

"How 'bout on the lips?"

Her first thought was: *Why not?* It was a red-dress kind of move.

Then she came to her senses. There was impulse; then there was crazy. "You're next," she said, pointing to the counter. "In line I mean."

They ordered and paid, and Scott turned to her to say, "You want to get a drink?"

"I can't. I'm..." *Sixteen.* "I'm with friends."

"Oh. Well, don't break too many hearts tonight." He touched his hand to his hat and showed his tooth gap. "Happy Thanksgiving."

"You too."

She got her candy and left the shop, smiling to herself, feeling elated, liking the sting of the cold air on her cheeks and the feel of the dress tight against her skin. The world was all possibility. Despite the increasing pain in her feet, she nearly skipped over to the bench to pass out treats to Reyna and Carson.

"Make a new friend in there?" Carson asked. He wore a half smile that she'd seen before, when he was irritated or perplexed about something, like when he'd gotten a B-minus on a history paper he'd thought was perfect.

He must have seen her kiss Scott through the shop window.

"This stuff is kind of nasty," Reyna said, tentatively touching a piece of rock candy with her tongue. "Like, how are you supposed to eat it? Pointy. I feel like I'm going to break a tooth." She definitely would have said something if she'd seen, too.

Lucy sat down. "That's why it's called rock candy."

Carson leaned forward on the bench so he could see Lucy and raised his eyebrows, asking a silent question. She shrugged. He bit into a pecan turtle and didn't say anything else.

"Let's go look at the water," Lucy said. "Maybe this is a good place for the ashes, after all."

"You left them in the car." Reyna was limping, holding one of Carson's arms.

They got to a railing and checked out the water below, lapping against the pilings, scummy at the edges. "It doesn't exactly say 'sacred burial ground,' I guess," Lucy said.

Carson disentangled Reyna's arm and climbed up onto the bottom slat of the railing and spit into the water.

"Gross!" Reyna exclaimed. "Why'd you do that?"

He stared down into the water. "I don't know."

"Sick."

Lucy, careful in her heels, joined Carson at the rail, climbing one slat higher than him. She leaned over as far as she could and spit, too, and then laughed because it all suddenly seemed hysterical. How could she have ever thought her grandpa, her mom, anyone but her had control over her life? She could make things happen, all on her own.

Reyna shrieked. "Did you just *spit*, Lucy? You guys are freaks! I don't know you. I'm walking away." She went about twenty feet down the railing and found her own section to lean on.

Lucy felt Carson's eyes on her. A gust of wind came hard and cold, blowing a curtain of hair over her face. When she lifted her arm to sweep it out of her eyes, she lost her balance and teetered forward, still high up on the rail. Carson grabbed her around the waist and pulled her down.

"Jeez, Lucy." He dropped his arms, letting her go. "What was that?"

She knew he didn't mean about climbing the rail. "Just showing my gratitude to our military forces. It's Thanksgiving, after all."

"Remember how I just saved you from falling into the water? Feel free to thank *me*."

She put her arms around his neck. "Cheek or lips?" she asked, still laughing.

He took her shoulders and pushed her back gently, unamused. "Don't do that."

She let go.

"You guys," Reyna called. "I'm sorry, but my feet."

♪

They drove out to Seal Rock—not a short trip. Reyna chattered most of the way, about how much her feet hurt and about how

133

she and Abby were going to have to leave Lucy's house early the next day to go to two separate family desserts. Carson spent most of the time looking stuff up on his phone, silent.

The night had gotten bitter. The same cold air that had made Lucy feel so alive at the pier now just hurt her face. The three of them went down the deserted stairs at the Cliff House to the overlook, Lucy and Reyna walking carefully without their shoes. "I'm getting frostbite," Reyna said. "My toes feel like they've been chopped off."

"You can't get frostbite in this weather," Carson said. "The temperature has to be at least literally freezing, which it is not." He consulted his phone. "It's forty-two degrees. You're good."

Lucy surveyed the beach, holding the container of ashes to her chest. High tide. The waves crashed, roared back, crashed again. "I'm going down to the water," she told Reyna and Carson. "You guys stay here." She took the next flight of steps until her bare feet hit sand, grainy and damp.

"Be careful!" Reyna shouted.

When she felt the sand harden and ooze seawater, she stopped. She opened the container. Her giddiness had turned to an ache, and she thought of something Grandma Beck had always said whenever anyone else in the family was all stressed out. *I tell you what my mother told me: 'Das wird sich alles finden.' Everything will be okay.*

Maybe it was true.

Lucy held the container to her body.

Her grandmother would like this. The wild wind, the waves. She'd even like that Lucy had kissed a sailor on this particular occasion.

And she'd like Will. Lucy was certain Martin had been right about that.

The edge of a wave swirled around Lucy's feet, numbing them, as she stared at the barely visible horizon. She inhaled and let the thick air fill her.

"Das wird sich alles finden."

She flung the ashes into the blue-black night.

18.

Lucy woke to the smell of turkey, and it made her happy. Thanksgiving, as holidays went, wasn't the worst. This year, especially. She'd get to eat, and hang out with her favorite people: Reyna, Gus, and, now, Will.

She closed her eyes and thought about that.

Okay, so maybe it was a little soon to call him a favorite person. She hadn't known him long at all. But that's how she felt. Anyway, there was the kind of bond that comes from years of spending time together and then the kind that was nearly instant, because you just knew.

When she rolled over and opened her eyes, there was the red dress, along with her heels and coat, piled by the bed. Had that really been *her*, in those things? She hung the dress in the back of the closet with Reyna's other clothes and straightened her room. After her shower she put on comfortable jeans and an oversize sweater and fuzzy blue socks with the little nubs on the bottom that kept her from slipping on the hardwood floors.

There were red-cocktail-dress days; then there was the rest of the time.

♪

Her dad sat at the kitchen island, talking to Martin and drinking coffee. He'd dressed almost exactly as she had: old jeans, soft sweater, slippers. She draped her arms over his shoulders from behind, and he patted her hand against his chest, the whole incident with his earbud-yanking and her refusing to say good-bye to her mom forgiven.

"Have fun last night?" he asked, and she pulled away from him, feeling caught at something.

"I was just out with Reyna."

He turned around and smiled. "I know. I saw your note. But did you have fun?"

"Yeah. I did."

"Good." He put his hand under her chin and studied her face. Like he could see something different there.

"What?" she asked.

"Nothing."

"Ohhhkay." Lucy went to the coffeepot. "Where's Gus?"

"Already at the Wii. I told him no limits today."

Martin touched her back. "Shall I make you a couple of eggs, doll?"

"No." Lucy's father got up. "Let me." Lucy and Martin exchanged a glance, as if to see if they'd heard him right. They had—he was shooing them away from the fridge and taking out eggs, butter, cream.

"Oh, I don't know if there's room. . . ." Martin said, nervous.

"Room for what?"

"For both of us in the kitchen?"

Lucy carried her coffee to the island, to get out of the way.

"Nonsense," her father said. "It will take me five minutes to make, take us two minutes to eat, one to clean up, and we'll be gone. The French invented the omelet, you know."

Martin backed away. "I surrender. I'll make myself scarce."

He left the kitchen, and Lucy watched her father set up across from her at the island and crack eggs into a bowl. He tried to do the first one using only one hand but dropped the shell. As he picked it out, he asked, "Did you call your mom?"

"No. But she didn't call me, either." Though she'd threatened to, there were still no messages on Lucy's phone.

"I want you to call her."

Lucy sighed. He ground pepper into the bowl and said, "Don't sigh at me, *poulette*. I want my family to get along."

"Dad, she—"

"She's my wife. And the mother of my two beautiful, talented children." He whisked eggs, and Lucy tried to imagine her mom as the object of his affection, his partner, the love of his life. "It hurts me," he continued, "that you can't get along. I don't want to take sides."

"Because you're scared of her. Them."

"No." He stopped whisking. "I'm the only one in this family who's not a musician, Lucy. I married into this . . ." He stared at the ceiling for a few seconds. "This incredibly beautiful world of talent and art that I don't even begin to understand. It's like magic to me. I feel lucky to be a part of it, to just be able to sit back and watch and listen and marvel: These are my children. That's my daughter. How did it happen?" He gestured at his bowl of eggs. "I can make an omelet. I can manage money. I can keep a calendar. But I'm not like your mom, or like you, or like

Gus. I'm not...special. Sometimes I'm not sure what I contribute."

"Half our genes, Dad."

"True, yes, thank you."

She'd never, ever given one brief thought to what it might be like for him as an outsider to music and their family in that way.

"What did you think," she asked, "when I walked off in Prague? What did you really think?"

He whisked. Poured in a little cream. Cleaned a drip off the rim of the bowl.

"Tell me," she said.

"I thought I should have never let you go onstage that day to begin with. I thought I should have told you about Grandma the second I knew. And I also thought you had the right to do what you wanted. Including quitting, full stop."

"You did?" That was news to Lucy. "You could have said so."

"I did," he said. "I talked about it with Mom."

"I wish you'd said it to *me*."

"Maybe I should have."

She watched him get out a pan. "All I'm asking from Mom is for her to...I don't know...acknowledge that it's *my* life. Like you just said, I had the right to make that decision."

He sighed. "Yes, I thought you had the right to quit if you wanted. But I wish you hadn't wanted that. Mom wishes you hadn't wanted that. She can acknowledge it's your life and still feel disappointed by what you choose to do with it. That's *her* right. Grandpa's, too."

Lucy stayed quiet while he made the omelet. Maybe she hadn't tried hard enough to see her mother's perspective. Her

139

grandfather's. She didn't want to apologize, exactly. She believed in what she'd done in Prague, and being sorry wouldn't change anything.

But her dad had a point.

They ate without saying much else, and when they finished, he reminded her, "Call Mom."

"They might not even be there yet."

"Leave her a message, then."

♪

"Hi, Mom. I'm sorry I didn't say good-bye to you and Grandpa. I hope you had an easy flight. I . . . everything smells really good. Happy Thanksgiving, okay? Bye for now."

♪

Reyna and Abby showed up around noon, and Gus took Abby straight to the Wii.

"You look fresh and innocent," Reyna said to Lucy, once they were alone in the foyer. "Carson told me you kissed some random sailor in the candy shop?"

"A cheek kiss."

"A stranger's cheek." She walked toward the kitchen.

Lucy followed her. "Wait. Are you *mad*?"

"No."

"Yes, you are. What?"

Reyna turned. "It's just . . . hearing all this stuff about my dad's affairs. Maybe that's how it starts, you know? Some girl in a tight red dress who thinks she's being cute kisses you on the cheek, and next thing you know you're cheating on your wife."

Lucy laughed. "That's... his girlfriend had just broken up with him. The sailor."

"So he said." Reyna sighed. "Sorry. Maybe I'm being too judgey. But also the thing with Carson. You shouldn't toy with him, because he actually likes you."

"Likes me how?" Lucy asked, confused.

"How do you think?"

She remembered his face when she'd put her arms around him. "He said that?"

"He doesn't have to. I have eyes."

"But he's always talking about who he likes. And my name hasn't come up."

"I know. Just... don't be that girl, is all I'm saying." She pulled Lucy's hand. "Come on. Let's forget it. I want to see Martin."

They made a big entrance into the kitchen, and Reyna gushed over Martin and the great smells coming from the ovens while Martin petted Reyna's hair jealously. "If I had your looks..."

He put them to work getting out serving platters and bowls, and chopping garnishes. Lucy thought back to the night before, how good she'd felt. How alive. She hadn't meant to hurt Carson or anyone else. Only to express... it wasn't happiness, exactly. More a kind of fullness. Like if she didn't do *something*, she'd explode. Like on the drive to Half Moon Bay.

Since quitting, she realized, she'd had nowhere to put that feeling.

And she was about to change that.

♪

When the doorbell rang, Gus came tearing down the stairs from the game room. "I'll get it!" Lucy and Reyna and Martin came out from the kitchen, and Gus pushed past them to fling open the door. Will and Aruna smiled big at him. Aruna held a potted plant and was gorgeous in a flowery kind of blouse that no one else Lucy knew could pull off without looking like an old lady. She handed the plant to Martin. "It's rosemary."

"It sure is," he said, smelling it. "Thank you."

They came in, and Aruna surprised Lucy by giving her a squeeze. She wore some kind of spicy perfume, not too much, just right. Will waved hello and stuck out his hand to Reyna. "Hi. I'm Will."

"Reyna," Lucy said, pointing at her. "Best friend."

"And best friend's sister," Reyna added as Abby sidled up to her. "Nice to meet you."

Gus dragged Will off somewhere, and Aruna went into the kitchen to hang out with Martin. Lucy's dad had gone to the wine cellar.

When Reyna and Lucy were left alone in the foyer, Reyna said, "*That's* the same guy from the Internet?"

"Will? Yeah."

"Cuter in person."

Lucy shrugged, and Reyna shook her head. "Like you didn't notice."

♪

An hour later they were all at the table, Martin too. Lucy's dad held up the bottle of wine. "It's the first Beaujolais," he said.

Then to Lucy, "I'd be betraying my ancestry if I didn't insist you have a glass. Only to sip from, to taste."

She didn't hesitate to hold out her glass, catching Martin's eye for a second to see if he approved. He made a noncommittal gesture. "It's Thanksgiving."

"Me too?" Reyna asked.

"If you call your mom and get permission."

"Never mind."

He tipped wine into Lucy's glass, filling it. More than a sip or a taste. "Make a toast, *poulette*. Earn your Beaujolais."

She held up her glass; everyone followed. The feeling at the table was about a hundred times more relaxed than it had been the last time Will and Aruna were there. Maybe Lucy should toast Mom and Grandpa, but she didn't miss them.

"To Grandma."

Martin touched his glass to Lucy's. "Hear, hear."

After they all sipped, Aruna said, "Tell us about her, Lucy."

"She..." *She was just here last Thanksgiving. She had on a blue dress. She loved me.* Lucy looked to Martin, hoping he'd see she couldn't talk. "Sorry." Her voice broke, and she found herself glancing at Will. He made a sympathetic face and very slightly lifted his water glass to her.

Martin and Lucy's dad talked a little bit about Grandma Beck; Lucy listened and sipped her wine, which was already making a warm path through her body. Martin told a couple of stories Lucy hadn't heard before; then Abby started to fidget, and Gus asked about dessert. Aruna offered to help Martin clear, insisting the rest of them stay put. Lucy's dad refilled her glass, then excused himself to get another bottle.

That left Will and Lucy, and Reyna and Gus and Abby, at the table. Reyna had gone shy around Will. "So how about you?" he asked her. "What's your thing?"

Reyna shrugged. "No thing."

Abby piped up in her adorably husky voice: "She can count backward from a hundred without even having to stop and think."

"That must come in handy," Will said.

"Yeah, well, I don't like to brag."

Lucy's father came back with the wine and spent what seemed like five minutes hunting for the wine opener until Gus pointed out it was in his shirt pocket. Martin brought out dessert: chocolate pecan pie, pumpkin pie, a fruit-and-cheese plate, ice cream. Three trips to and from the kitchen. "This one is vegan," Martin said, indicating the pumpkin pie.

"Thank you," Will said. "Looks great."

While dessert got passed around, Lucy caught Gus gazing at Will with complete adoration. Starstruck. The way Will fit right into things so quickly, without any kind of effort or drama, was a miraculous occurrence for the Beck-Moreaus. As a teacher, great with Gus. Nice to Lucy's friends. He didn't treat Martin like the help. He didn't kiss up to Lucy's dad.

And he was willing to be Lucy's friend.

The wine made her tongue pleasantly dry and her thoughts a little gooey. She watched him dig into his vegan pumpkin pie with a wink at Abby.

He was kind of perfect.

♪

Reyna and Abby left around seven. "And now we have to go to two more desserts," Reyna said. "One with my dad at my aunt's house, and then with my mom at ours."

"Aw, *ma chère*," Lucy's dad said blearily. "I'm glad you could be with us today." He gave her a Euro-style kiss on both cheeks, his French manners coming out with the Beaujolais.

Lucy, too, felt bleary. The cartilage in her knees had been replaced with wine. Her head spun a little, and she gave Reyna a long hug and a wet kiss on the neck. "You're my best friend," she murmured.

"Yeah, I know," Reyna said, pushing her gently away.

"Nice to meet you guys," Will said.

When the door closed behind Reyna and Abby, the rest of them loitered awkwardly in the foyer until there didn't seem to be anything to do but migrate to the piano room. Somehow, Lucy was leading the way.

"I've got cleanup," Martin said, excusing himself to the kitchen.

Gus stopped in the hall and said, "I don't want to play."

He'd never said *that* before.

"Come on." Lucy nudged his shoulder and immediately wanted to take it back. She'd never, ever cajoled him about piano.

"It's my day off."

Maybe now that Grandpa Beck and Mom were away, she was seeing the real Gus. Maybe he'd been faking his willingness all along. *Impossible*, she thought. *I'd* know. She looked to Will.

"Yes, it is your day off," he said.

Lucy's dad had already sunk into Grandpa Beck's chair. "Do whatever you want, Gustav."

"Can we play Wii tennis?" He had turned to ask it of Will, who groaned and patted his stomach. "No chance. How about something that doesn't require me to move, like chess?"

Gus made a face. Lucy smiled. Maybe because of being around Abby for half a day, or maybe for other reasons, he was being a normal, annoying, ten-year-old boy, and she liked it. He asked their dad, "Can I go watch TV?"

"Of course."

Aruna put her hand on Gus's shoulder. "That sounds great, actually. Can I come?"

He grinned hugely, and they went off together, and that left Lucy and her dad and Will in the piano room, with no real reason to be there. "My grandma would like you," she blurted out to Will, who sat on the love seat. "Don't you think, Dad?"

"Oh yes, most certainly. And you," he said, pointing at Will, "would fall madly in love with her. She was a charming woman. Lucy has that, Hannah's charm."

Lucy swayed a little when she turned to her dad. "I do?"

"I think what Lucy has is a need to sit down," Will said.

He was right.

The piano bench didn't look uncomfortable.

She glanced over her shoulder and saw her dad's head resting on his chest, though he still had a tight grip on his wineglass. Will had gone to the bookshelf and studied it as if looking for something specific.

Lucy lowered herself onto the piano bench and touched her fingers to the keys. They were smooth and responsive. Inviting. Like they'd been waiting for her.

She closed her eyes.

The first thing that came out was a phrase from the ricercar Gus had been working on, the Bach. She fumbled it badly. Will was right—that diminished seventh was weird. Lucy closed her eyes and did it again, still missing about half the notes. Then again, at a more restrained pace. Searching for the shape of it, making the music.

Better.

Her fingers started to limber up, but what came out of the piano still lacked what you'd call artistry. She hadn't expected to be *great*. It didn't work that way. If you neglect your gifts, they shrivel up and die, and you don't deserve them. At least, Grandpa Beck had said that once.

But as she played she knew: Nothing had shriveled up and died. It had only been resting.

Her fingers still had the gift of translation that Grandpa said they did.

Her heart still understood what the music wanted her to do.

Her blood: wine and warmth and life.

She gave up on the Bach when she couldn't recall anything from the second half and moved on to Saint-Saëns's *The Swan*. This one came easier, and her body moved in its old way, rocking forward a bit with certain phrases, her arms light, like a dancer's.

After that she went into a little Duke Ellington riff from a song she'd forgotten the name of.

"...*some kiss may cloud my memory...*"

Her father, suddenly right behind her, was singing. And she remembered she wasn't alone.

It was like being forced out of a good dream when someone snaps on a bright light.

147

She jerked her fingers away from the piano.

"No, no, keep playing," her father said, leaning his weight on her shoulder. "Please." Then he tried to put her hands back on the keys. A few ugly notes filled the room.

"Dad, don't." She stood up, too fast. The room spun, and her stomach turned; she sat back down and pulled the piano lid over the keyboard. *That looks like a good place to rest my head*, she thought, and did, its old wood cool against her skin.

What had she just done? Yes, she'd wanted to play again, but not like this, not so...exposed. It was supposed to be only her and the music.

Another hand touched her shoulder now, a lighter one.

"Are you okay?"

It was Will.

"Try sitting up, Lucy." He eased her shoulders back. "Let's walk around."

His voice was so nice.

"I don't want to walk around. It spins."

"I know."

With Will's help she stood. After a woozy few seconds, she found her feet and walked across the room while he stayed right by her. "Where's my dad?"

"Bathroom. I'm thinking he might be in there awhile." He touched her arm. "Speaking of which, do we need to find you an empty bathroom? Sometimes it's good to just, you know, hurl."

She shook her head. Getting up had helped.

They walked around the room again, in a circle, and Lucy joked about it being like a Jane Austen novel; then Will said she seemed all right, and they could talk a little bit, if she wanted.

They sat on the love seat. Will took off his glasses and put them on top of his head. His wonky eye looked more normal without them. He smiled. "So. You're full of surprises. How did that feel?"

Now she smiled. "Good."

"I could tell."

"You could?"

He nodded. "You're rusty, of course. But for someone who hasn't played in almost a year..."

"Eight months," she corrected.

"But who's counting?"

"Not me."

"Really, Lucy, wow. The Saint-Saëns...you talked to that piece like it was an old friend."

Remember that, she thought.

Mr. Charles appreciating her classwork had been a nice substitute, but it was merely a shadow of what it felt like to be noticed for music.

She'd missed being heard. Known. By others. By herself.

She put her head in her hands, overwhelmed.

"Lucy?" Will asked. "Are you okay?"

"Yeah. It's..." She lifted her head. "I forgot. How it feels."

"I know."

"No. I mean to be me."

He touched her shoulder, like he had at the piano. She let herself lean against him for just a few seconds. He smelled clean and good, and a little bit like pumpkin pie. When she straightened up, she said, "I can't believe I did that in front of my dad."

"He won't remember much."

"Yes, he will."

She got a little spinny again and closed her eyes. "What now?"

"Let's talk about it when you're not about to fall over."

Then they heard Gus and Aruna in the hall. Will stood and met Aruna at the doorway; they kissed. Aruna said, "We heard you playing a minute ago, babe. Sounded great."

They'd thought it was Will. And smooth, instant, like it was the truth, he said, "Thanks. Just noodling."

Lucy stared at the back of his head and thought: *He's on my side*.

19.

Waking up the next day was not pleasant.

Lucy had a flu-y, hot headache behind her eyes. Staying in bed didn't feel good; neither did getting up. On her way to the bathroom, she nearly tripped over a lump on the floor. Gus.

"Ow," he said, in a croaky morning voice. "You stepped on my leg."

"Well, what is your leg doing there?" She gave him a gentle kick.

"You said I could sleep in your room."

"I did?"

"Yeah."

"Hm." She went to the bathroom, saw her empty retainer case, and realized she had no idea where the retainer was—not in her mouth, which tasted nasty. She brushed her teeth and tongue and wet a washcloth with cool water. Maybe she'd forgotten about Gus sleeping in her room, but she hadn't forgotten about anything else. Not the playing, not Will, and not what her father had said to her when he'd finally emerged from the bathroom, pale and clammy-looking.

"You break my heart, you know." And he'd made a motion with his hands, of snapping something in two.

Now she stretched out on the floor next to Gus and draped

the cloth over her eyes, pressing down on it. His sleeping bag made swishing sounds as he rolled over onto his back. "Want to share my pillow?"

Lucy scooted closer; their heads touched. After a minute of silence, Gus said, "Don't be one of those people who drinks."

God, was I that bad? She tried to make a joke. "Ever? The whole rest of my life?"

"Will doesn't. You don't have to. Not everyone has to."

"It's a holiday, Gus."

"So?"

With the cloth still over her eyes, she felt around at her side until she found his hand through the sleeping bag. "You're right. But Dad kind of made me; you saw."

Gus wasn't having it. Lucy heard and felt him sit up. She took the cloth off and looked at him, the sleeping bag bunched around his waist, his curls sticking up everywhere. "He can't *make* you. Remember how you told me people can't *make* you do stuff. Like they couldn't *make* you keep playing. Like that."

Even though he was using it against her, she was pleased to know that he remembered their conversation six months ago, when she'd felt it her sisterly duty to inform Gus that he had a choice about piano, too, always. "You're right," she repeated. "I chose to. And the way I feel now, I probably won't choose to ever again." She jostled his hand until he withdrew it from the sleeping bag and touched hers. "I'm sorry, Gustav. Forgive me?"

"Yeah."

He took the cloth from her and arranged it back over her eyes.

♪

Martin had made the kitchen spotless, like Thanksgiving had never happened. He sat at the island, writing—a letter it looked like—and Lucy greeted him with a wave before zeroing in on the coffeepot.

"I like having you here all the time," she said, after she'd gotten her mugful. "You should just move in permanently. Mom and Dad never save me any coffee in the mornings."

"*Mm*. How are you feeling?"

"Fine."

"Really?" He put down his pen and watched her pour her cream.

As she put it back, she held the fridge door open and pointed into it. "You're amazing, you know." All the leftovers had been stored in square glass containers, labeled with a label maker, and arranged in rows and stacks. "Did you stay up all night doing this?"

"It's past noon, hon. And don't change the subject."

"Where is everybody?" She'd fallen back asleep, hard, after her talk with Gus that morning. When she'd woken she was still on the floor, the washcloth by her ear, drool on the pillow, and no sign of Gus. "I feel fine. I mean, headache. But this coffee is unbelievably good."

"Your dad took Gus to a movie. Some big superhero thing. Why don't you sit down? I'll make you a turkey sandwich."

That sounded perfect. She finally felt like she could eat again, and eat a lot. "I can do it."

"I can do it better, and as a bonus, not make a mess."

She sat and watched him while she drank her coffee, and soon had a masterpiece of a sandwich in front of her: whole-grain bread, turkey, mayo, salt and pepper, and a thin layer of cranberry sauce. "Thank you."

Martin got himself a slice of pecan pie and more coffee and sat back down. He folded his glasses, laid them on top of his writing materials, and stared at Lucy.

"What?" she asked, uneasy.

"I heard you last night," he said. "At the piano."

"That was Will," she said reflexively.

Martin shook his head and laughed. "It was you, Lucy. You think I don't know what you sound like, after hearing you play nearly all your life?"

She swallowed her bite of sandwich and took another one without tasting it. When she'd swallowed that, she said, "I felt...festive."

"Oh, I see. A onetime Thanksgiving show, and then it's *really* the end?"

Lucy folded down the corner of the paper towel Martin had given her to use as a napkin. Then folded again and again, until she had an accordion of folds in front of her. "Don't tell them I played," she said. "Mom or Grandpa. I don't want anything to change."

"You don't? You're completely content with things as they are?"

She pinched a little bread off her sandwich and put it in her mouth, though her appetite had retreated. "No. That's not what I mean."

"Your mom, even your grandpa, in his way, they want you to be happy."

"No, they don't," she said sharply, certain.

"Lucy."

"They want me to achieve something or at least not publicly embarrass them. My happiness is beside the point." She got up with her plate and began to wrap the rest of her sandwich the way she knew he liked her to: tight, with the self-sealing plastic wrap.

"I know it feels that way," he said. "You have to trust me. I've known them longer than you have."

There wasn't even a space in the fridge big enough for her sandwich half. "You're not their daughter." She felt helpless, lost. "Where should I put this?"

He came over to her, took the sandwich out of her hand, and made a perfect little place for it in one of the drawers.

"Please," she said. She held on to his forearm, pleading, after he'd closed the fridge. "What happened last night, it was..." She searched for the word. "Private."

"It's hard for me to understand, Lucy."

"You understood when I quit."

"I understood your protest against what happened with your grandma. I didn't think, all this time later, you'd still be protesting. You made your point, Lucy, very well. You don't have to keep making it."

"Grandpa wouldn't—"

"Oh, stop with that," Martin said. "The man isn't God, even when he thinks he is. He doesn't run your life, or your mom's, nearly as much as the two of you tell yourselves he does."

She let go of his arm.

"As a person whose major talents are cooking, cleaning, and

organizing leftovers," he continued, "I don't know why someone who can make such beauty would run from that."

She wanted to tell Martin that being on the other side of this thing, to be the one with the talent or the gift or whatever you wanted to call it, it wasn't like he thought. There was this pressure, this expectation that somehow you owed it to the world to do something you weren't sure you wanted to do, at least not in the way the world wanted you to do it.

But she knew that kind of talk only sounded ungrateful. "I *am* thinking of playing again," she confessed. "Only thinking. And I don't know how it will all work. So I don't want to tell them yet. Or Gus, okay? Until I'm ready."

A smile spread across Martin's face.

"*Thinking*," Lucy reiterated. "I want time. To sort it out." Time, and help.

"Okay, Lucy. Our secret for now." He held her shoulders and stepped back, looking proud. "Your grandma would approve."

♪

They were alone in the house, Martin and Lucy. She left the kitchen. Her sock feet led her to the practice room. The piano lid hadn't been moved since she'd put it down the night before. Lifting it, Lucy drew a deep breath.

The night before, her playing, even in the moment of it, had the quality of a dream. Full of food and Beaujolais and the sense of freedom from her grandpa being half a world away, she'd been almost in a trance. Like it had happened underwater, the people and things around her muffled and distant.

This time there was no wine fuzzing the edges of the moment.

Instead, what coursed through her was a sense of familiarity, of home.

It made her lips curl into a smile.

This was for real.

The keys under her fingers and the bench she sat on had substance, resistance. She felt sharp and awake and conscious of herself moving across a threshold.

Okay, Kristoff. Here we go. The memory of Grace was there, too, and the spirit of Temnikova, both insisting she properly warm up.

She ran some arpeggios. Her hands still had good stretch to them; she could span the intervals without too much fumbling. After a few minutes of concentration, she realized she'd become slumped and paused to straighten out her back and go at it again. Once she felt sufficiently warmed, she looked through Gus's music and chose an unfamiliar Chopin waltz to try.

Her sight-reading hadn't deteriorated. It did take a couple of measures for the head knowledge of what she was seeing on the page to travel down into her hands, but then the muscle memory kicked in, and the more she played the less she had to think.

And not thinking was...spectacular. She'd forgotten this part. How your brain stopped grabbing on to every thought that floated by, stopped gnawing on every bone your subconscious tossed at you.

When she finished the Chopin, she rolled her neck a few times and got up. She wanted to be out of there before Gus and her dad got back from the movie. She closed the lid again, put Gus's music exactly as she'd found it, scooted the bench under the piano, and left, shutting the door behind her.

♪

Lucy tried to put some time into her Alice Munro paper but felt highly in need of distraction. She texted Reyna.

How were 2nd & 3rd desserts?

awkward

Sorry. fwiw wine gods are punishing me w/massive headache. Sorry if my dad was embarrassing.

There was a long delay before Reyna's answer came.

I know it's not perfect but you have a really nice family. Gotta go.

She was upset, Lucy could tell. Reyna only said "gotta go" when she didn't have to go but wanted to.

Call me if you need to talk

Reyna didn't respond, and Lucy kept checking her phone just in case she wasn't hearing it, until finally she silenced it and stuck it under one of the pillows on her bed so she could concentrate. Her head had begun to hurt again, worse than it had in the morning. That had been an "I need food and coffee" headache. This one was here to stay.

She Googled some stuff about Munro, did a tiny bit of paraphrasing, and called it a day, homeworkwise. She'd clean up the paper on Saturday and get it in good-enough shape for draft form, then do history reading on Sunday, and continue to neglect precalc for as long as possible.

When she closed up Munro, she retrieved her phone and, in the process, found her retainer, sticky and lint-covered. She set that aside and got on her unmade bed, shoving her feet under the blankets for warmth, and texted Will.

Hi. Talk now? Or later?

There was no reply and no reply and no reply. Didn't anyone want to text her back today? She decided it was time to eat again. She took her phone with her, and on the way downstairs, a text did come in. It was Lucy's mom.

**Got your msg. Travel nightmares & much to do.
G-pa worn out. Will call later.**

It wasn't exactly "Happy Thanksgiving to you, too," but it was something.

♪

She'd just come out of the kitchen with the leftover half of her sandwich and some pie when Gus and her dad finally got home. The sensitive brother who'd placed a cool cloth over her eyes that morning had been possessed by the annoying ten-year-old-boy Gus. Who she didn't like as much as she had last night. He tried to reenact a fight scene from the movie by pretending to roundhouse kick her in the side and karate chop her neck.

"Stop it." She pushed him away, harder than she needed to. "You're going to make me drop my pie."

Her dad had his phone to his ear—listening to messages, it looked like. Gus still danced around her, quoting some dumb thing she could only assume was also from the movie.

"You should practice, Gus," she said on her way up the first flight of stairs. She only meant it as a way to get him to leave her alone, but hearing herself made her wince. It was exactly what she told her mom she wouldn't do. "Or not," she said, and turned to look down at the landing where Gus stood, touching the banister and staring up at her.

"I will," he said, defensive.

"Never mind, you don't have to."

"Lucy's right." Her dad pocketed his phone. "Try to get in an hour or so, yes? To stay on track. The showcase is—"

"—in three weeks," Gus said. "I know."

"Another day off won't be the end of the world, Dad," Lucy said. "Overpreparing is as bad as underpreparing."

"You're the one who just told him to practice!"

Gus looked at him, then at her, and then stomped off to the piano room.

Lucy leaned over the banister, feeling a little bit sorry for her dad. By his own admission, he didn't get what it meant to be a competitive musician trying to master a piece, not on the inside.

"Dad."

He looked up.

"Go sit with him while he plays."

"Really?"

"I mean, don't stare at him or anything. Take a book. Or your laptop or whatever. Just...be there. It's lonely sometimes." Going over and over and over the music. Imagining an audience and a critique. Losing all perspective, not being sure if it was getting better or worse. "Trust me."

He nodded. "I do."

♪

Will called while she sat on the bed eating. She counted two rings plus a half of one then picked up. "Hi."

"Hey."

There came the awkward pause of people who've never talked to each other on the phone before, then they each said, "How are you?" at the same time.

"You first," he said. "How are you feeling?"

"Kind of sick this morning, huge headache, but I got extra sleep and a lecture from Gus about drinking. Feeling a little better. Eating pie." She took a final bite and set her plate on the floor.

"Ha. Martin's cooking was a major topic of conversation on our way home. But I meant about the you-know-what. Starts with a *p* and ends with *iano*?"

"Ohhhh, *that*," Lucy said. "Well. I played again today. Chopin. While Gus and my dad were out."

"And?"

"Awesome." Lucy reclined on her bed and ran her hand over the comforter. "You know how when you're playing, and everything else disappears?"

"Yeah, I don't get that very often anymore, myself."

"Why not?"

He considered. "I'm not sure. Maybe it's part of getting older. That's why I like to work with young musicians. You're still alive in that way."

"I wasn't, though. For like a year or something before Prague. I was like . . . piano zombie."

"Bet you no one could tell."

"I could. And it felt really different from that last night, and today."

"It makes me happy to hear that, Lucy."

"Me too." It made her happy to say it, and to feel it.

She listened to his breathing until he asked, "So what's next?"

"I was hoping you'd tell me."

"Ah. See now," he said, "I assumed part of the deal with this was *not* having people tell you what to do."

"Oh, yeah."

"Try this: Sometimes if I'm having trouble knowing what I want, I think through what I *don't* want and see what's left."

That made enough sense. Lucy sat up straighter on the bed. "I know I don't want to compete." She didn't want her mom biting her nails over the repertoire and asking anxious questions about it all the time. She didn't want Grandpa Beck obsessing over where she ranked and pushing her to perform as much as possible, compete, record, to build her reputation. She didn't want the competition juries, mostly wrinkled and sour, watching and listening for reasons to downgrade her existence.

"How about performing?" he asked.

"I don't know," she said.

"In some ways that's the point, right? To share your love? Complete the circle?"

The way he put it sounded a little kumbaya, but it wasn't that different from what Grandpa Beck said about translation. Who were you translating for? Only yourself? No. All the great composers wrote music that was meant to be heard. The musician, the person at the instrument, was the bridge between the composer's head and the listener's ear.

"Yeah," she agreed.

"Have you thought about conservatory?" Will asked.

"Like for college? Music school?" She had, once upon a time, assumed that would be her path. Then it was like she woke up one day and had turned pro.

"Yeah. Or even the Academy now."

"Oh, no Beck-Moreau will ever go to the Academy here. Over Grandpa's dead body. He literally said that once."

"Eventually you'll have to stop blaming him and decide what *you* want to do, and just accept you'll never get his approval," Will said. "Listen to your old pal Will. I've had my own losing battles with that. Just step out of the fight."

There was a knock on her door. "I have to go," she said. "I mean, thank you. I have to think."

"Go enjoy the rest of your weekend. I'll be around on Monday, if you want to talk."

"You're, like, here all the time lately." Not that she was complaining.

"Your mom e-mailed to ask for extra hours. Grandpa's orders."

"See?"

He laughed. "Uh, yeah."

They said good-bye, and Lucy went to answer her door. Her dad stood at the top of the stairs with his arms folded, and Lucy worried for a second she was in some kind of trouble. Then he said, "I just talked to Mom. She said you called her. Thank you."

"She didn't want to talk to me?"

"She didn't talk to Gus, either. Things sound crazy over there. The connection was bad."

She shrugged and tried not to let it bother her.

"Is there anything you want to do this weekend together?" he asked. "I took Gus to the movie. I'm available for you, too, chicken."

Lucy grimaced at her nickname. "That sounds better in French, you know." As usual his timing was terrible. All she wanted to do was sit and think over what Will had said. "I have a lot of homework. And a *hangover*," she added, giving his shoulder an affectionate push.

He held up his hands. "My fault. My fault. Okay, I'll leave you alone. Sweet dreams." He leaned in for a kiss, then went downstairs.

She returned to where she'd been sitting on the bed and pulled a pillow into her lap. What Will said about conservatory—music school—wormed its way into her. It hadn't occurred to her that she could still go. The idea of it, the idea of even the remote *possibility*, changed everything.

What could any conservatory possibly teach you? It was her grandfather's voice. The voice of pride and ego and worry over what people would think. With her performance and recording background, wasn't she beyond music school? Would it be going backward? Evidence of some kind of defeat?

If Will thought so, he wouldn't have suggested it.

And the Symphony Academy would be a way to dip her toes in before she made any huge decision about college. She could figure out what she wanted. Maybe what she wanted wasn't even about playing piano. Maybe composing. Or teaching, like Will did. Trying other instruments or even studying music history.

If she went that route—the Symphony Academy—she wouldn't be able to keep it a secret much longer.

Lucy, eight years old, sitting between Grandma and Grandpa Beck at the symphony hall.

They were there to hear Leon Fleisher, a pianist who had been famous when her grandparents were young. He'd been a child prodigy, making his public debut at eight, Lucy's age, playing with the New York Philharmonic at age sixteen, and traveling the world.

Then, at the height of his career, his right hand stopped working. Just ... stopped.

"But he kept playing," her grandmother told her, while they waited for the concert to begin. "He kept making music. He conducted; he taught; he developed a repertoire using only his left hand."

Grandpa Beck had been reading his program without comment. Lucy's grandmother leaned forward, so he would hear her, and said, "Your grandfather thought he should have given up. He predicted Fleisher would never be able to play with both hands again. He thought it undignified that he kept going."

"You say that as if I were the only one," he said, flipping the page of his program.

"Well," Grandma Beck said to Lucy, settling back in her seat with a smile. "Here we are. And here he is. With both his hands after forty-some-odd years of only the one, older than me."

Lucy watched the performance, watched Fleisher's hands for any sign of imperfection. At one point her grandfather whispered to Lucy, "There. He missed a note in that phrase."

She hadn't noticed. It sounded beautiful to her, and she liked the way he sat relatively still on the bench, did not make huge flourishes or use dramatic head movement. He let the music speak. Lucy always remembered that and tried to do the same when she performed, and aside from the subtle rocking she couldn't quit, stayed still for the music, let it speak.

The audience stood for him for a long time, and Grandma Beck one of the first ones up.

"A pity ovation," her grandfather said, but when Lucy looked at him, there were tears running down his face.

20.

On Saturday Reyna texted Lucy that they should work off some pie. Lucy walked to her house; Abby answered the door. "Is Gus with you?" she asked.

"Hi. No, sorry," Lucy said. "He's chained to his piano. Where's your sister?"

"Asleep."

"Uh-oh." She jogged up the stairs and found Reyna in bed, listless and dazed.

"I guess I fell back asleep after I texted you," she said.

Lucy pulled the covers off of her. "What do you want to wear?"

"Yoga pants. Hoodie. You know the socks I like."

Reyna didn't move while Lucy got her clothes out and tossed everything on the bed. "I'm not going to dress you myself."

"I need coffee."

"You can have coffee after we walk," Lucy said, hoisting her up by the forearms.

"Why are you so mean to me?"

♪

The day was cold and overcast, not the best walking weather. And Lucy had a new headache, this time concentrated at her left temple in a way that made her want to push her fingers into it to stop the throbbing. When they were out on the street and halfway up the first block, she said, "So after you left on Thursday, Aruna and Gus went—"

"Who?"

"Aruna. Will's wife?"

"Oh yeah."

"She and Gus went to the TV room, and the rest of us went to the piano room, and I was like, I don't know..." They were breathing hard, pumping their arms. "I *sat* there at the piano and—"

"Oh my God." Reyna yanked Lucy's hand and pulled her toward the curb. "We have to cross the street. That's one of my dad's girlfriends."

Lucy looked at the figure coming in their direction from over a block away. When they got to the other side of the street, Reyna said, "They're everywhere. I feel like we have to move to another state or something."

"Don't move. Okay, so I don't know what came over me, but—"

"Are you talking about the pier? Because I don't know, either."

Lucy stopped walking and folded her arms against the wind. "No, I'm talking about Thursday. Are you even listening?"

"Yes?" Reyna had stopped, too.

"No, you're not."

"Sorry," Reyna said with a shrug, and started walking again. Lucy didn't follow right away. When she did she walked at a slower pace than Reyna, forcing her to turn around. "Wednesday night was a little *weird*, is all. You didn't even ask if you could wear my dress."

"You said it was okay! You didn't want it. You were going to throw it out."

"You already had it on! What was I supposed to say?" They were at an intersection. Reyna jabbed the walk-signal button about ten times in quick succession.

"And then at Thanksgiving you were...I don't know. You're not *you*."

The light turned, and they crossed. "I'm me. How was I not me?" They walked in silence for a couple of blocks. "And what if I *am* different?" Lucy asked. "A lot happened to me while I was out of school. Maybe the me who came back last spring wasn't really me. I don't know."

They stopped at another crosswalk, stepped off the curb, and almost got run down by a car making a right turn. "Asshole!" Reyna shouted. Then said to Lucy, "A lot happened to me, too. And I wish you'd been there."

"Well, me too."

When it was safe, they crossed. Reyna had led them to Peet's Coffee, and now they stood outside the door and could see their reflections. She said to Lucy's, "Of course you can change. But tell me. Like if you're going to go back to how your life was before, give me some warning because...it was hard."

They stepped apart to make space for a man who came out with a coffee cup in his hand. When he'd passed through, Lucy said, "I'll never go back to how it was before. I promise."

"Okay," Reyna said quietly.

♪

On Sunday morning Lucy helped Martin drag the Christmas decorations out of the huge closet under the staircase, and they adorned the banisters with garlands and put together the artificial tree for the foyer. The rest of the day passed in a haze of homework. Lucy decided that reading about the Middle Ages was almost as excruciating as living through them. It made her actually enjoy doing her precalc.

Gus came up to her room once to use the laptop, which he took over to the bed while she sat at her desk. He recited his day's activities: He'd spent two hours with the Wii, watched about five episodes of some horror show, and binged on pie.

"Now that's a day off," Lucy said.

"I saved you the last piece of the chocolate pecan."

She turned in her chair. "Really? That's your favorite."

"Yours too." He typed something into the computer.

"What are you looking up?" she asked. Wii cheat codes, she figured, or clips from the movie he and their dad had seen.

"Nothing."

She went over to him, to make sure he wasn't looking at anything little boys shouldn't be looking at. "Who's Kim Choi?" she asked, when she saw the list of results on the screen.

"Someone I'm playing against in February. It's a he. Grandpa said he's really good."

"So are you."

Gus shook his head. "He's better."

Lucy closed the laptop, barely giving him a chance to snatch his fingers away. "Don't think about it like 'playing against.' Don't even think about it at *all*. It's in February."

"February is close." He reached to reopen the screen; she clamped down on it.

"Gus," she said, "do you want to end up like me?" She pointed at herself and made a face.

"Yyyeah," he said carefully.

Lucy sat there, her finger suspended in midair and still pointing at her chest, a host of reactions coursing through her. "How do you mean?"

"Like how you worked hard and won things and got to go around the world and stuff. And then if I don't want to do it anymore, I'll quit. Like you."

She put her arm down. "I wasn't happy, Gus." She'd explained this to him after Prague.

"I know. You had to."

"But you won't have to," she said.

"Only if I want to."

You're so good, though, she caught herself thinking. She immediately corrected the thought. Being good wasn't a reason to keep doing something you didn't want to do. The voice in her head, sounding exactly like her grandfather, countered, *You're ten. How can you know what you want?*

She imagined Gus quitting. Walking away, suddenly, as she had. She could understand a little more why everyone had been so let down. Maybe her family's reaction hadn't been *all* about Grandpa Beck wanting to avoid embarrassment or claim her success, or about her mom making up for her own failure. It was like her dad had said, and Martin, about how playing the way she and Gus could was a gift. Common between the two of them but rare in the world. And hearing Gus say, so easily, "Only if I want to," made her also realize that maybe jumping ship at Prague hadn't *all* been about her grandma. Maybe it was, in part, as simple as a ten-year-old's reason: I don't want to.

"It's normal to need a break," she told Gus. "Like today. But do you ever? Want to quit?" She braced herself.

"No," Gus said. "Now I have Will."

Lucy picked up the laptop and went back to her desk. She didn't want him to see her relief and adjust future answers to that question to anything but his own feelings.

Yeah. Now we have Will. Maybe she should tell him, as long as they were having this deep brother-sister talk, about her own conversations with Will. "Gus..." she started.

"I think he's my best friend."

She turned. He looked so sweet and sincere. She could tell him all the reasons his grown-up piano teacher could *not* be his best friend. No one he'd known such a short time could be.

But that would make her a hypocrite.

"Okay," she said. "Just promise me you'll stop Googling the competition."

"Promise."

21.

Nonspecific holiday decorations had gone up at Speare over the weekend. Apparently the least potentially offensive thing about December was snow, not that it would ever snow in San Francisco. There were sparkly Styrofoam snowflakes hanging in the hall, and cutouts of cheerful snowmen on various classroom doors. The one on Mr. Charles's door had been enhanced with a drawn-on Shakespearean-era ruffled collar.

"Merry whatever, I guess," Lucy said to him, feeling a sense of satisfaction at turning in her second-to-last Munro draft. He'd like it, she was sure. He took the paper from her, surprised. "This draft isn't due till Wednesday, you know."

"I know. I'm ready for your notes." She stayed by his desk for a few seconds while other students came in. "How was your Thanksgiving?"

"Nice. Turkey. Same as ever." He put her paper in his in-box. "How about yours?"

"Ditto. Sort of."

"Looking forward to reading your paper."

♪

Carson was at their table in the second-floor lounge at lunch, and Lucy paused, wondering if she could turn back without him noticing. She didn't know how to act, if what Reyna had said about him liking her was true.

"Hey, Luce," he said, barely glancing up from his phone.

"Hiii." Lucy approached the table with caution. "Is Reyna coming?"

"Meeting with Ms. Spiotta." Spiotta taught Reyna's English class and was the head of the department. Carson leaned to reach one hand into his backpack, on the floor next to him, while still operating his phone with the other hand. "I got you a Heath bar."

Her favorite item in the machine at school. She took it from him and sat down. "Sometimes I forget how awesome you are, Carson Lin."

"Yes, you do."

Lucy ripped open the candy-bar wrapper, forgoing the real lunch of leftover turkey and roasted veggies Martin had packed for her. She slid the Heath out on its cardboard tray and offered Carson half. He shook his head.

He was a great guy. And she wouldn't make the whole thing worse by giving him the You're a Great Guy speech. All she could say was, "Sorry if I was kind of crazy on Wednesday."

He finally put down his phone. "It's okay."

"It's been a weird time for me," she said, biting into the thick toffee of the first half.

"I know. For you, for Reyna, for the Lakers, yeah. No one ever asks if it's a weird time for *me*." He changed his mind about the chocolate and put the entire second half of it in his mouth at once.

"Is it?"

He chewed, and chewed some more, and swallowed and said, "I think life is just a weird time."

"Ha. Yeah." Lucy finished off the Heath. "Can I tell you something?"

"No. Kidding! Yes."

She could practice the words on Carson before she tried them out on her mom. "I started playing piano again. And I think I might want to go to music school. *Might*."

"Like make a comeback?" he asked. "Be all famous again and whatnot?"

"No, not like that. Definitely not like that. More like because . . . I just want to. It's what I love. I think."

"Like I love Apple products and plan to camp out at their offices this summer until they give me an internship, even if it means not bathing for a month and living on Slim Jims?"

"Like *that*," Lucy said, pointing her finger at him. "Well, maybe not exactly. But that's the gist of it."

"You didn't love it that way before?"

"I don't know." She thought how she could explain. "Okay, remember how your grandma was freaking out at you about your grades the other night?"

"No, I totally forgot about that." He rubbed his chin, fake-professorially. "But I'm intrigued. Go on."

"Multiply that by a factor of, I don't know, fifty?"

Carson pretended to write an equation on the table with his finger. He studied the blank surface. "Ahh."

"So I don't know if I loved it. I don't know if I got the chance. I mean, you shouldn't have a 'career' by the time you're eleven, right?"

Carson got serious, staring at the table and spinning his phone on its back, over and over. "I wish I'd known you then. I wish I'd heard you play. I don't know anything about that kind of music. Do you think I could hear you someday? Play that stuff? I mean obviously I've stalked your past on YouTube, but in person?"

"Yeah," Lucy said, touched that he wanted to. "Someday."

"Cool."

"You know what?" she asked.

"No. What?"

"I wish I'd known you back then, too."

♪

When she got home, she saw Will's car parked a little ways down the block. She came into the house quietly, through the back. Martin had left a note on the island—he was doing errands, and her dad was at his downtown office, which he didn't really need but rented to keep from going stir-crazy in the house.

She detoured to the bathroom, to wash her hands and check the mirror. Her hair suddenly struck her as...excessive. The hair of a teenage girl who thinks hair is more important than it actually is. She smoothed it down and pulled it over one shoulder, which helped some.

Gus and Will were in the music room working on the piece for the showcase. Gus's playing sounded slightly lethargic at first; then Lucy realized Will was probably having him go through the piece at three-quarter time, a kind of deliberate and extremely focused practice Grace Chang had used with her when prepping for a performance or competition.

This time she wouldn't barge in on the lesson and send Gus out. She stayed in the hall awhile, listening. She remembered what Gus had said about Will being his best friend. And about wanting to be like her.

She had to tell him what was going on, before he heard it from their dad or Martin or figured it out on his own. They'd been in this thing together nearly their whole lives; she couldn't go rogue now without letting him in on it. She waited at the kitchen island and tried to focus on homework until Gus and Will took their break.

About twenty minutes later, they came into the kitchen, Will first. Lucy touched her hair and felt surprised to realize how happy she was to see him. "Hi."

"Just the lady I'm looking for," he said.

Gus opened the fridge and asked, "Why?"

"Because Lucy's my buddy, buddy." Will chucked Gus on the back of his head gently. "Do you want to go back to the music room? Or upstairs? Or take a walk?"

"Why can't I stay with you?" Gus closed the fridge, a couple of cheese sticks in his hand.

"Because," Will started, but Lucy cut him off.

"You can," she said. "Here." She hooked her foot around the stool next to her and pulled it out. Gus sat, and Will went around to the other side and leaned on the island. It occurred to Lucy that she should talk to Gus alone, without Will there. It was kind of between them. But Gus liked him so much, and everything just sort of seemed to *work* when Will was around.

"So," she said to Gus, "I have to tell you something. Kind of a secret. I don't want Mom or Grandpa to know. Yet."

"What about Dad?" Gus peeled back the wrapper of one of his cheese sticks.

"He knows. Sort of. Martin too."

"What is it?"

"Um. Okay. I..." She glanced at Will. "I've been thinking about playing again. And I sort of have been. Playing again."

After a pause Gus said, "Piano?"

"No, trumpet."

He didn't laugh. "Since when?"

"Thanksgiving," Will said. "While you and Aruna were downstairs. Cool, right?"

"You know, too?" He looked from Lucy to Will and back to Lucy. Confused.

"Well, he was there." She left out the parts where she'd already been talking to Will about it before that, that he was the one who'd brought it up in the first place.

"But...yesterday you said how you weren't happy."

"I wasn't. Before."

"Grandpa's not going to let you." He said it like it was the end of the conversation.

Lucy's face heated with frustration. Grandpa was thousands of miles away but still there. "I'm not asking Grandpa's permission. It's not going to be like it was. Will's helping me and—"

"Have you been...teaching her?" Gus asked Will.

Her.

"No," Will said. Lucy confirmed it with another no, and her eyes met Will's. *Say something,* she thought. *Say something to make it better.* "Be happy for her, Gustav."

That wasn't it. It sounded parental and disappointed. Gus

179

turned red. "But...you're..." He jumped off his stool and stalked out of the room, leaving his cheese.

When he'd gone Lucy said, "Well, that sucked."

Will rubbed his hands over his face. "Let me go talk to him. Unless you want to?"

"No, I think you."

"Okay. Then do you have time to grab a quick coffee when I'm done here? We can debrief."

"Yeah. Just...don't tell Gus."

♪

They walked to a coffee shop on Fillmore. "Is he okay?" she asked.

"He'll be fine." Will hunched his shoulders in the cold. "I'm kind of surprised how he reacted. Were you guys really competitive or something?"

She shook her head. "I don't think he's mad about me playing."

"Fooled me."

"He's mad that you and me...have been talking. He didn't know. Yesterday he called you his best friend." Then, feeling she'd told a secret, immediately added, "Forget I said that. Okay? Seriously. I'm the worst sister."

He touched her arm. "No, you're not. Like I said, he'll be fine." Then he added, "God. That's really sweet, him saying that."

"I know."

They went into the crowded café, and Lucy ordered off the holiday menu, something called a Mega-Minty Mocha.

"Whipped cream?" the barista asked.

"Oh, probably not?"

"Come *on*," Will protested. "If you're getting *that*, you gotta have the whip. This is no time for restraint."

She said yes to the whipped cream, feeling her mood lighten, and they waited for their orders. "I can't believe it's December already." It was the first holiday season in forever that Lucy hadn't had a dozen benefits and recitals to do. She wouldn't have to bust out a green velvet dress this year.

"Wait till you're my age. There's one of those every day. 'I can't believe I'm thirty already.' 'I can't believe it's tax time already.' 'I can't believe I'm tired already, it's only eight!' Et cetera."

Lucy cracked a smile. "But you get to do what you want."

"Doing what you want still affects others. At any age. As we have just experienced. Here." He pointed to a vacant table. "Go get that. I'll bring our coffee over."

She hung her coat on the back of the chair and sat down. When Will put her Mega-Minty Mocha with its tower of whipped cream in front of her, she groaned. "This is mortifying. I'm a real coffee drinker, you know. Not a fake."

"I'm not judging." He sat across from her with his soy latte. "So. Other than the Gus situation, how are you?"

How was she? She felt good to be there with him. Bad about Gus. Happy about playing. Worried about her mom and grandpa coming home. "Confused," she said.

"That's okay." He hovered his spoon over her whipped cream. "Do you mind?"

"Whipped cream is vegan?"

Sheepish, he said, "It's my weakness."

"Go for it."

He scooped off the top and stirred it into his latte. "You'll get used to being confused. Adulthood is a perpetual state of confusion."

"Is this supposed to be a pep talk?" Lucy asked, taking a cautious sip of her drink.

"How is it?"

"Minty. Mega-Minty."

"Okay," Will said. "Here's a question. What do you love?"

"What do you mean?" she asked.

"What do you mean what do I mean?"

"I mean it's a broad question."

"When you're trying to figure out what you want," he said, "and you sort of know what you *don't* want, it helps to know what you love. So what do you love?"

"Gus."

"*Hm.*" He touched two fingers to his mouth, then said, "No people. People are complicated. What do you love, uncomplicatedly?"

"Chocolate."

"Goes without saying. And?"

One of Will's hands rested on the tabletop, the other on his mug. Lucy focused on his hands and thought about what she loved. *Loved* loved. What gave her joy. "Well, music."

"Come on, Lucy. Obviously. What *about* music?" he pressed. "*What* music?"

She took a deep breath, thinking. "Okay. Beethoven's Fifth.

You know how you're not supposed to say that one? I mean that might be the only classical piece half the world knows, so if you're . . . you know, if you're *us* . . . you're supposed to have a better, cooler, more obscure answer. But I freaking love it."

"Hey, there's a reason it's so popular."

"That part in the third movement when the cellos have been playing and then the horns come in? And that clarinet stuff in the second, when they're running counter to the flutes. Love."

"Me too. It's perfection."

"And Vivaldi's 'Winter.' First movement. *Major* love." Her excitement grew. She forgot about Gus being mad at her and listed more moments and minutes of favorite pieces, stuff she'd played and stuff she hadn't. The whole time, he watched her intently. She'd never felt someone so focused on her. Even a concert hall full of people didn't feel this way.

"What else?" he asked.

"Do you know Ryan Adams?"

"A little."

"There's this one song with a simple guitar intro and these two little drumbeats . . . or, wait." She pulled out her phone, found the song, and played the first ten or fifteen seconds through the speaker.

He bent forward to get his ear closer to her phone. "Nice."

She stopped, overwhelmed with example after example that came to mind. Not only music, but also nature, food, and even though they were complicated, people. Like Carson, being so awesome to her today even though he'd been hurt, and Reyna and her willingness to show up wherever, whenever. People like Gus. People like Will.

"Why do people...we...why do we drag around like life is so awful?" Why did they forget that there was so much to love?

He took off his glasses and rubbed his eyes. "I guess... because there's also a lot that *is* awful. That's the struggle of getting old. To make sure you don't let what's hard or painful or whatever obscure the beauty."

"You're not old," Lucy said with a laugh.

"No. But I'm old*er*. Than I was. Than you."

She looked at her Mega-Minty Mocha, which was turning into a lukewarm sludge of sugar and cream. "You're lucky. Sixteen is hard."

"I know. But you'll get through it. We all do. Your mom, your grandfather. Me."

"My grandfather was sixteen?"

"I'm not saying I'd put money on it, but the odds are in my favor."

She smiled at him, thinking how lucky *she*, of all the people in the world, was to be sitting at this coffee shop right now with this person who made her feel so totally good.

He finished his coffee, put his glasses back on. "So. I like your list. When I'm feeling confused, creatively or generally, sometimes it's because I don't know what I care about. I forget, like you said. And I think if you can remember what you care about, or at least remember how it felt to care about *anything*, well, it helps. Keep thinking about that."

"Okay."

"And Lucy, Gus will come around."

She nodded. She didn't want him to go.

"All right." He got up and put on his coat and smiled down at Lucy, the multicolored Christmas lights around the café window framing his head, and she knew she'd passed from look to stare many seconds ago. "What?" he asked.

"Nothing," she said, and lifted her hand in a wave. "Bye."

"Talk to you soon, Luce."

22.

She walked home in a slight daze, emotional, light-headed. A menorah in a neighbor's window was so pretty, it almost made her cry, and the rising moon in the dusk was just barely a sliver, a new moon, and she had to stop to marvel at it.

What is this? she asked herself, putting her hand on her stomach.

She knew the Mr. Charles kind of feeling and the stalking-Joshua-Bell feeling and the crush-on-her-tutor-Bennett feeling.

Joshua Bell was a stranger. Bennett was gay. Mr. Charles liked her and everything, but when she compared him to Will, she could see that no matter how many times Mr. C said "friends," it all really boiled down to him being her favorite teacher, and her being the teacher's pet.

This was not that.

When she got back from the coffee shop, she considered going straight to Gus to try to talk to him, but she wanted to be alone. Needed to. She spent a little time up in her room making attempts at homework. At one point her phone beeped a text message, and she lunged for it, thinking it could be Will.

Reyna.

Sick. Nastiness. Food poisoning or flu.
Did I catch it from you?

Lucy replied:

Not that I know of. School tomorrow?

No way in hell.

They exchanged a couple more messages, then the smell of food drew Lucy down to the kitchen, where she found a note taped to the oven in Martin's loopy, purple-inked script:

Eat it all.
I do not have room for leftovers.

The downstairs felt hollow and deserted. "Dad?" she called up the stairs. She climbed up the first flight and repeated: "Dad?"

Then up the second.

"Hello? Gus?"

She paused at the door of his room. He rarely closed it all the way, as it was now. "Gus?" She knocked. "Can I come in?"

Very faintly she heard, "If you want."

He was lying on his bed reading, and didn't deign to look at her.

"Do you know where Dad is?" she asked.

"Racquetball."

"Did you hear me calling?"

"Yes."

"Were you planning to answer at any point?"

He didn't say anything. It occurred to Lucy that this must be how her mom felt whenever she stood in Lucy's doorway, trying to have a conversation Lucy didn't want to have. She took a few more steps toward Gus. "Are you hungry? Dinner is ready."

He didn't say no. He didn't turn any pages. Lucy got closer and took the book out of his hands. He sat up, lightning fast, and grabbed for it. "Don't!"

She held it over her head. "Come down and eat dinner with me. Then you can have it back."

"Give it, Lucy!"

But he stopped grabbing and sat there, a kind of hurt fury in his eyes. Still adorable, though, with his curls all disheveled from bed-head. Lucy had to force herself not to touch them, which would surely piss him off even more.

"Come on," she said. "Everyone's gone. Just you and me."

He stared at her for a good minute, and she no longer had the urge to cuddle him or ruffle his hair. Now she just felt scared, that Will was wrong, that he'd stay mad. She held out his book.

"Here. I'm sorry."

Leaving her standing there with her arm outstretched, he got up and walked around her and out the door. "Only because I'm hungry," he said.

She placed the book on his bed and followed him down.

"Why can't we eat in the kitchen?" Gus asked, watching Lucy set the table.

"When have we ever had the whole dining room to ourselves?

It'll be like a celebration. The official end of Thanksgiving. Sit down; I'll do everything."

She got them each a glass of water. She served the food—a vegetable frittata—and toasted some baguette slices and put a ton of butter and garlic salt on them the way Gus liked and their mother rarely allowed. They ate, and through it all Gus didn't say a word. When he finished his food, he put his napkin on the table and got up. He had to pass Lucy to get out of the dining room, and when he did she was ready. She grabbed his forearm.

"Gus."

He didn't jerk away but wouldn't meet her eyes.

"Did Will talk to you?"

He nodded, and Lucy dipped her head so that she could see his face. She realized he was close to tears, and her heart crumpled. She wanted to pull him into a hug but resisted, as it was clear he did not want to be hugged. Her fingers, around his arm, loosened into something more tender.

"I want to play again," she said, her voice low. She knew it wasn't about that, him being mad, but she also wanted him to understand this part of it. "For me. I think I want to go to music school. I'm not totally, totally sure, and I don't want Mom or Grandpa to think this means whatever it is they'll think it means."

He looked at her. "You can't have Will."

Lucy let go of his arm. "It's not—"

"I had Temnikova for six years. She wasn't like Grace Chang. She wasn't *nice*."

"I know." She tried to come up with words that would make him feel better, and fumbled. "I'm not doing anything official with Will and piano. We're just … he's giving me a small amount of advice, is all." She said it with as little gravity as she possibly could, which wasn't easy.

Gus frowned. "Don't do anything to mess it up," he said.

"Mess what up?" she asked, though she could guess.

"Me having Will."

They both heard their father come in the front door, and Lucy stood to clear the table. "I won't, Gus." When her dad made it into the dining room, she asked, "Did you win?"

"Nope." He grabbed the last piece of baguette from Lucy's plate and crunched into it. "And why would you ask me that when you know I never win?"

"Belief in the possibility of change?"

He pushed his lower lip out and shrugged, as if considering the truth of that. Then he looked from Lucy to Gus and back to Lucy. "Everything okay here?"

They both nodded.

"Then why so serious!" As he said that, he grabbed Gus into an affectionate headlock. Normally, Gus liked to tussle with their dad, and they hadn't done it much since they'd broken some Beck family heirloom in the foyer.

But now Gus said, "Don't."

Their dad took it as an encouragement to scuffle harder.

"Dad, don't!" Gus repeated, and tore himself away, breathing hard. He whirled around and left; Lucy and her dad listened to his angry footsteps on the stairs.

Baffled, Lucy's dad turned to her. "What's going on?"

She shrugged.

"Please don't tell me he's turning into a teenager already."

"I don't think that's it." She added, "We saved you some food. It's in the kitchen," and made her own exit.

Later, up in her room, Lucy texted Will.

Gus is still mad.

She lay on her bed with the phone on a pillow next to her. Emotional again, the same as she was on the walk back from coffee. She didn't want to mess things up for Gus any more than Gus did. But she did want this friendship with Will.

He reminded her of her grandma. Funny like her. Attentive. Not a fan of small talk—instead someone who wanted to discuss the important things, like how it felt to be alive. *Let the world talk about the weather,* she'd said once. *You and I will talk about you and I.*

And of course there were things about Will that were decidedly not grandmalike.

She rolled over and closed her eyes.

She didn't just want the friendship with him. She needed it.

23.

Lucy overslept.

Shit, she thought, when she realized Gus was at her door. *Why today?* Her mother and grandfather were coming back in the afternoon; she'd wanted to start over. To care about things again, like Will had said. Things such as being at school on time.

Gus helped her get her stuff together. "Thanks for waking me up," she told him. Her retainer felt glued to the roof of her mouth; she took it out and tossed it into the case without rinsing it.

Gus watched and made a grossed-out face. "Dad made me."

Lucy pulled on her socks. "Well, thanks anyway."

Downstairs her father stood at the door, dressed and thumbing something into his phone, only slightly less displeased than her mother would have been. He expressed himself more efficiently, gesturing to the door with a pointed finger and saying, "Out. Now."

He walked fast to the car, which he'd brought around to the front and double-parked. Gus jogged to catch up, his backpack bouncing on his shoulders, Lucy behind him. "Sorry," she said to her dad. When they were all in the car and buckled in, Lucy leaned forward from her spot in the backseat and said, "If I ever, *ever* do that again, leave without me, okay? I don't want to make Gus late."

She'd never thought to say that to her mom on any one of their many rushed mornings; the routine seemed written in stone. But nothing was, really.

"And what about *you* being late?" her dad asked.

"I guess that's my problem."

She could imagine how her mother would respond to that. *No, Lucy. It's everyone's problem, because it reflects on the family and disrespects Speare and the money we pay for you to go there.*

Her dad said simply, "Fair enough."

"When I get my license, I can drive us. Right, Gus?"

She longed for him to turn his head and make eye contact. He stared out the window. "If you want."

"Whatever is going on between you guys, we don't need to see that tonight when Mom gets home, okay? Be the charming children I know you can be."

"Charming," Lucy said, glancing at her phone to see if Will had replied to her text from the night before. He hadn't. "Got it."

♪

Outside Mr. Charles's room, she braced herself to be given the boot again. She'd worked up an excuse-free apology. She'd throw herself on his mercy. But when she opened the door, he waved her in without comment.

The plan for the day, which he'd written, as always, on the whiteboard, was for the class to work in their usual groups to come up with some *Othello*-related hypotheses and criticisms.

Lucy joined her group: Marissa Karadjian, Jacob Fleischacker, and Emily Steerman.

"I'll take notes if you want, since I'm late," Lucy said.

Marissa flipped through her *Othello* paperback. "Yeah, okay. Um, how about something related to what we were saying the other day about love and possession in the context of the culture back then? Like women as possessions or whatever?"

"Too obvious," Jacob said.

"Fine." Marissa closed her book. "You come up with a plan."

Jacob and Emily brainstormed, and Lucy took notes until Mr. Charles appeared at her shoulder and told the group, "I need to borrow Lucy for a sec."

She followed him out into the hall. Back in the day—okay, just a few weeks ago—she would have been ecstatic at a special class-time hall conference. This time she knew he was going to call her out on her lateness, maybe even ask her to leave his class permanently. But as soon as he turned around and held up what she realized was her paper, she knew it wasn't about being late.

"I'm a little confused, Lucy."

Whenever adults used that phrase, it didn't go anywhere good. She waited for more.

"Is this all your own work?" he asked.

"Yeah. Well." She shifted her weight and glanced away from him, a queasiness growing in her stomach as she thought about the fast paraphrasing she'd done when putting together the draft, the little bit of cut-and-paste from the Internet. "I mean . . . when doing research, you know, it's easy to . . . it's a draft."

He looked down at the paper, flipped about two-thirds into it, and handed it to her. "Listen." The tone of his voice changed.

Softer, gentler. "I can understand, because of your feelings—I mean, how you look up to me and everything—maybe you thought if you put some of my ideas into your paper, it would make me—"

"Wait. What?" Lucy read the page.

Mr. Charles pointed to a paragraph. "This is from my grad-school thesis. Verbatim."

Her hand flew to her mouth. *No.* "I . . . I did a little Googling, but I swear I didn't know that." At the same instant, what he'd just said about her "feelings" sank in. The words on the page blurred, and she didn't know if she was more embarrassed by her semiaccidental plagiarism or by him saying that. She didn't want to double both humiliations by crying. "It's out there on the Internet without your name on it. I would have noticed. So it's probably been used a whole bunch of times."

He sighed. "Great. Okay, but that doesn't make it all right."

"I *know*."

"I'm giving you an incomplete on the draft. So the best grade you can get on the final paper is a B." Then he touched her arm. "I'm sorry."

She shoved the paper back at him. "Don't be. It's my fault. I'll start over."

"You don't need to do that. Just fix the parts I marked."

"And I don't . . ." She shook her head. How could she have thought he didn't *know*? Pumpkin bread and little notes on his desk and hanging around his classroom so much when she didn't have to. It was all so obvious and pathetic. Was she being like that with Will? That even her ten-year-old brother knew something? *Don't do anything to mess it up*, he'd said.

"I don't feel very good." Her voice trembled. "There's something going around."

Instead of returning to the class, she strode down the hall, toward the girls' room.

"Let me at least write you a pass..." His words faded behind her.

♪

She called her dad to come pick her up, claiming the same stomach bug Reyna had. Then she spent all the time she would have been at school writing a new draft of her paper and checking her phone for replies from Will. She wondered what he did during the day when he didn't have Gus. Did Aruna work? Lucy suddenly had a million questions about them and their lives, wanted to know everything.

This was *not* a Mr. Charles situation, she'd decided. Will wasn't her teacher and was really her friend, and a *good* friend at that. He knew her and her world and knew what she needed right now.

But she had to stop looking at her phone. She put it on vibrate and zipped it into her book bag.

She got in a solid hour of focus on her work, then checked her phone again. There was a reply from him, finally.

Sorry re Gus. It will get better. Call me for a sec?
I have an invitation for you.

An invitation? He answered after half a ring. "Lucy, hiya. I thought you'd be at school."

"I came home sick."

"Too much Minty Mocha?"

"It's . . . maybe."

He paused. "Or are you that upset about Gus? Or something else?"

See? Friends. He knows me. "Something else."

"Want to talk about it? I mean, I'm on my way out, but if you want to tell me I can listen for a minute."

"It's okay." She didn't think she could explain about Mr. Charles without feeling stupid. "What's the invitation?"

"We're having a little get-together at our house this weekend. A sort of a party. We do it almost every Friday, actually. Musician friends. I think you'd like them. Totally different crowd from what you're used to."

"Oh." She bit her thumbnail and stood to pace her room. "Why?"

"Why come to a party?"

"I mean why are you inviting me? Won't it be all . . . people your age?"

"Yeah," he said. "The old folks."

"Ha-ha."

"No, I know what you mean. I thought you could see normal people with noncelebrity lives in music. These are working musicians and teachers and people who do it for fun. Something new, right?"

A party. He was inviting her to a party. "Can Reyna come?" She wasn't sure why she asked that. It wouldn't be Reyna's kind of thing, but the prospect of having her along felt like a comfort. Maybe it would be the kind of adventure that would bring them closer. Also it would solve transportation issues.

"If you want. I don't know how much fun she'd have, but sure."

"I'll ask."

He gave her his and Aruna's address. They lived in Daly City. Lucy couldn't picture Will and Aruna in a gray place like that. She'd assumed they lived somewhere hip, like Cole Valley or the Haight.

"I hope you'll come," he said.

♪

When her dad checked later to see how she felt, she told him it must have been something she ate and that she felt fine now.

"I'm leaving for the airport in about fifteen minutes," he said. "Do you want to ride with me?"

"Too much homework."

He touched her forehead with the back of his hand, then cupped her cheek. "You made it a good Thanksgiving for me, *poulette*. Special. Hearing you play again. That made my year."

She put her hand over his and pressed it against her face. They hadn't talked about it since that night. She'd half-hoped the wine had made him forget, but now she was glad he remembered and had been thinking about it. "Did you tell Mom?" she asked.

"No."

"I know I need to talk to her," she said. She took her father's hand from her face but held on to it, separating his fingers one by one as she spoke. "I'm going to. I'm not sure exactly when."

He nodded. "Okay."

"And you contribute, Dad."

"What?" He smiled, perplexed.

"Not just half the genes."

He pulled her head to his chest. "I could have done better. Now you're all grown up."

♪

Lucy put on a dress her mom had bought her a few months ago. It wasn't so much Lucy's style—a little too Young Professional for her. But her mom liked it, and Lucy wanted to show effort.

She looked in the closet mirror and thought, again, *Too much hair.* She should get it all cut off. Or at least half of it. Donate it to one of those cancer-wig charities. Only, she wanted it gone *immediately*, and she did have a fairly sharp pair of scissors in her bathroom drawer that she used for trimming her bangs. The idea caught hold, and she peeled off the dress to avoid covering it in hair.

Staring in the bathroom mirror, she wondered why anyone would want hair this long. She was always having to pick strands of it off her sweaters and clear it from the shower drain, and sometimes on a warm day it felt like a wool blanket against her neck.

She took up the scissors, knowing that Reyna would advise against this. Lucy wouldn't be dumb; she did just an inch or two at a time, not one big dramatic "I'm a pixie now" chop, like so many celebrities did.

She got it up to her shoulders in something like a shaggy bob.

It didn't look bad. It didn't look *good*, either; she'd have to get it fixed. But it had the effect she wanted, which was: something different. Something to mark a change.

She put the dress her mother liked back on and realized it

didn't look right with this hair. In her closet she slid hanger after hanger across the rod—no, no, no, no. Then she hit the little group of items she'd held on to for Reyna. Not only the infamous red dress but several other things. That whole day—at Reyna's house, the drive to Half Moon Bay—seemed far, far in the past.

Lucy's black pencil skirt with a plum sweater would work. The high neckline of the sweater complemented the shorter hair. Her mother would choose heels, or maybe a low wedge, with this outfit, but Lucy put on textured tights and her flat brown boots. And earrings, dangly silver ones.

She was a different person than she'd been when her mom left the week before. Now she looked it.

It would still be a little while before they all returned from the airport. Lucy sat at her desk and put some finishing touches on her paper, including a short note of apology to Mr. Charles for being lazy with her research. *About what you said,* she added at first, *I wouldn't call them feelings, at least I wouldn't say*

She backspaced over it all. The thing with trying to say you didn't care was that saying it meant you did care. The appropriate weapon of not caring was silence. She kept the note formal, student to teacher.

A knock on her door. "Come in."

Her heart leaped to see Gus. His eyes went wide when he saw her hair. "That's short."

"It's not short. It's medium-length."

He got closer, right up to her chair. He circled her slowly, and she could feel his breath on her cheek and then on her newly exposed neck.

"It's kind of medium-short."

Lucy fought off a smile, because she didn't know why this should make her smile, then didn't know why she was fighting it, and grabbed Gus around the waist while she had him near. She hugged him rough and tight, the kind of hug he claimed to hate and always struggled against. Not this time, not much. He held on to her for a second.

Then he said, "They're home."

24.

They went downstairs to greet their mother and grandfather. Lucy, suddenly sure her mother would hate her hair, wished she'd at least waited to change her whole look until after they'd had a chance to talk. Her voice-mail apology was a start, but there was a lot left to say.

She clutched Gus's hand, then let go. When they got to the last flight of stairs, Grandpa looked up. His face brightened.

He's happy to see us, Lucy realized with some wonder. Why it should surprise her, she wasn't certain. But his happiness worked on her, and she found herself smiling back at him. In his smile she caught a glimpse of a gentler reality of him, a person whose major crimes against her were based on something good: pride in the accomplishments of his offspring. Maybe pride gone extreme and overfed with money and status, and damaged along the way because of those things, but still: pride that she was his granddaughter.

He, Lucy's parents, and Martin were all crowded into the foyer with luggage and other bags and what looked like a case of wine. Lucy and Gus stopped on the bottom step and each accepted a hug from their grandfather, and Lucy also got a kiss on the cheek. "You look lovely," he said to her.

That made her mother, who'd seemed to be aggressively fussing with luggage in a specific effort to *not* look, finally do so. She studied Lucy as if trying to figure out what was different.

"Lucy," she finally said, "that's . . . very you. I wonder why we didn't do that sooner."

Lucy chose to ignore the "we" and went to her mother to hug her. She smelled different. Airplane upholstery and some new perfume. "Welcome home," Lucy said.

Her mother let go and indicated a couple of bags to Martin. "That's all food. Special ingredients you can only get in Germany, Grandma always claimed. The wine comes from a family vineyard in Lössnitz."

"Let's open a bottle," Grandpa Beck said, "and eat."

♪

Lucy sensed her mother's eyes on her throughout dinner. She resisted touching her hair but felt it brushing against her neck in different ways as she ate. Martin had put out some of the preserved sausages with dark German bread that had been in one of the food bags. There was also potato-and-leek soup and arugula salad.

"I can feel winter coming," Grandpa Beck said. "There's an edge in the air."

"We could make a fire later," Lucy's father said.

Her mother interrupted their visions of a cozy evening. "And how did your studies go, Gustav?"

"Fine." He sounded disinterested, occupied by trying to discreetly eat around his leeks.

"Fine?" Grandpa Beck asked. "Better than that, I hope. How is the preparation for the showcase coming?"

Lucy's dad chimed in. "He worked hard. You'd be proud."

Gus let his spoon go and gave Grandpa the attention he demanded and the answer he wanted. "Will says I'm ready. That it's already great. We'll make it perfect."

Grandpa smiled. "Good. Then we have to start thinking about the Swanner. Let's get Will over for dinner soon. I want to talk to him about that."

"Aruna too?" Gus asked.

"Of course."

They finished eating, and Lucy waited for them to mention Grandma's family and whatever kind of ceremony there'd been when they'd spread the ashes. It hadn't even been a week since Lucy's own little ceremony, if you could call it that, at Seal Rock. A week. Eight months of what felt like virtual sameness had flown by, then suddenly there'd been this eternal weeklong stretch in which nothing remained untouched and unchanged.

Except Mom and Grandpa. Exactly the same, discussing Gus, schedules, upcoming holiday obligations. Lucy looked around the table at her family.

Life couldn't be all about achievement. Proving some indefinable thing to unnamable people on arbitrary timelines.

She wanted more for herself, for them.

She set down her spoon to ask about the details of their trip, then lost her nerve when Grandpa Beck looked at her, still gentle, still happy they were all together.

Tonight was good. Tonight, she wouldn't make waves.

♪

After everyone was in bed, she put on some Matt Haimovitz cello suites—not too loud—and pulled every article of clothing she owned out of her closet and drawers. With her entire wardrobe piled on the bed and floor, she sorted. Aside from her school khakis and polos and sweaters, she tried on every piece and asked her reflection, *Is it me?*

The answer, usually: *No.*

It was like what Reyna had done with her post-divorce closet purge, though that had been about ridding her life of evidence of her dad.

For Lucy, it was more like what Will had said, about discovering what you want and care about by knowing what you don't.

She wanted to chip away at everything that made up her life now and see what was left. She'd find the real life beneath, the one waiting for her.

25.

Lucy had put her phone as far away from her bed as possible so that she couldn't snooze. Alone in her room in the quiet of the morning, starting again with her mother seemed simple: a face-to-face apology to add to the voice-mail one, and she wouldn't be defensive no matter what her mom said. Then she'd make a choice to get along. People in a family who cared about each other should be able to work this kind of stuff out. Plus, the holidays were a natural time for reconciliation. Maybe they could go Christmas shopping together.

Lack of cooperation from her hair almost made her late despite waking on time. When it was long, the weight of it helped it hang right no matter what she did or didn't do. Now the shaggy layers were a mess, and not in a good way.

There wasn't time for vanity. Products and bobby pins and a little more makeup than usual, and she was out the door and down the stairs, ready to meet her mother with a smile.

But it was only her dad and Gus getting ready to go and signaling to Lucy to be quieter on the steps. "Mom's asleep," her dad said. "She'll probably be catching up with that all day. Ready?"

Lucy nodded, disappointed in herself to feel relief.

♪

She placed her Munro draft in the in-box on Mr. Charles's desk, a few minutes early to class, CC's coffee in hand. He nodded at her. "I'm glad you're feeling better," he said, then did a double take. "Did you change your hair?"

"Yeah." Did he like it? Hate it? "I'm sorry about yesterday."

"I know." He picked up her paper, and she watched his pale eyelashes as he scanned the pages. "That was fast work."

"I wanted time to get your notes before doing the final draft."

"I'll look at it while you guys work in your groups."

Lucy couldn't concentrate or contribute, knowing Mr. Charles was reading her paper. She could see him up there at his desk, flipping through it, his face showing nothing. She imagined the moment he'd come across her note and partly wished she'd included that more personal thing after all.

At the end of the period, as students left the room, Mr. Charles stopped her. They stood in the doorway together. "Good work, Lucy." He handed her the paper. "I made a few notes on one of your central hypotheses, but you're on the right track."

And despite the embarrassing mess that had gone on between them yesterday, those words still meant so much, and Lucy found herself smiling at him, if not quite meeting his eyes.

"The new hair is cute," he added, giving her a little bump on the shoulder with his knuckles.

"Thanks." She got out of there before she said anything else.

In her next class she looked through the paper, skimming only for his handwriting, especially at the end where she'd written her apology. He'd written just beneath it: *Life is long. A lot happens. We learn.*

♪

Lucy had texted Reyna earlier to see if she'd be at school today— she would—but didn't warn her about the cut. She wanted her unedited reaction. Carson saw it first. They ran into each other on the stairs to the second floor at lunch. "You chopped it off! Holy..." He jumped up a couple of stairs above her, then down a couple of stairs below her, to get all the angles. "You chopped it off."

"It needs professional help." She felt nervous all of a sudden about what Reyna would think.

"You did it your*self*?"

"Kind of on impulse."

"Not baaaad." Carson held up his hand for a high five.

She slapped it and laughed. "I think that's my first high five for a haircut."

They sat at their table, and Lucy assessed her food situation. She had only an apple and half of an old protein bar, misshapen from being at the bottom of her bag for too long. She was starving, but when she thought about the options on campus, nothing sounded good. "I want a burrito," she announced. "Not a school one, a real one."

Reyna's unmistakable shriek interrupted Carson's response. Lucy turned in time to see her rushing over with her hands out. "Your hair!" Reyna sank her fingers into Lucy's choppy layers.

"We're gonna go get burritos to celebrate," Carson said.

"Celebrate what?"

"Lucy's hair, obviously."

Reyna went around to the other side of the table and squinted at Lucy, as if deciding whether the haircut was something to celebrate or mourn. "We can't. There's no way we'd make it back by fifth, and I can't miss again. Plus my stomach is still weird."

The apple and warped, linty protein bar would have to suffice. Lucy knew she shouldn't miss class again, either, after faking sick the day before.

"Seriously, though, Lucy, why did you do that?" Reyna sat down and studied Lucy's head.

"Is it bad?"

"Nnnoo. It's kinda..."

Carson sliced his hand through the air between Reyna and Lucy. "Now I have burrito on the brain. School burrito better than no burrito. I'll leave you ladies alone to discuss hair."

"Bye, Carson." Lucy lifted her apple to him. When he'd gone, she told Reyna, "I know. I didn't plan it. I'm going to get it fixed."

"I think it'll look good."

Lucy could see that Reyna was tired, still, from being sick. "I think it's part of what we were talking about on Saturday. Change. All of that."

"Well, it's hair. It's not supposed to stay the same."

"The other thing we were talking about," Lucy said. "Piano? I never got to finish."

Reyna folded her elbows on the table and rested her chin on them. "Tell me."

Lucy went backward, starting with how she was thinking about music school. She told Reyna in more detail about playing on Thanksgiving after she and Abigail had gone home, and then went all the way back to Prague—Reyna already knew what happened, of course, but they hadn't discussed it in depth because, at the time, Lucy didn't want to.

"In the moment, I never thought that would be the last time I played," she said. "I hadn't *felt* like playing since my grandma died. Now I do, and it's amazing to have that again. But it's also a little scary, because of how intense my family is about it, you know? So I haven't told my mom or grandpa yet."

"Don't you think... I mean, wouldn't they be kind of happy?"

"My grandpa basically told me I quit forever. He's not over it." She wished she could get that Pier 39 feeling back, when the idea of Grandpa's power seemed actually funny.

Reyna lifted her head. "Don't take this the wrong way."

"What?"

"Do you think it's *possible*, a tiny bit, that maybe you're the one who's not over it?"

"But you don't—"

"I know, I don't understand. I don't live there, and I'm not a musician, and I don't get that world or whatever." Reyna smiled. "Buuut I've known you forever. And you didn't have a problem with your family being 'intense' until pretty recently. *You* were intense."

Reyna wasn't wrong. She also wasn't right. "Only because I didn't know it could be any other way. I can see now, how Will is with Gus, that it—"

"Oh, *Will*. Right."

"What now?"

"Just what I said before." Reyna widened her eyes. "About being *careful*."

The lunch period was almost over. Lucy hesitated a moment.

If she wanted Reyna to understand the music stuff, and how Will was helping, she should attempt to show her what it all meant, up close. So: "Speaking of Will. He invited me to this thing this weekend. He said you could come. You should go out with me to this thing, and then you could sleep over at my house."

"What's the thing?"

"Sort of a party. With all these musicians and stuff. Will and Aruna's friends," Lucy said. "And you'll see what I mean about—"

"Adults?"

"Yeah."

"Musicians?" Reyna said it with more than a hint of misgiving.

"Mostly, I guess." Lucy pled, "Come on. Please?"

Reyna sighed. "Okay, yeah, we could check it out. I want to see Will and Aruna's house."

"It's ... in Daly City."

"They live in *Daly City*?"

"I know."

♪

Her mother was still sleeping or sleeping again when Lucy got home from school. Her grandfather, though, was up and in his office, sorting through the mail that had come while they were gone. She watched him from the hall. Either the trip had aged him, or Lucy hadn't taken an honest look at her grandfather in a long time.

Sensing her there, he glanced up from his work. "Lucy." He removed his glasses. "Come in."

He gestured to the chair across from his, on the other side of his desk, and she sat. "Are you..." She searched for something to say to him. "...unpacked already?"

"Yes. I like to be settled." He shuffled some mail. Picked up his glasses. Put them down again. The hair on his hands was white, the skin in wrinkled, spotted folds. "And Thanksgiving went well for you?" he asked.

"Yeah. Fine. How was the memorial?"

He set his fingertips on the desk and seemed to waver, his torso swaying slightly, head down.

"Grandpa?" Lucy said.

When he lifted his head, she could see that his eyes were watery.

"It must have been sad," she ventured.

He straightened himself, made his back rigid. "Oh." He waved his hand, a gesture somewhere between disgust and impatience. "People with their sentimental memories and religious comforts. When I die, I hope—" He stopped abruptly.

She couldn't imagine it, even with his noticeable aging. He was too stubborn, too busy, to die.

He picked up his glasses once more and put them on, examining his mail with intense displeasure. "They all want my money." He held up a piece of mail. "The Society of Lithuanian Oboists. Ha! They haven't done their research." He tossed the mail away, shaking his head. "Oboists."

Lucy smiled.

She wouldn't ask him about Grandma's ashes or demand an apology for what happened in Prague or for anything else. And he'd be upset about her playing again, and upset if she didn't, because either way it wouldn't happen according to his plan, and it was too late for it to be his anymore. Or Great-Uncle Kristoff's. Or whoever's. Yes, he was busy, and he was stubborn, but he wasn't that strong. He'd leaned heavily, his whole life, on these things that weren't his own.

Lucy added that to the list of things she *didn't* want for herself.

And her grandfather to the love list, the one she made at the coffee shop for Will, even though, as he said, people were complicated.

26.

Wednesday came and went, and Lucy still didn't talk to her mother. They exchanged words, about practical things and insignificant things, but they didn't *talk*. There'd been chances. But when those chances presented themselves, the words Lucy had practiced in her head wouldn't come out of her mouth.

Will didn't come; he had some commitment he'd made before taking the job with Gus.

Lucy and Will had an ongoing text conversation. They asked each other about their days, sent their status updates. Wednesday night he sent her a picture of a vegan cupcake he was about to eat, and she sent him back a picture of the page in her pre-calc book she was stuck on.

She'd hoped to have some time with him on Thursday, while he was at the house. I'm home if you want to say hi, she'd texted, but he didn't reply, and she hadn't heard from him since his good morning text, so she called him around the time he'd be driving home while she lay on her bed with the lights out.

"Lucy Luce," he said, when he picked up.

"So we're coming to that party thing. Me and Reyna."

"Good! Hey, sorry I didn't see you today. Gus wanted to talk."

"About what?"

He paused.

"Never mind," she said. "None of my business."

"You sound a little down."

"I guess. Stuff with my mom. We kind of had this fight right before she left town, and we haven't talked about it." She waited for a piece of advice or encouragement. He didn't say anything. "Hello?"

"Had to make a left turn."

She didn't really want to talk about her mom, anyway. She focused on Will's voice, which, she'd noticed, sounded younger on the phone than in person. Like he could be her age. "What were you like in high school?" she asked.

"Um . . . dorky. A bit overweight."

"Really?" He was so fit now, and Aruna so gorgeous.

"Yeah. I was a lonely kid. Well, you know how it is. Being great at classical music doesn't go far, socially. Even if you're mildly popular, you're not really *there* to enjoy it."

"Wait." Lucy propped herself up on one elbow. "Were you like me? I mean, and Gus? Did you travel and perform and stuff?"

"Yep."

She didn't remember any of that from when she'd looked him up that first night he came over. "What happened?"

She heard freeway traffic, Will breathing. "Nothing happened," he said. "I . . . well, I saw I wasn't going to make a career as a performer. I started teaching. I had the show for a while. And . . . here I am."

"How come you didn't tell me this before?"

"*Hm.* I guess I thought you knew."

"Did you tell Gus?"

Will paused. Then: "No. It's all on my résumé."

"But don't you think he'd like to hear about that stuff? More directly? I mean—"

"Lucy, do you like to talk about your glory days? Does your mom?"

After taking a second to get over her surprise at the frustration in his voice, Lucy said, "I guess not, but..."

"It's like this for most young musicians, you know. You aren't the only one who's been through some version of this. We grow up, and we aren't so special anymore."

"I didn't—"

"Look, it's been a long day." He waited for her to say something, but she didn't know what. "And I'm pulling up to my house," he said.

"Oh. Okay."

There was another silence, then he said, "I'm sorry, Lucy."

"It's all right." What else could she say?

"No, it's not," he said. "I don't want to be like that. Cynical."

The suspicion that he hadn't actually wanted to talk to her hurt, but she didn't want to make him feel bad. She wanted to make him feel better. "At least you're honest. It's better than pretending."

"Maybe. Maybe not." He sighed. "I'm glad you're coming to the party."

Lucy lay back down. "Wait, what should we wear? Me and Reyna?"

"Trust me, it's not the kind of party where people think that hard about what they're wearing. Wear whatever makes you comfortable."

They said good-bye, and Lucy dragged her laptop into bed and reresearched Will. This time she went past the first couple of pages of links and found some references to William Devi, young performer from the midnineties. There hadn't been much written about him. At least, it wasn't on the Internet.

She found one blurry old picture, probably scanned from a newspaper, of him, fourteen, receiving a plaque. Lucy smiled at his hair in a top-heavy nineties style that didn't exactly help him look less chubby. His facial features were unclear; zooming in only made them worse. She saved the picture to her computer, anyway, and thought about Will existing before she'd known him.

Glory days.

That made it sound like it was all behind her, when in fact having Will around had finally given her something to look forward to, faith that happiness was ahead. At the Academy, or wherever. But it didn't sound like he believed that for himself.

She texted him:

I think you're still special.

He replied simply:

:)

♪

After school on Friday, she took a bus to Laurel Heights, where she'd made an appointment to get her DIY shag fixed.

"You didn't screw it up too bad," the guy said, examining chunks of it as Lucy looked at herself in the mirror. She'd been wearing a little more makeup since changing her hair, mostly darkening her eyes with shadow and mascara. As she watched herself now, the nylon cape up to her neck, the stylist bobbing his head to the dance music on the radio and half-holding a conversation with the stylist next to him, she could see a little bit of her mother in her face. Her coloring was more like her dad's— neither dark nor light, just sort of generically Caucasian—and she'd always liked to believe she favored him, but her reflection didn't lie. The shape of the mouth, the depth of the eyes, even the way her shoulders had edges more than slopes, all said Beck more than Moreau.

She could almost see the woman she might become. Physically, anyway. And maybe she'd gotten too much like her mom in other ways already. Holding things in and holding on, like Reyna said. Letting Grandpa dictate how she felt about herself.

At the same time, her mother was worthy of admiration. She was smart. She worked hard. A lot of moms of Speare kids managed to make full-time jobs out of shopping and getting massages and undertaking unnecessary redecorating projects. Lucy's mother never slacked at managing the household and all the details of Gus's career and helping Grandpa Beck with his charitable trusts and the family trust—the one he'd be passing on to Lucy's mom and, maybe eventually, to Lucy.

"If you get one of our other services today, it's thirty percent off," the stylist said, rubbing something between his palms, then spreading it through her hair.

"Like what?" Lucy asked.

He talked to her reflection. "Color. Manicure. Lash tint. Brow wax. Whatever."

"How long does the lash tint take?" She could shave a few seconds off her getting-ready-for-school time if she didn't have to bother with mascara.

"Fifteen or twenty minutes."

"Okay."

She also ended up getting a manicure and spent way more time and money looking at and buying hair products than she'd planned.

The last, accidental glimpse in the salon mirror as she paid astonished her.

The haircut had changed her face. Or life had changed her face. Or her face always was like this and she hadn't noticed. All she knew was that there was little sign of the girl she'd been a couple of months ago, or at least of the image of that girl she'd carried inside her all this time.

She waited for the bus home, her eyes watering from the lash dye. It was dark now, dark earlier and earlier these days, but there were no calls or texts on her phone from her parents or Martin worrying over her. She hadn't told them about Will's party. They were letting her lead her life.

She felt unmoored, like some kind of last, invisible cord between her and them had been cut in those few strange days of Thanksgiving weekend, without it being officially decided or talked about.

That was what she'd wanted, she guessed. Permission to do

what she needed to do, for herself. Not to be an extension of the whole Beck-Moreau thing that had felt like such a burden for so long. To grow up.

This evening, this moment, standing in the increasing fog and cold, she thought maybe Will was right: *We grow up, and we aren't so special anymore.* It wasn't cynical. It was just true.

♪

The house felt achingly silent. A note on the entry-hall table said that her mother and father had gone out to dinner, and her grandfather had taken Gus to hear a string quartet at the Herbst. She stared at the note, thinking, *I like string quartets. He knows that.*

She went to the kitchen, pulled some pieces off the roast Martin had made the night before, and ate a handful of nuts and a few spoonfuls of leftover rice.

In her room she put on music to get ready by. Reyna would be picking her up at eight. None of her usual choices inspired the mood she wanted—fun, confident Friday night party with her best friend but not in some kid's garage. She scrolled and shuffled and played and skipped and paused and found nothing.

She got dressed in silence, putting together an outfit of dark skinny jeans, the flat boots, and a long coral sweater with a hood. The sweater had been another item her mom had bought for Lucy when Lucy wasn't with her. At the time it had seemed too long and drapey for her taste. It had an uneven hemline, and no one she knew wore uneven sweater hemlines, so she'd stuffed it into her drawer without even clipping off the price tag: $389. For a sweater.

Now she could see why her mother had thought it would work on her. It hung perfectly on her tall body, skimming her curves in a way exact but subtle. And the color did something for her skin. Maybe, after she talked to her mom, Lucy would ask her to go shopping for more stuff like this.

The text alert on her phone jangled her out of her mirror trance. Reyna was waiting outside in the car. Lucy got all her stuff together, left a note for her parents, and went out to meet her. "You look really cute," Reyna said. "Supercute."

"Thanks."

"Do I look like I've been crying all day?"

"Nope. Well, let me see." Lucy turned on the car's interior light and pretended to scrutinize Reyna. "Gorgeous, as usual."

"'Cause I have."

Lucy didn't have to ask why. They held each other's eyes in the yellowy glow. "Do you want to..." *Cancel?* She couldn't say it, couldn't give Reyna the chance to not go to the party. If she didn't see Will tonight, it would be two more whole days before she did, which felt too long. "I'm sorry," she said. "We'll have fun tonight. Promise."

"All right," Reyna said, turning off the dome light. "Let's go show those Daly City people how it's done."

27.

Will and Aruna's house actually had some character and charm, considering it was basically a stucco box, like every other house in the neighborhood. The paint job—cream with brick-red trim—helped, and so did the plants on the stairs leading up to the front door, which had a nontacky Christmas wreath on it.

Lucy reached for the doorbell; Reyna grabbed her hand. "You don't ring the bell for a party. You just go in."

"At my house you ring the bell."

"Nothing that has occurred at your house could remotely be called a 'party.'" Reyna opened the door, then stepped behind Lucy and gave her a push inside.

The house didn't have an entryway or hall. They were suddenly right in the living room, which was filled with people ranging from more or less like Will and Aruna—youngish, cool—to those older, grayer, or geekier. A few of them turned to look at Lucy and Reyna.

It wasn't like making an entrance to a music-festival party or benefit reception. Lucy had no certainty of belonging, no sense of her place.

"I don't know how long I'm going to last here," Reyna whispered.

Me neither, Lucy thought, but she wanted them to try. "You'll be fine. There's Will."

Lucy pulled Reyna toward the other side of the room, where Will stood. He looked good: jeans, a light-blue T-shirt that had been washed into comfortable perfection, and a soft-looking navy cardigan. He hadn't shaved; his stubble had a bit of red in it, though his hair was nearly black.

"Hey, I'm so glad you came. You look lovely." He gave Lucy a kiss on the cheek, right in front of everyone. The stubble left a scratchy warmth. "Can I take your coats?"

Lucy handed him hers. "Mine's in the car," Reyna said. "And thanks for inviting me."

"Sure." He turned his attention back to Lucy. "I'll go put this down, then introduce you around."

"Cheek kiss," Reyna said to Lucy. "Is that what you guys do now?"

"We're friends." He'd never actually done that before. She resisted touching her face.

Will came back before Reyna could say anything else, and for the next ten minutes or so, he introduced Lucy to his guests. And she noticed: They knew who she was. Not everyone, and no one said anything obvious about it, but as Will took her from person to person and introduced her by her full name—Lucy Beck-Moreau—she saw it happening: extra attention suddenly paid, a few *ohs,* the sincerity behind the *nice to meet you*s.

When they got through the living room and made it to the kitchen, Lucy sensed eyes following and people talking in lowered voices. Then Will had to excuse himself to greet someone else who'd just gotten there.

At least half the people they'd just met were women, but Reyna misread the stares, anyway. "Why do I suddenly feel like a massive hunk of jailbait?" she muttered.

"It's not that."

She peered back through the kitchen doorway and wondered what they were saying about her. Maybe that she was a has-been. Or a spoiled brat in a four-hundred-dollar sweater who'd thrown away the life they would have treasured.

Then Aruna came into the kitchen, dressed in faded jeans and silver sandals and a flowy top, and opened up her arms. "Hey, my girls!" She gave them each a hug, then held up a bottle of gin. "Anyone? No, what am I saying? I guess you'd better not."

Aruna chatted away while mixing up a pitcher of martinis, raving about Martin's cooking at Thanksgiving. "I don't know how you don't weigh three hundred pounds, Lucy. But you're..." She looked Lucy up and down, holding fast to the gin. "Wow, young lady. Did you change your hair? Tell me about your dozens of boyfriends."

Reyna, examining the nonalcoholic drink options on the table, said, "Lucy's hot but doesn't try at school. Plus she has a thing for older men."

Thanks, Reyna.

Aruna poured a few careful drops of vermouth into the pitcher. "Oh, I understand that." She glanced up toward the doorway as someone walked in. "Here's an older man for you now. Julian, Lucy. Lucy, Julian."

"And Reyna," Reyna said.

"Nice to meet you both," Julian said. He stood close to Aruna

224

and touched the back of her hair. "And I thought I was a *younger* man."

"To me you are. Not to them." She tilted her head toward Reyna and Lucy, and walked out with the pitcher.

Julian had longish hair and a sandy-brown goatee and was taller than Will. "I'm not that old," he said. "I'm twenty-two. Same as you guys, probably." He stooped down to dig in a cooler under the table and retrieved a beer.

"Yep." Reyna looked at Lucy and rolled her eyes. "Close."

"I'll be right back," Lucy said. She wanted to find Will.

Reyna coughed conspicuously into her fist. Lucy knew that meant she didn't want to be ditched with Julian, but then a couple more women came into the kitchen and Lucy repeated, "I'll be *right* back."

The living room seemed to have twice as many people in it now, and Will was clear on the other side of it, by the bay windows, with his arms folded talking to some middle-aged lady in a saggy dress. Crossing the room daunted her. She turned and retreated into the hallway.

She didn't want to go back to Reyna and her anti-party attitude. The door at the end of the hall had been left ajar. A dim light—a night-light, maybe—emitted a kind of faint welcome. An invitation. Lucy checked over her shoulder, then peeked inside. It was Will and Aruna's bedroom. She went in and closed the door behind her.

Lucy hadn't exactly spent time imagining their bedroom, but if she had she wouldn't have pictured this. She would have figured them for a simple and clean IKEA-looking setup. Instead it was lush, and a little cluttered with books and clothes and shoes. The bed, in the center, was a low platform, covered with the coats and purses of party guests and a lot of throw pillows with exotically embroidered covers.

The room smelled faintly of the spicy perfume or lotion or whatever it was Aruna wore. Lucy went to the dresser to see if she could find out what it was. She'd never had her own signature scent; maybe she should.

With an eye on the door, she dug through a shallow, rectangular basket that contained that kind of stuff—lipsticks, lotions, perfume samples, bracelets, hair clips that still had strands of Aruna's dark hair attached to them. Nothing that smelled like Aruna. Then she saw, just behind a framed picture of a dog, a slender bottle. She uncapped it and sniffed. Yes, this was her. Lucy positioned the bottle near her wrist.

Don't be an idiot, Lucy. Like no one would notice you reeking like her.

She put the perfume back and instead slid open the small middle top drawer of the dresser, not sure what she was looking for.

There were voices in the hall, and she froze for a second, but then the voices faded. She couldn't stop now. She moved to the bedside tables—one a mess of books, magazines, more lotions, reading glasses, a dirty coffee cup. A red scarf had been draped over the lamp. That had to be Aruna's side.

On the other, Will's nightstand was nearly bare except for one book, a small notepad on top, a pen on top of that, and a bowl of change by the lamp. Lucy wanted to see the book; one single book compared to Aruna's leaning pile must mean something.

A mystery novel; no big revelation.

In the change bowl, nail clippers. If he was like every other pianist she'd known, he trimmed his nails obsessively so he wouldn't feel them touching the keys.

Voices in the hall again made her jump. Lucy grabbed the clippers and shoved them into her jeans pocket, then pretended to be looking for her coat on the bed. A couple came into the room—Lucy had a random jacket in her hand, the clippers in her pocket. She attempted a smile as she put the jacket back down and walked out.

♪

When Reyna saw her emerge from the hallway, she grabbed Lucy's wrist, hard. "Where were you?" she asked through gritted teeth. "You left me there with creepy whatshisface and his salsa breath."

"Not alone. Anyway, I thought maybe you liked him," Lucy tried.

Reyna dropped Lucy's wrist. "Yeah, because you know how I love gangly college music nerds."

Lucy looked over Reyna's shoulder, searching for a glimpse of Will in the living room. The nail clippers in her jeans pocket made a comforting pressure on her thigh. "I want something to drink. . . ." She moved away from Reyna, toward the kitchen.

"I don't want to go back in there!" she hissed. "What if that guy wants my number or something? He was giving me *looks*. Can we just go?"

Lucy turned around. "We've only been here, like, half an hour."

"It feels longer."

"Another half an hour." Reyna made an anguished face as if Lucy'd just requested one of her kidneys or something. Frustrated, Lucy said, "I never ask you for favors, Reyna."

"Yeah, except for when you need a ride somewhere. I know that's the only reason I'm here tonight."

Lucy pressed her lips together and went to the kitchen.

There were a few people getting drinks. Lucy found some sparkling water and studied the pictures on the fridge, trying to guess who were friends and who was family. There were a lot of shots of Will and Aruna together, dressed up at various events.

And one of Will with a young Asian girl, maybe nine or ten, in concert attire. Lucy had known he must have other students. She just never pictured them as actual people. Kids, and maybe students her age or older. Girls. Women.

Did he go out to coffee with them? Ask them what they loved? Text with them?

Someone touched her shoulder. She turned. It was the lady in the saggy dress who she'd seen talking to Will earlier. "Lucy. It's so great to see you here. I'm Diane Krasner."

They shook hands. Lucy knew exactly who she was, though they'd never met. The name Diane Krasner had been spoken in their house for months; she'd put together the showcase Gus was preparing for. "Nice to meet you," Lucy said. "Gus is really excited about his piece."

Immediately she wanted to take it back. She had no idea if Gus was excited. But schmoozing was habit. This was exactly the kind of fake life she didn't want to go back to.

"Excuse me," she said to Diane, in hopes of escape.

"Wait, I'd love to hear what you've been doing," Diane said.

She had gray hair cut into a chin-length bob, large black-framed glasses, and a thick coat of red lipstick. "Is it true you haven't touched the keys since Prague?"

"Yeah, I..."

"Until now, I mean." A slow smile formed; she had a smudge of lipstick on one of her top teeth. "What made you decide to go back to it?"

A flicker of shock zipped through Lucy's brain. Will had told people? She stammered out an "I don't know."

Then Will came into the kitchen, and Diane grasped his elbow. "Let's get Lucy into the showcase," she said to him.

"Oh," Will said, glancing at Lucy, "no. It's so soon."

"From what you told me, she's ready enough. It would be such great publicity."

Lucy watched Will's face. From what he'd told her? She waited for him to say something, like what a ridiculous idea it was. He held up one hand and brought it toward her shoulder, but she stepped back.

"Um, I have to go find Reyna."

Will's and Diane's voices faded, and Lucy found Reyna sulking in the hallway, one shoulder resting against the wall as she stared toward the living room. Lucy was ready to say, *Come on, I'm going to get my coat and then we can go*, but when Reyna saw her, she said, "Do you want to hear my theory about you?"

"Your theory about me about what?" she asked, distracted. Maybe she should go back to the kitchen, tell Diane directly that no, she had no interest in the showcase.

"Men. This." Reyna gestured to the living room. "That thing at the pier."

"Not really." Lucy turned toward Will and Aruna's room to retrieve her coat. Reyna grabbed her arm from behind; she yanked it away. "Fine. Tell me your theory."

"You miss having an audience."

Reyna said it with a sly smile, like they could be, possibly, joking around. Lucy put her hand on her chin and nodded and made her eyes wide—exaggerated, fake listening. "Tell me more."

"See, you got screwed up by performing so much as a kid. You were, like, conditioned to be on stage. Now you want a round of applause for, I don't know, writing an English paper or showing up at school or wearing a sexy dress."

Lucy dropped her hand from her face.

"Guess what, Lucy? You're just a normal, boring person like the rest of us. No one cares about this stuff except, like, the six people in your world. And now you think Will's gonna—"

Then Lucy put her hand over Reyna's mouth and pushed her against the wall. She glanced toward the kitchen. "Don't." And they stood in a lock, bodies pressed together, close enough to kiss. Something in Reyna's eyes clicked on. Lucy took her hand away.

"You like him," Reyna whispered slowly. "As in you actually think...I told you to be careful and—wait. Wait. Are you guys..."

"It's not like that. He believes in me."

Reyna laughed. Lucy felt the gust of it on her face. "He believes he's going to get some teen-girl action." Reyna tried to squirm away, but Lucy was stronger and kept her pinned there. She wouldn't let Reyna make it all into a dirty joke.

"Ow, Lucy!"

"You know what? Lots of people's parents get divorced, and *they* don't start acting like assholes."

Then Reyna gave Lucy a long look before shoving back so that Lucy hit the opposite wall of the hallway. "Trust me. I know men a lot better than you do. I've had *real* relationships and nonrelationships with *real* guys, and no matter how 'nice to you' or whatever they seem, how 'special' they make you feel, they're all the same when it comes down to it. My dad. Every guy at school, maybe even Carson. Will."

They were leaning on the walls across from each other now.

Someone walked between them to get to the bathroom. "Excuse me."

Lucy knew that Reyna didn't want to be there. And that the stuff between her parents had been brutal, the knowledge of her dad's affairs crushing. But Reyna was wrong. About men. About Will.

"If that's what you think, you should probably leave," Lucy said.

Reyna laughed. "Without you?"

"I'm not kidding. Leave."

Reyna pushed herself off of the wall and turned away. "Have fun with your new best friends."

Lucy let her walk down the hall and disappear around the corner, and waited until enough time had passed for her to have gone out the front door. Then she went to the living room and tried to ignore the fact that people were watching, noticing that Reyna had left upset. She pulled back the edge of the curtain and looked out the window. Part of her hoped Reyna's Mini would still be parked there, Reyna leaning on it, maybe, waiting to see if Lucy would come out. All she saw were the car's taillights retreating into the foggy night.

She let the curtain fall back into place.

Then she realized Aruna was standing behind her, watching over her shoulder. "Do you two fight a lot?" she asked, her breath on Lucy's cheek.

"No."

Aruna put her arm around Lucy. The weight of it was uncomfortable, but Lucy resisted shrugging it off. "It's hard at this time of life," Aruna said. "You're both changing. I remember. So much happens at your age. You're becoming the people you'll be."

Alcohol turned people into philosophers. She'd seen it with her dad, and sometimes her grandfather, the way they'd make trite statements sound like the wisdom of the ages after a cocktail or two. But she knew Aruna was right.

28.

After Reyna left, Lucy wasn't sure what to do with herself. Will seemed to always have people around him. She stayed on the edges of the room, wondering how she'd get home, what Will had said to Diane Krasner, if Reyna would ever talk to her again, and if she cared.

She noticed a girl sitting on the floor nearby and held in a little gasp when she realized it was Felicia Pettis. Felicia was a few years older than she was and had always been the one taking the prizes that Lucy won, after her, and doing the tours that Lucy did, before her. They'd never actually been in the same place at the same time.

She saw Lucy watching and waved. Lucy went over, pushing aside all thoughts of Reyna.

"Hi," Lucy said. "I hope this isn't weird, but ... okay, I probably shouldn't start a sentence like that if I don't want it to be weird, but ...." She put her hands on her cheeks. "I can't believe I'm finally getting to meet you. I didn't see you when I first got here, I—" She didn't want Felicia to think she'd been ignoring her on purpose or something, out of jealousy or an old sense of competitiveness.

"I blend in," Felicia said. She was petite and smooth-faced, and she scooted over on the floor to make space for Lucy. "Sit down."

"Thanks. I'm . . . I'm Lucy."

"Yeah, I know," Felicia said with a laugh. "I love that sweater."

"Oh, thanks. My mom picked it out, which is ironic, because . . . well, I don't know why it's ironic."

Felicia sipped from her beer bottle. "So. I have *just* learned tonight about what happened in Prague. It shocked me, I have to say."

Lucy inched closer. "You really hadn't heard?"

She shook her head. "I took myself out of the loop a long time ago. I went off Facebook, I went off Twitter, I don't read the blogs, the industry news, any of it."

"Yeah, you sort of dropped off the face of the earth. The last thing I heard about you was at the Himmelman, like, three years ago."

"And what did you hear?" She held up her hand. "Never mind. I don't want to know."

Lucy laughed. She hadn't heard anything definite, just everyone wondering why Felicia wasn't there and trying to make guesses ranging from the flu to that she'd run off with some conductor from Spain.

"I used to watch your YouTube videos all the time," Lucy said. "Especially that Liszt one?"

"Oh, God. I begged my dad not to record that recital. I had this massive cold sore. . . ."

"I didn't notice. I was too busy obsessing over your interpretation of that piece. So original."

"Thanks."

"Do you . . ." Lucy paused and reframed her question. "I hate it when people ask me this, actually, because it feels personal, but now that I'm asking you, I guess I understand why they ask me. They really just want to know if I play anymore, that's all. I read too much into it," she said, shaking her head. "I get, I don't know. All defensive. But: Do you play anymore?"

Felicia nodded. "I do."

"Just for you? Or?"

"No, I'm still on the whole circuit or whatever you want to call it. I just don't *win* now or place very high or do publicity stuff, which is why you thought I dropped off the face of the earth." She was matter-of-fact and didn't seem embarrassed about being at the middle or the back of the pack or wherever she was.

"Oh." Lucy didn't know what else to say.

"And I work part-time doing data entry at a place that allows me flexible hours," Felicia said. "I live in West Portal with two roommates. I'm taking some classes online at State. You know. Just being twenty." She smiled and held up her beer. "That's my little speech. I have to give it every time I run into people who remember me from back then."

Lucy wondered what her own defense would be, the lines she might wind up repeating over and over to explain her choices.

"How do you know Will?" she asked Felicia.

"Everyone knows Will. I was on his show way back. We stayed in touch. He's a sweetie."

"Oh, yeah, totally," Lucy said, trying to sound as casual as Felicia did, like Will didn't mean anything special to her.

"Earlier tonight he was telling everyone you were coming and that he'd heard you play, and you were still great even though you hadn't played for a while and all this stuff. So congrats on that."

Lucy leaned forward, not sure she'd heard. "What?"

"It's cool, making a comeback. I mean *I* didn't know you'd left in the first place, but whatever makes you happy. Will's just a teeny-tiny bit excited. It was cute."

Okay, Lucy thought. It didn't sound totally terrible or anything. Still. It was their secret, she'd thought. She stood up. "It was nice to officially meet you, finally. I should..."

"Hang on." Felicia pulled out her phone and handed it to Lucy. "Put your number in. And I'll do mine."

Lucy took her phone out of her pocket and gave it to Felicia. "Thanks."

"Seriously, we should hang out."

"Thanks," Lucy said again, and put her phone back in her pocket, next to Will's nail clippers.

♪

Ten minutes later Will finally got away and found her, back in the kitchen, sipping more bubbly water and reading the label on a box of crackers. "Hi," he said.

"Hi."

"Reyna left you."

"I told her to." She set down her water. "Where's your piano?" she asked him. She was tired. Drained, emotionally, from the fight with Reyna and now trying to figure out why Will was telling people she was making a comeback.

"I don't have one here. There's no room. My piano is at my folks' house in Sacramento."

"Sacramento. That's a long way to go."

"Ha, yeah, well, I don't go." He smiled. "Don't look so sad. My viola is here. In a closet. I have plenty of access to pianos, don't worry."

It didn't seem the same to Lucy, and she wondered how much he actually played other than with students. "I think I'm going to call my mom to come pick me up," she said.

"Let me give you a ride. I want to explain about Diane, and . . ." He scratched at his stubble. "Or try to."

He sounded defeated, and Lucy knew she wasn't mad about him telling a few party guests, didn't really care, and just wanted to be able to talk to him without all these people around. "You can't leave your party," she said.

"It's my party, I can leave if I want to," he sang. "Sorry. Now maybe you can imagine the dorkiness that was me in high school."

"A little. I guess I should say good-bye to Aruna?"

He looked toward the living room. "You can give it a shot. I'll meet you at the door."

Aruna was sitting on the floor in front of the couch, her martini glass still held loosely in her hand though it was full of olives now and not gin. "Lucy!" she exclaimed, loud enough that everyone turned around. "Come here, beautiful."

"Thanks for having me," Lucy said, squatting next to her, smelling that exotic perfume.

"God, those are great boots." Aruna squeezed Lucy's calf, pulling her off balance; she half-fell, half-sat on the floor. "You should spend the night. I can't believe Reyna ditched you!" She reached over her shoulder and patted the couch. "Right here. This is our guest bed."

Will called from across the room. "I'm taking Lucy home, babe! Don't do anything crazy."

"I'll wait till you come home to get crazy," Aruna replied. To Lucy, she said, "I hope you had a good time, not counting Reyna."

"I'm glad I came," Lucy said. "Thanks."

She stood up, waved good-bye to Felicia, and at last got out the door. When Will closed it behind them, he exhaled hugely and said, "We made it."

They trotted down the stairs, into the Daly City fog.

♪

Before they'd even driven the first mile of the fifteen they had to go, Will said, "I talked. About you. I spilled the beans." He shook his head. "When we agreed to keep it a secret, I mostly thought about your family. I got excited and mentioned it to one or two people."

Lucy played with the hem of her sweater and felt the bump of the nail clippers in her pocket. "It's a small world," she said. "I mean, Diane Krasner. She's only one degree of separation from my parents."

"I know. I guess I wanted to impress her."

She looked over at him. His profile, lit every few seconds by headlights, was elegant, strong. "Why? You don't have to impress anyone. You're you."

He laughed. "Oh, sure, just say my name, and the red carpet rolls out."

"My parents think you're impressive. Everyone knows you're

a great teacher. My grandpa wouldn't have hired you if you weren't somebody, trust me. You had that TV show and—"

"Right. *Had*. Canceled after two seasons."

She watched the road, Will making the turns that would take them onto the highway.

"I interrupted you," he said. "I'm sorry. Yes, I'm a good teacher. Thank you. Anyway, I don't need to talk about this, the main point is I shouldn't have said anything to anyone without asking you first. If you don't forgive me, I understand."

He usually seemed so confident and comfortable. She wanted him to see himself through her eyes.

"You impress *me*," she said. "You, being yourself. From when I first met you. And I didn't even know all that stuff about from when you were my age."

"Back in the olden days." He smiled and glanced at her. "I'm sorry. I'll stop with the self-pity. Thank you, truly. That means a lot. You impress me, too. Not just with your musicianship. Now that we're real-life friends, there's a lot more to be impressed by."

Real-life friends.

"Like what?" she asked, thinking she shouldn't but unable to stop herself.

He contemplated the question. "You're very poised, obviously. Smart. I think you're brave to do what you're doing. Inertia is a son of a bitch, you know? Once you stop something, it's hard to restart. Especially something that requires hard work."

"Yeah."

"Also you must know you're beautiful."

Lucy looked at her hands in her lap. Her mom and dad had told her that. Her grandma. Reyna. Sometimes she thought it about herself. This was different. "I'm not mad that you talked about me," she said quietly. "I have to tell my parents, anyway. This will help make me do it."

"Oh, God, thank you," he said, relief in his voice. "When I saw the look on your face in the kitchen with Diane, I thought I'd really effed it up."

Their freeway exit loomed. She imagined herself home, with her family, telling them. Tomorrow?

"No," she said. "Maybe it's not even that big of a deal. Maybe I'm the one who's been making it harder than it needs to be. Reyna said something like that...."

"Is that what you were fighting about?"

"That's...too hard to explain."

"Okay. I won't pry."

He drove exactly the speed limit and not one mile-per-hour over. "Hey," he said, "mind if I take Portola? I know it's the long way, but I love the view."

"Me too."

He rested his elbow on the driver's side door and touched the hair at his left temple. "About impressing people...I guess I've been feeling old lately. I can see my future, being an old guy who teaches. You know, never having my own success again."

She'd been watching him talk, the shape of his jaw as it moved around his words. She was losing track of the conversation and of her own thoughts. The experience of being in the car with him had become more physical than mental. She was aware of everything he did with his hands, mouth, voice. And noticing her own body, the grip of denim on her thighs and the sweater hood behind her neck, prickling.

They passed the School of the Arts, and that brought her back to her mind.

When Lucy was in eighth grade, she'd asked her mother about going there for high school. She'd been looking at the school's website. The kids seemed like they were having so much fun.

Her mom had laughed the idea away with one sentence: *You're overqualified, to say the least.*

Lucy asked Will now, realizing it had been her turn to talk for a while. "Is it dumb to go to music school when I already kind of...know everything?" Then she covered her eyes. "Um, that sounded awful."

Will chuckled. "You're great, Lucy. But nobody knows everything."

"I just mean—"

"No, I know. Listen." Will pulled over, turned off the engine. The car was cool and dark, the spectacular lights of the city before them, and a dizzying wave washed over Lucy as he leaned into her space a little bit to turn on the stereo and mess with some buttons.

Then it started, a piece she knew and loved: the four opening notes of the woodwinds, the build of the timpani, strings. The piano came in. Skillful. Expressive.

"Do you recognize that?" he asked.

"Mendelssohn. Concerto number two."

"It's you."

"What?"

"It's you, Lucy."

She stared out at the famous view she'd been seeing her whole life—the Transamerica Pyramid, the string of lights across the Bay Bridge. Yes, it was her. She remembered: the hours in the music room with Grace Chang sitting near. She remembered the day she'd nailed this piece, found the music in it, made it a part of her. How it had landed, finally, not in her head, where it had been confounding her for months, but in her heart, where it belonged.

She'd flown with her mother and grandparents to Ohio to record it with the Cleveland Orchestra. She could smell the rehearsal room—rosin and old paper.

"My grandma came with us when we made the CD," she told Will, still staring out over the city. "I think she was my lucky charm, because the whole thing went so well. No drama. I was happy. I was good. I—" She stopped talking, so she could listen and resurrect the sense she'd had at the time of being one with the orchestra, and with herself, the way everything that wasn't the music had run over her like a distant, quiet stream.

She didn't just remember the love she'd had as she played. She felt it, now. Love. Like falling.

"It's damn near perfect," Will said quietly. "God. Listen to that."

She turned away from the skyline and looked at him. They listened and stayed face-to-face, and the moment was a window, inching up, and she went through it, his eyes pulling her along, seeing her, and seeing her, and seeing her.

He broke his gaze abruptly and pointed at the stereo. "*That* is the point of music school. To bring that Lucy back. Because you need to separate all the family shit from *that*. And I think, for you, school would be the best road to take. If you do it the old way, you're going to wind up in the old traps."

Lucy tried to hear his words through the moment, through feeling so close to him and to herself.

"School will still push you," he continued. "It'll be demanding in a different way than you're used to. But it will be your teachers and mentors and advisers and peers who push you, which is, I don't know, just healthier for it to be those people and not the ones you really need love from. I mean your family."

She swallowed, to clear the pressure that had been building in her throat. "That makes sense." Her voice came out unsteady.

"Are you okay?"

She nodded and let their eyes meet again.

"Should I get you home?"

No, she thought. "What . . . ?" *is happening?*

He thought she hadn't heard him. "You're tired," he said. "Me too. I'll get you home."

He started the engine and continued on to Lucy's house. He'd turned off the CD. Quiet filled the car.

She felt him glance at her once or twice, but he didn't speak. When they stopped in front of the house, she delayed saying good-bye by moving as slowly as possible. She went through the steps: took off her seat belt, turned her body toward the passenger door, opened it.

Then she turned back. She reached across to hug Will.

She held on a second, and a second longer.

Don't make me let go. Her breath caught, like she could cry, her heart full.

"All right," Will said quietly, patting her back. "I know, Lucy."

She moved her hand and felt the skin of his neck under her fingers, warm.

"Okay," he said, pressing his palm to the back of her head. He took her hand off his neck and lifted it to his face. He held it there a moment, grazing it with his lips, before saying again, "Okay."

She let go and got out of the car, went to the front door, and waved to him to show she'd got it open and was safely inside.

III.

Con Brio, Con Fuoco

(WITH SPIRIT, WITH FIRE)

29.

Lucy didn't send Will any texts on Saturday; she didn't understand what had happened or how to act. He didn't send any to her, either. She stayed in her room, neglecting her homework in favor of making a playlist for him. His Christmas gift. It included some of the music they'd talked about at the coffee shop. She titled the list: "What I Love."

That distracted her for several hours. Because once she started listening to something she loved to see if it belonged on Will's CD, she couldn't just stop in the middle of it. Love meant paying attention, so she sprawled out on the floor with her good earphones, trying to hear every song as if for the first time, falling in love with each one over again. And certain songs brought back memories, like being little and riding in the car with her mom, and the B-52s coming on the eighties station, and her mom singing along. Where'd *that* Mom go? Lucy didn't know what her mother listened to now, what made her sing with the radio.

The B-52s brought her back to reality. She needed to prepare herself for the talk with her mom that *had* to happen this weekend.

Because she was actually doing this. If she'd had any doubt left, Will erased it when he made her listen to herself with the

Mendelssohn. She wasn't afraid anymore about what anyone else would think.

But when Will called her on Sunday, when she was coming in from a walk, she almost didn't answer, suddenly shy and uncertain at his name on her phone's screen. Finally, after ring number four, she picked up and began the climb up to her room.

"Hi."

"Hey," he said. "Everything okay over there?"

"Yeah. Good. How about you?" She took the stairs two at a time, glancing in Gus's room on her way. He was lying on the floor, reading a comic book or a magazine or something.

"Good. Spent yesterday recovering and cleaning up from the party, then we went to a student's chamber-music recital."

We. Him and Aruna. His wife. "How was it?" She'd made it up the attic stairs and closed her door behind her.

"Fine. That's actually why—well, part of why—I'm calling. Diane Krasner was there. She was serious about the showcase, Lucy. She said they'd make a space for you."

"What? No. I told her no."

"Actually, *I* told her no. You ran off."

"Same thing," she said. "Because, no. Obviously I'm not going to play the showcase." She paused. "Right?"

"Well. I think you should seriously consider it."

"It's in, like, two weeks!" Lucy sat on her bed and rested her head on her hand, confused. "And . . . *why*? Wouldn't that be the 'old way'? Like you said? The old traps?"

"I thought about this all night," he said. "I promise I don't recommend it lightly. But listen: What's going to happen when you tell your family you want to go to music school?"

248

"I don't know. I guess I'll find out soon."

"You'll get push back. That's my guess."

"Push back is an understatement." Her grandfather would more than balk at spending that kind of money on something Lucy had already quit once. She'd had her chance, he'd say, and she'd discarded it.

"And it's what you've been afraid of. What's been keeping you from telling them what you want. Right? You're afraid they'll say no and that them saying no will deter you somehow. Mentally."

"And also I didn't know what I wanted."

"You do now." His words slowed down, quieted. "I felt it in the car on Friday, Lucy, how you connected to the self, the you who made the recording."

She slid off the bed and sat on the floor. She dug into her pocket for his nail clippers, which she'd been keeping with her at all times.

"I do," she said. "But not..."

"I know what you're going to say. But performance is the language your grandfather speaks. Your mother, too, because of him. You playing the showcase would make a statement they'll understand." His voice gained excitement. "It would prove you *mean* it, Lucy. That you can't be talked or, I don't know, *shamed* out of it. And it being so soon is a plus. You can't stress yourself out too much with preparation, and this whole thing will be dealt with by the New Year, and you can start...fresh."

A grand gesture, an echo of the drama with which she'd quit, only in the reverse. And without the distressing shock/embarrassment factor, because her grandfather would know about it ahead of time.

"I don't know." What would her grandmother think? "What about Gus? Isn't that kind of stealing his spotlight or something?"

"It's a feel-good holiday concert. Not a competition. Plenty of spotlight to go around."

When she didn't say anything, he continued: "I get that you're unsure, and I wish you had more time to think about it. But Diane needs to know by tomorrow. If you say yes, they want time to add your name to the advertising."

There wasn't any point in delaying the inevitable. Left to her own timing, she might never take any action, period. Doing the showcase would get all the pain over with at once: Gus would be mad for a while. Grandpa would fume.

She'd rip off the scab of the last eight months with one good, hard yank.

"When tomorrow do I have to decide?"

"As early as possible. I think this is good," he said. "Trust me, okay?"

"Okay." She opened her hand and looked at the nail clippers on her palm. "Okay."

Neither of them spoke for a few seconds, then Will said, "I guess I should let you go."

They said good-bye; then, remembering the beginning of their conversation, she texted him to ask, **That was part of the reason you called. What was the other part?**

She lay on the floor, her phone in one hand, the clippers in the other, until he finally replied.

To tell you that Friday night was special to me.

The words were a current, electric and bright, that traveled through her bloodstream, into her heart and back out to her fingertips, that typed: **Me too.**

After a second he replied: **xo**.

♪

She found her mother in the parlor reading the Sunday paper in one of the armchairs and drinking coffee. With her feet up, her hair in a simple pony, and wearing stylish reading glasses, she could have been the star of a catalog shoot for some perfect J.Crew late-Sunday-morning lifestyle spread.

"Hey," Lucy said, to announce herself. She picked up the arts section, which her mother had tossed aside along with sports and business. She sat in the other armchair.

"Hi there." Her mom nudged the ottoman so that Lucy could share it.

"Thanks." She pretended to read the paper for a while and waited for her mother to ask her something. Like how school was going, for example, or where she'd been Friday night, or maybe she'd offer some little bit of conversation about the trip to Germany. When it became clear her mother wasn't going to talk, Lucy said, "I'm sorry again about what happened before you left."

Her mother let a corner of the paper fall down so that she could see Lucy better. "I know. Me too. It was bad timing." Then she straightened the paper back up and kept reading.

"Mom."

"Mm?"

"That thing Grandma used to say, what her mother told her,

that German phrase? That everything will be okay? How come you never say that?"

Her mother put down the newspaper and took her feet off the ottoman. She set her reading glasses on top of the paper. "I don't know. Maybe I don't believe it."

"I do," Lucy said. "I think I do. Mom, I need to talk to you."

She could begin with a statement, something attention-grabbing. *I'm playing in the showcase* and backtrack from there. Or she could return to the beginning, to the first moment she'd started to feel like the playing wasn't for her anymore. But she couldn't rehash every hurt, every disappointment, every moment that felt like betrayal, and expect to arrive anywhere good.

"I'm sorry that I quit."

That was the sum of it, and she meant it in every possible interpretation.

"Oh, Lucy, that's long past us." Her mother's voice was tired. "I should have handled the whole thing differently. We shouldn't have made you go to Prague. I should have put my foot down with Grandpa. I should have listened to your dad. I thought about it on the trip, and . . . well, it's just so complicated."

"It's not past us, though. It's not past Grandpa. And it's not past me, and I—" Lucy moved to sit on the ottoman, now close enough to rest her head on her mother's knees.

"Your hair is so short now," she murmured, putting her hand on Lucy. "I've always wanted to try short hair. I'm too scared. I'm a coward, Lucy."

"You're not."

"I do want to believe that everything will be okay."

"Mom," Lucy said. "I want to play again. I might want to go to music school." She lifted her head; her mother drew her hand back. "Mom, I miss it so much."

Her mother stared for a few moments. "Oh. That's...not what I expected."

"Me neither."

"Are you *sure*, Lucy?"

"I'm sure right now. I'm not saying I'll be doing it in ten years. I can't..." How could anyone be expected to plan their whole life at any given moment, say "I promise" forever, see into the future? There always had to be room for uncertainty, for change. "Yes. I'm sure for now."

"All right," she said. "All right," she repeated, more definite this time. "Let's talk."

♪

Even after their long talk, Lucy couldn't have imagined the strength her mother would show at dinner.

"We're going to discuss Lucy's future," she said as soon as the food was on the table. She laid out the facts plainly and unemotionally. She didn't look at Grandpa Beck the whole time and didn't let him interrupt, though he tried more than once.

Lucy talked, too, about how she'd missed playing but not the way her career had gotten, holding everything else hostage, the relentless pressure.

"If you can't handle *pressure*, you shouldn't *play*," Grandpa Beck said.

"*Why?*"

"Stefan," her father said, "are you listening? She doesn't want us directing or interfering."

"'Interfering'? Oh, is that what we've been doing, giving her this life?"

Gus stayed quiet, his eyes shifting one way, then the other, following the conversation.

"She doesn't know exactly what she wants to do yet," her mother said. "Music school is definitely on the table. Even the Academy if—"

"Absolutely not," Grandpa Beck said.

"*Even* the Academy, if that's what she decides is best and—"

Lucy raised her hand. "Hi. Sitting right here."

"I will never give one cent to those people!"

"—I will pay for it," her mother said, "out of the money Mother left me. Marc and I discussed it, and we agree she would approve. *If* that's what Lucy wants."

Lucy couldn't remember the last time her parents were so united, in support of her, and not backing down from Grandpa. Gus might be another story. She braced herself for his reaction to what would come next. She'd thought about telling him herself but had chickened out. Her mother broke the news:

"Will has arranged with Diane Krasner for Lucy to be in the showcase."

Lucy wished she could have said it without invoking Will's name, because that was what would hurt him the most. "It was more like Diane came to him," Lucy told Gus.

"Why?" he asked her, his face reddening.

"How can she be ready for a showcase after nine months away?" Grandpa Beck said, confused. "You'll only embarrass yourself, Lucy."

She ignored him, kept her eyes on Gus. "It's complicated.

She brought it up, and Will thinks it's a good idea. So I can prove something to myself."

Her grandfather threw down his napkin over his unfinished food. "You think you can waltz away and then waltz back on a whim?" He turned to Lucy's mother. "Will is involved in this? I hired him for Gustav."

"It's not fair," Gus said.

Lucy's dad, seated next to Gus, told him gently, "It isn't fair or unfair. It's just what's happening. It's like before, when you first started: Lucy was always there, too. You liked that."

Her dad thought it was all about the playing. He didn't get the Will part.

"But she quit."

"She changed her mind."

"But..." Gus's face went red, then he shoved back his chair and got up to run from the room.

"This is insanity," Grandpa Beck said. "Music school? You've played at the biggest festivals all around the world! What can music school do for you now? What is your *goal*?"

"I don't know," Lucy confessed.

"You don't know."

"Maybe I'll teach."

"*Teach*?" He laughed. "Do you know what teachers are? They're failed performers. Even your precious Will is only teaching because he tried to make it as a professional and he failed to rise above the competition. Teaching isn't a *goal*. It's a defeat."

Lucy opened her mouth to defend Will, but her mother jumped in first.

"Dad, that simply isn't true!" Her face was flushed. "I wish I'd

255

kept playing. I *wish* I'd had the chance to teach. I wish I played for a church choir. I wish I accompanied amateur, wannabe Broadway singers. Any of those things that you believed were a fate too humiliating to contemplate, I *wish* I'd done, to stay connected to that part of myself. A part that *you* gave me."

Lucy's dad put his arm around her mom.

"Katherine," Grandpa said, "it was different. You weren't—"

"I wasn't good enough. I know. All of Lucy's life, you've been saying that you didn't want her to end up like me," her mother said. "Neither do I."

Her grandfather got up, and he stormed off, too, leaving Lucy at the table with her parents. "I'm sorry," she told them. Quitting had caused conflict in her family in a way she'd never wanted. Now unquitting was doing it, too.

Her father patted her hand. "So are we, *poulette.*"

♪

At ten fifteen she called Will. She figured, at this hour, it would go to voice mail, but she at least wanted to tell him yes, she'd do the showcase, and if he answered she could give him all the gory details of what had happened at dinner. Maybe he'd have advice about how to deal with Gus, too. She didn't want to hurt him, but she had, and there was no way out of it.

Aruna answered.

She didn't say hello. She said, "Kind of late, Lucy."

"I'm..." Lucy took a second to gather her startled self, a buzz of adrenaline shooting through her arms. "Sorry, I thought the phone would be off."

256

"That doesn't explain why you're calling my husband in the middle of the night."

It's just after ten, she thought. "I'm sorry. I'll call back tomorrow."

"I'm sure you will." Then Aruna hung up.

Lucy rose from the bed and paced the room, sick to her stomach.

She saw, in her memory, the way she'd held on to Will in the car, on and on. Touching the skin of his neck. Will's lips on her fingers. The pull of his eyes. The feeling of falling. All of their texts.

And what Reyna had said. Not at the party, but before. *Don't be that girl.*

30.

She didn't sleep. All night she worried about Aruna.

Maybe she'd tell Will he couldn't be friends with Lucy. Or, worse, that he couldn't come to the house anymore at all, even for Gus.

She remembered Gus's face when he'd told her not to mess anything up with Will. And she'd told him she wouldn't.

Nice job, Lucy.

But what was she supposed to do? Pretend like there was no connection? She knew he was married; she wasn't going to *do* anything. She needed his friendship, however she could have it. Someday Gus would understand, when he went through this himself.

This. Whatever this was.

♪

She didn't want to face Gus in the morning.

Before he got up, she double-checked the bus route, went downstairs to eat a bowl of oatmeal, wrote a note for her mom, and quietly left the house in the December morning dark. The stillness, the aloneness of the time of morning, the reviving snap in the air, were all what she needed. Forget the bus; she'd walk to school.

The building had a dim and lonely look to it when she got there, but the doors were unlocked. Lucy went in and sat on the floor outside Mr. Charles's room, curled into her coat and holding her phone in her hand, eager to hear from Will and also scared.

She'd have to see Reyna today, too. And apologize or not apologize or...whatever. She wouldn't change what she'd done on Friday, but she also didn't want Reyna to be mad.

It felt like every time she tried to do something that was best for herself, it meant some other relationship got damaged.

She stood when Mr. C. came down the hall, and he clutched his heart with exaggerated shock and made a show of looking at his watch. "What is this vision before me?"

"Hi."

He opened the classroom door. "Come on in, Lucy." He unpacked his bag onto his desk, and she sat at Mary Auerbach's, which had faint pencil doodles on it, swirls and lines. "Did you know Mary Auerbach is a vandal?" she asked, pointing to the desk.

"Don't worry. I'll get her expelled." He patted his chest pocket like he was looking for something. "Is everything all right?"

She couldn't answer. Instead she asked, "Do you want me to clean off the whiteboard?"

"Um, sure." He got the spray bottle and towel out of his drawer and set them on his desk. Lucy cleaned the whiteboard, and he dealt with some papers. After a while he paused and looked up. "Whatever it is," he said, "it'll be okay."

With one final wipe, she got the last of Friday's assignments off the board. "You're a good teacher, Mr. Charles."

♪

Reyna and Carson were at the table in the second-floor lounge. Lucy watched them from where they wouldn't see her and considered her options. She could dump her stuff on a chair and sit with them and act like everything was okay, maybe make a joke.

Except she couldn't think of one.

She abruptly turned and went down the stairs before they felt her watching. And though she still had three more classes, she found herself walking out of the building. Walking and walking.

She could still back out.

She could call Will and say no, she'd decided not to do the showcase. She could make sure not to run into him at the house and not text him anymore. Things would be good with Gus again. Ironically, changing her mind would probably only make her relationship with her grandfather worse. He'd say, *I told you so*, that he knew she wasn't committed.

But she didn't want to back out. And she didn't want to avoid Will.

She didn't want to run away from this, from herself.

She only needed to make the call, to tell him yes.

First, one more thing.

She boarded a bus to the Richmond District.

♪

Grace Chang's apartment building didn't quite match up with Lucy's memories of it. But then, she'd only been there a couple of times: once when Grace had invited Lucy's whole family over for dinner to meet her parents, who were visiting from Washington, and once when she'd had only Lucy over. They'd walked a few blocks to Grace's favorite dim sum shop and had loaded up on shrimp cakes and sausage buns and *char siu*. Back at the apartment, Grace had made tea.

Lucy couldn't remember now the point of that afternoon, like if Grace had wanted to talk about something specific, or if there had been some music-related purpose to it, or if they were just hanging out, the way Will sometimes did with Gus. She mostly remembered the food, so delicious eaten straight out of the greasy, white bags at the small, round table in Grace's kitchen.

There was no reason to think she'd be home in the middle of the day. She probably had students. *Of course she does*, Lucy thought, feeling dumb for even thinking it could be otherwise. Just because Lucy had quit didn't mean Grace would have totally changed careers.

She found the doorbell for Chang. Her finger hovered over it a few seconds. Longer.

They hadn't talked since Prague. Obviously, Grace had heard what happened, all sorts of versions of it—from Lucy's parents, from other people who had been at the festival, from the blogs. She hadn't heard it from Lucy.

Lucy had still been in shock at her own actions and her grandmother's death and the way her parents and Grandpa Beck had handled everything. She'd shut down. So she wouldn't take Grace's calls. When she'd listened to the voice mails, tears sprang up in some kind of Pavlovian response to Grace's voice, which Lucy had always loved. Soft, but not hard to hear. Light, but assertive. A trace of the particular kind of accent that San

Francisco first- and second-generation Chinese Americans have—clipped consonants and a few dropped letters on certain words.

"What happened, Lucy?" she'd asked in one of her messages.

Lucy had meant to call her back. And maybe it wasn't too late to tie off this remaining loose thread, before at last moving forward.

She depressed the doorbell and waited a reasonable amount of time. Pressed it again, waited again. Grace wasn't home. Lucy could probably find her number somewhere, or e-mail her. Maybe.

Lucy wandered around the neighborhood for a while, looking for the particular dim sum place they'd gone to. It had a dragon on the awning, she remembered. Unfortunately, several of them did. She thought she found the right one somewhere on lower Clement, but as she walked down the street eating shrimp cakes from the bag, she could only think, *Doesn't taste the same*.

31.

Martin caught her on the way in the back door. "The jig is up, doll face. School called; I had to report you to the authorities." He gestured with his eyes toward the main part of the house. "She's in her office."

"Thanks for the warning."

"And I heard about your little announcement last night." He leaned against the kitchen island. "Boy, when you decide something, you move fast."

Lucy held her book bag in front of her. "Gus hates me."

"Oh, I doubt that."

"No. He does."

Martin tilted his head. "For playing the showcase? A competition would be different. But it's you and Gus and eight or nine other people, right?"

"It's not that. It's..." She looked at Martin. If she started talking about Will, even said his name right now, he'd see exactly what was going on, with his spooky intuition. "Anyway, we'll work through it."

"Yes, you will." He opened his arms. "Come here. Give old Martin a hug."

She did. He squeezed her close and said, "Your grandma

would want to be here to see all of it. She didn't want to miss a thing."

Lucy nodded and pulled back. "You'll come to the showcase? Since she can't?"

"It'll be my pleasure."

♪

She passed the music room on her way to her mom's office. Gus's and Will's voices, mixed with piano notes, came from behind the door. So Aruna hadn't banned him from the house. Lucy felt mild relief.

Her mother was working at her laptop with a calendar open next to her on the desk, a smaller desk than her grandfather's and more ornate, Victorian. It suited her mother's classic style.

Lucy didn't even wait for a reproachful look or an accusation. "I cut most of school today. I ..." She hadn't planned what to say after that.

"Yes, I know."

"I'll get detention. But if there's anything else you want to ... you know, *do* to me ..."

Her mother, with intent focus on the computer, said, "I don't think there's anything I could do to you that would make any difference."

"I've been fighting with Reyna. I couldn't stay. I—"

"I thought we were turning things around, Lucy. Remember yesterday?" She closed her laptop. "*Yesterday*. I just want to know what to expect. Are you going to commit to this and then back out? Am I going to spend my money to send you to music school only to find out a semester later you want to be a geologist?"

"No, I don't know. I mean no, I don't want...a geologist?" Lucy laughed. She was tired from her walks, her bus rides, her thoughts. "But if you need me to say 'forever,' I don't think you should spend your money. I'll..." *I'll what?* "I'll figure out something else."

"Oh, you will."

"Yeah. I will."

They stared at each other until Lucy's mom put her face in her hands and rubbed her temples. "Don't prove my father right, Lucy. Please. That's all I ask."

♪

The knock on her door came about an hour later.

It would be Will.

Lucy, I need you to not contact me anymore.

But when she opened the door, he was smiling. Warm, winning. He didn't seem upset at all. "Hi," he said.

"Hi."

It was the first time they'd seen each other since Friday night, in the car. Her head felt floaty and peculiar, as it had then, and she realized she'd missed him. She almost said it. *I missed you.*

"Have you decided?" he asked. Then held out his hand and said, "Don't tell me! I mean, don't tell me what you decided. Just *if* you did."

"I did."

"Come downstairs with me?" he asked.

"Okay."

He started down the first, narrow attic stairs, then stopped, turned, and looked at her; their eyes met for a second. He didn't move. The space was small; they were close. He touched his face and seemed about to say something. She let her eyes meet his again, and her head spun. "What?" she asked.

"Don't worry, Lucy," he said, his voice low. "About what happened last night. The...phone thing. You haven't done anything wrong. I promise. I'm sorry I didn't call you about it earlier today. It's been busy, and I wanted you to see my face." He pointed to himself. "See? My face?" Then he drew his finger in an X across his chest slowly. "I *promise*."

Lucy bit her lip to keep her nervous tears in and nodded.

"Okay. Come on."

In the music room, Lucy first sat on the love seat. Will closed the door behind him and sat on the piano bench. "Over here," he said, patting the bench and making room.

She got up, walked over, settled in next to him. Their legs touched.

"I want to play something with you," he said. He shuffled through some music on top of the piano, found a few sheets, and put them up while Lucy warmed her fingers with arpeggios.

She smiled when she saw the piece. "I love Prokofiev."

"I'll start. When it splits off here"—he pointed to the middle of the page—"you do this part."

"I know this one. It wasn't written for four hands."

"No, this is my arrangement. But no one does it quite right, the way I hear it in my head. Obviously what we really need here are two pianos, but let's try. I'll do the pedals."

He began, and Lucy felt right away, listening, what he wanted from the piece in this arrangement. Less bounce than the way it was usually played. *Con vivace*, with life, but not so much life that the music got lost in the performance of it. Her cue came, and she joined in. Her left hip was against Will's right, on the small bench, but she only felt the notes.

There were a few spots when they got out of sync, and Lucy would say, "Whoops," or lean forward to squint at his handwritten music and ask "Is that a triplet?" and Will would answer or give a little instruction, and at times their hands collided, but they didn't stop until the end.

They both let their fingers rest on the keys for a few seconds. Then Will, smiling at her, said, "Wow. It's like you're in my head."

"This is a good arrangement."

"Thank you." He played a few phrases of something Lucy didn't recognize. She stayed on the bench, next to him. "Can I tell you something?" he asked her, still playing.

"Yeah." She put her right hand back on the piano and added a little to what he played.

"What I said last week on the phone, about growing up..."

"And not being special?" she asked, with a small laugh.

"Yeah. I want you to forget I said that. I wish I hadn't."

"Why? You were right."

"No." He shook his head and stopped playing, turning slightly toward her, still so close. "That's not how I want to be. Maybe at home. When you're married to someone, they're used to seeing you at your worst. But you shouldn't have to hear that stuff or believe it when you're sixteen. I'm usually more careful about letting that side of me come out around my students."

She kept noodling on the keys. "I'm not your student."

"I know. Can you stop for a second?" He lifted her hand off the piano and set it onto her lap before letting go. She looked at it, an alive thing with a nerve system that in this second seemed connected to every other part of her body. "I like the idea of being the best version of myself when I'm with you."

She nodded. "Okay."

"I could have at least waited a *few* more weeks before show-ing you Mr. Hyde and his bleak, cynical thoughts."

"Who?"

Will gave her a half smile. "Dr. Jekyll? Mr. Hyde?"

"Oh yeah. I always forget which is which." She tilted her head, watching his eyes. "It doesn't matter. You should just be yourself with me."

His smile went away, made his face serious. Then he sprang up off the bench and gathered his sheet music. "Now. Tell me what you decided about the showcase."

"I'm going to do it."

His face changed again, to satisfied. "Great. Let's call Diane."

♪

That night, before bed, Lucy knocked on Gus's door. He'd com-pletely, expertly ignored her at dinner, right down to asking her dad to pass the salt when Lucy'd just had it in her hand. Grandpa Beck, too, had not spoken to her or about her. Somehow it was even worse than when she'd quit.

Now Gus didn't answer. "Come on, Gustav," she said, pleading. Nothing.

She lay down in the hall and put her lips as close to the crack between the door and the frame as she could. "Gus. I love you.

Okay? You're my brother, and I love you. I'm so proud of you. I'm *so . . .*" Proud didn't even describe it. "I look up to you, actually. How hard you work and how you're not scared of that. Hard work. You're brave."

She waited, imagining that any second she'd see the shadows of his feet coming toward her head, and the door would open.

She waited and waited.

"And I want to be brave, too," she finally said. "This is how I can do it. I don't know how else, right now." She waited a few minutes more. "And I'm sorry."

Then she gave up and went to bed.

32.

At school on Tuesday, Lucy passed Reyna in the halls twice, and twice Reyna looked the other way. Feeling bold, Lucy took her lunch to their usual table but wound up alone and reading a book until Carson came up and dropped his backpack onto one chair and sat in the other. "Reyna texted me to say don't eat with you, so I thought I better come eat with you."

She absorbed the sting of Reyna doing that. Then, filled with appreciation for him, said, "Thank you. You are an awesome friend, Carson."

"It's true. You should take advantage of me more." He pointed a cautionary finger at her. "And not like *that*. I won't stand for it."

"I'll try to keep it clean."

"What. Is going on?" He wiggled his phone at her and made a show of turning it off. "Look. I'm even disconnecting myself from all my important business. So talk to me. I mean, I turn my back for one second, and everything falls apart."

There was no way Lucy could explain to Carson what her fight with Reyna had really been about. She closed her book. "You know how she gets in her divorce moods."

"Yyyyeah, but that's old news, and we always deal with it."

"I guess I lost patience and said something mean."

"What did you say?"

"I don't remember specifically." Like she'd ever forget.

"Right," Carson said.

"But she said stuff, too."

"Bet you remember *that*. And then you kicked her out of some party? Some party *I* was not invited to, I might add?"

The way he described the situation did make the whole thing sound kind of like Lucy's fault. Maybe it had been. "You would have hated this party."

"Carson Lin hates no party. Anyway, if it was so terrible, why did you stay after Reyna left?"

"I said *you* would hate it. Not that it was terrible."

He straightened in his chair. "I don't want to take sides. You need to make up, so I can feel normal again."

"Well, Carson," she said affectionately, "it's not about you."

He squinted at her. "*Hm*. If you say so."

"Speaking of *you*, let's . . . speak of you. I only ever talk about myself lately. If I start doing what Reyna's done, with the divorce, tell me."

"Um, you've been doing what Reyna's done with the divorce."

"Oh. Ouch. Okay. The topic of Lucy is officially banned for the rest of lunch."

They talked about his week, his Thanksgiving, his plans for next summer. She listened, and he made her laugh, and she wished Reyna were there with them.

♪

On Wednesday Lucy swallowed her pride and sent one text to Reyna to test the waters.

I think maybe possibly I could have handled things better.
Hope everything is going ok for you.

She never got a reply.

♪

Then it was time to put Reyna and Carson and Gus and everyone else out of her mind and start working with Will on her showcase piece. She focused on herself, and on the piece, and on Will.

They were texting every day again. Usually they started with some thought or question about music and ended up on something else: school—Lucy's experience and Will's memories—or movies or books, or parents. Usually just…life. How it felt to be a person. How it felt to be them.

Like: They discovered they were both scared of those music-festival cocktail parties, even though they could both fake small talk and turn on the charm pretty well. "I know it wasn't a *party* party," Lucy said, "but were you scared at my house that day we met?"

"Yes! God, your grandfather and his twenty-thousand-dollar conductor's baton."

"Seventeen thousand."

And: Will told her that Aruna had been his first serious girlfriend. He didn't meet her until he was twenty-four, and that made Lucy feel better about being a late starter compared to Reyna.

At the same time, she didn't like to hear about Aruna. It hurt her in a pointless way, the kind of hurt she had no legitimate right to and that had no cure. It was easier to pretend that there was no Aruna. Lucy only texted or called when she knew more or less where Will was, and with whom. Never when he was at home.

Every day that he came over to work with Gus, he stayed after, on his own time. Gus would leave the music room, and Lucy would go in. Gus wasn't giving her the total silent treatment anymore, but they hadn't talked much, either. Grandpa Beck still wasn't happy about the whole thing. He didn't think Will should be working with Lucy under his roof, but her mom defended their right to do it.

Will's coaching of her piece—a reasonably uncomplicated Brahms sonata—was illuminating. He heard things she didn't, and that taught her to hear things *he* didn't, and together they found a shape and character to it that felt right, and exciting. She wasn't crazy for the piece, but she liked it and did it well, and Will said it would fit nicely into the rest of the program.

They sat together on the bench a lot. He could have helped her from anywhere in the room, but they stayed close. Sometimes she feared she'd lose herself totally, and pull a Pier 39 right there at the piano, only worse.

She contained her energy, put it into the music.

Each time he left, Lucy had some of this energy left over, and she didn't know what to do with it other than play more. She worked on a couple of other pieces on her own—the Chopin she'd pulled out the day after Thanksgiving and a Philip Glass series of pieces, *Metamorphosis I–V*. Back in her previous career, there had always been something to prep for, a recital or competition or recording, and no time to work on whatever else she might have wanted to; it had felt like cheating.

Now that she wasn't keeping her playing a secret from her family, and no one was telling her what to do, she was a glutton. She binged on piano. She played every single thing that interested her, everything that crossed her mind to try. The Brahms would be fine; she didn't need to work it to death.

It was all for her.

Except sometimes she thought about what Reyna said, about Lucy needing an audience. Maybe she did. Not an auditorium full of people. Just Will.

Because every thought she had, everything she observed around her, every conversation, every experience, everything that made her laugh—she imagined telling him, or him watching. She wanted herself, the particular way he saw her and the way she liked to be seen by him, reflected back, over and over.

It was like there was this letter to him in her head that she was always writing and never getting to send.

It reminded her of being a kid and making a new best friend, how the two of you made your own world with just that person, and never wanted to leave it.

And though she'd never been in love, it reminded her of that, too.

33.

The weekend of the showcase, a climate of agitation took over the house. Lucy had never seen Grandpa Beck so uptight about a performance, especially one that wasn't going to have winners and nonwinners—also known as losers. At dinner on Friday night, he gave Gus the third degree about his piece, how many hours he'd practiced that week, and even about his hair. "You'll have it cut before Sunday."

Gus glanced at their mom. "I will?"

"I actually think his hair is fine, Dad," her mother said.

"I find the curls insouciant." Grandpa Beck's fork clattered to his plate.

Lucy pressed her lips together and looked at Gus, but he was refusing to look back. How could he not share a laugh with her? It was possibly the most ridiculous thing Grandpa Beck had ever said. She didn't even know what it meant, which made it even funnier. Gus, stubborn, kept his eyes fixed on his food.

"All right," their father said. "A new topic, please."

No one asked how Lucy's piece was coming. There'd been some kind of official or unofficial pact, apparently, to not talk about it in front of Gus or Grandpa Beck. Her mother or father or Martin asked her about it a couple of times when they were alone, but it was otherwise an impressive feat of group pretending.

And, after a couple of weeks of feeling good and sure about what she was doing, nerves were creeping up. She'd had too much time on her hands since school went on break. On Saturday her own tension about playing and not wanting to have any awkward run-ins with the members of her family who were angry led her to sneak around the house like a burglar, trying not to see anyone or let anyone see her. In the morning she went out shopping, in search of the perfect thing to wear at the showcase instead of the stiff dresses heaped in a pile in the back of her closet since the day she'd purged her wardrobe.

At a consignment shop on Union, she found it: a simple vintage dress, cut in the style of the twenties. The color was very close to the coral of the sweater she'd worn to Will's party, with seed-bead detailing. Totally wrong for the time of year but exactly right for how Lucy wanted to feel while she played.

The same shop had a basket of old bow ties on the counter. She couldn't resist buying a kid-size one to give to Gus, for good luck. Of course, she had no idea how she'd give it to him if he continued to avoid her like the plague.

That afternoon, Reyna called.

Lucy didn't answer. She was up in her room, stretched out on the floor with her phone next to her, trying to just breathe, in and out, and bring her anxiety under control. And if Reyna was calling to tell her what a shitty friend she was, she didn't need to hear it now. She had enough of that going on in her own head.

The phone rang again. It was Will.

"Talk me down," she said, by way of answering.

"What's going on?"

"Oh, just that I can't breathe is all." She rolled over onto her stomach.

"Well, it so happens that I *predicted* you'd be having a little difficulty breathing. And what does Lucy like when she's feeling that way? Coffee."

"Yes, she does."

"Let's go get some. To talk through it and, mostly, to celebrate. That you're really doing this. Which I know hasn't been easy."

"You'd drive all the way here for coffee?" she asked, knowing he would.

"I'm way ahead of you, Beck-Moreau. Already in the neighborhood."

She sat up. "Christmas shopping?"

"Uhh..." He did the chuckle she'd come to think of as his for-her laugh. "You know I haven't seen you in two days?"

She did know.

"Meet me on the other side of Alta Plaza," she said. Gus was hurt enough by all the time Will was spending with her at the piano. They didn't need to rub their extra hanging out in his face.

She crept down the stairs and slipped out the back door, closing it quietly behind her. She dashed across the street, up the stairs to the park, walked through it, and sat on a bench at the top of the stairs to wait for Will.

The neighborhood had gone nuts for Christmas wreaths and lights. She'd been so out of it lately, so wrapped up in her own life, that other than helping Martin with decorations on Thanksgiving weekend, she'd barely noticed the holiday happening all around her. Life, turning cold and bright in that Christmas way.

She didn't want to miss it. She didn't want to miss anything, ever again.

She'd be careful this time to not let music become more important than people, than sanity, than joy. Whatever had the potential to obscure life that way, to the point that her own grandfather would look her in the face and say her grandmother was fine when she wasn't . . .

Then Will was there, coming up the street. She loved the sight of him, his slightly awkward turned-out walk, the one that could help her see the chubby teenager evidence suggested was once him. The way he scrunched his hands down into his pockets.

The way he smiled at her when she ran down the stairs to meet him.

♪

They had coffee over in the Haight, far away from places where she might run into people she knew. They talked about the Brahms piece for a little bit, and Lucy shared the thoughts she'd had while waiting.

"Sometimes I think trying to be *so* good at something . . . like, maybe it isn't the best thing for a musician, or probably any artist. When it takes over your life like that? I don't want it to stop me from seeing," she said. "You know? People or the world or whatever."

"Nothing will stop *you* from seeing, Lucy. The fact that you're even aware of it being a danger, already at sixteen, is part of why you don't need to worry about it."

"I do worry about it, though." She sat back in her chair. "Look what happened with my grandma. What I missed. Why they lied."

"You all learned from it. You showed them and yourself where the priorities should have been."

She explored her thought some more. "Maayyybe," she mused, "maybe for the first couple of years of college I'll stay general. Undeclared. I want to have my eyes open to everything."

Will's brow, above the frames of his glasses, furrowed. "Are you changing your mind about music school?"

"No. I mean, you know, just thinking." She shrugged, smiled, happy to be with him and happy to be drinking good coffee. She didn't really want to be undeclared; music school was still *it*. It felt good, though, to be free. To give herself permission to not think about forever. "I should probably get home," she said, noticing the growing dark through the café window.

Will turned in his chair to get his coat from the back of it. "I can see, a little, why this has driven your mom crazy."

Lucy laughed. "What."

"This. The waffling. One minute you love music, and the next you're talking like you could do anything else, and meanwhile you have no clue how many people would cut off a limb to have what you do."

He was smiling. Sort of. But also, sort of, frustrated. With her. Like on the phone that day when he'd defended himself for not telling her, or Gus, about his "glory days."

She tried to make a joke. "That would be dumb. Cutting off a limb. Especially if the thing you wanted was to play an instrument."

They were both standing now, their coats on. He stepped close to her in the small coffee shop, and they were eye to eye. "Okay. It's your life, Lucy. I know. Okay?"

She wanted to touch his face. She had never wanted to touch anyone's face before, hold it between her hands. Run her thumbs along the eye-socket bones, or whatever those were called, feel the lips...

"Don't be mad at me," she said, quiet so no one in the shop would hear.

"I'm not."

"Promise?" Her eyes filled.

He nodded. She didn't believe him.

She pitched herself forward so that her forehead rested on his lapel. He patted her back a couple of times and then put his arms around her and held her close. "I'm not," he whispered. "I'm not."

♪

On the ride home she was a little weepy, brushing a tear away every few blocks. They didn't talk. He stopped the car at the same side of the park where they'd met. The neighborhood sparkled. "Lucy," Will said, "it's hard for me, I guess. Spending so much time with you, and Gus, how good you are, how *much* you are. And how much you have in front of you."

She remembered what he'd said that night in the car, on the

way home from the party. About being an old guy who teaches. "You don't like your life?" she asked him.

He sighed and leaned his head back on the seat. "It's not that I don't like my life. It's . . . You'll understand when you're my age. I know that all you want now is to not be sixteen. But it's a great age, when you're looking at it from the other side of thirty."

"You make yourself sound all old."

He was quiet.

"You're not," she added.

"You'll see. Youth and beauty. When you're getting older, when you know there's no going back, something about it hurts."

They were both concentrating on the dashboard.

"It hurts in the way an incredible composition or performance hurts," he explained. "Do you know what I mean?"

She remembered the drive to Half Moon Bay with Carson and Reyna. The dazzling ocean and the sense that she could explode out of her skin from the beauty of it all. "I think so."

"*You're* beautiful, Lucy. Inside and out. And that hurts, too. It hurts more specifically. More personally."

Lucy's hands were folded in her lap. She needed to wipe away more tears but was afraid to move them. They would go to Will's arms, his face.

"I understand," she said. "I know you think I don't. But I do."

They sat in the car, quiet, only the street noise around them.

"Hey," he said, making his voice bright, "I have a little Christmas present for you. Do you want it now?"

"Yeah!" She matched his tone. "I have something for you, too, only I didn't bring it."

He smiled, then reached into the backseat and produced a flat package. She tore off the wrapping. It was a notebook, covered in dark red leather.

"Open it," he said.

It was filled with music manuscript paper. And there was a pen loop and a pen.

"Martin helped me. I told him I wanted a special pen for a special person. And he knew where to get the best paper."

She ran her hand over the smooth, blank pages. "Thank you."

"Maybe, when you get to school, you'll enjoy doing some of your own arrangements. Or even composing. You could. You have such a great ear."

"Thank you." She closed the book and turned to him for a hug. A thank-you hug.

"You're going to do great tomorrow," Will said.

And, like she had the last time, she held on. This time it was her lips, not her fingers, that found his neck and rested against it. For a second. Two seconds. Feeling warmth, feeling the fine hairs. He made circles with his hands on her back.

They stayed like that, until Lucy got out and ran back home across the park.

Spinning. Cold. Ready.

34.

What am I doing?

Lucy sat in the front row with all the other musicians who would play that night. The concert hall, overheated and filling with people, had been decorated with holiday lights that cast a warm yellow glow over everything.

Cozy, if you weren't fifteen minutes away from being on stage for the first time in almost a year.

The ride to Davies had been quiet, the family divided up into two groups: She came with Gus and her dad, because she didn't want her grandfather to stress her out, and because her grandfather refused to ride in her dad's small car. She'd thought about calling a cab, to avoid her family entirely, but she wanted to show Gus that though he was still mad at her, she didn't feel the same toward him.

Martin would be in the audience. Convinced Reyna hated her, she'd been too nervous to text her again. But she'd invited Carson and hoped he'd tell Reyna, but she didn't know if they'd come.

Their dad had dropped them off so he could go park the car. Outside, Lucy'd taken Gus by the shoulders and forced him to look at her. His curls were gone, per Grandpa's instructions. "You're already in your suit and probably don't want this, but..."

She pulled the little bow tie out of her dress pocket, the same pocket that held Will's nail clippers, for good luck. "You could be like a mini Grandpa." She wiggled it at him, hoping for a smile.

"I don't want to be like him." He'd totally lost all sense of humor.

"You're not," she said, shoulders sagging. "You won't be. It's a joke."

Gus started to walk away; she wouldn't let him. "Gus. You are amazing. *Be* amazing tonight. I love you no matter what."

His eyes knifed into hers. "You took him," he said. "After you said you wouldn't."

She dug through all the things she could say about freedom and fairness and being older, being a grown-up, and who had a right to do what, and she knew they would all sound like excuses and justifications. Maybe they were. "Forget about me," she said. "Just think about yourself right now. Grandpa Beck makes everything into a contest, but in real life it's not. It's not."

Gus turned around and walked toward the doors. Lucy let him go in on his own, like he wanted to. "You're going to like me again someday," she called after him.

Now, sitting in the front with a queasy stomach, Gus five seats away, sweat dampening the armpits of her vintage dress—she doubted everything, everything that had happened in the last month.

Gus was right. She shouldn't be here. It wasn't fair. The family name had pulled strings. Will had pulled strings. Diane Krasner was a publicity hound, and Lucy hadn't earned this like the other performers had, not this year. She checked the program for the millionth time. She'd go fourth.

In her peripheral vision, she caught and felt the presence of Will. He'd come down to the front row and now crouched in front of Gus, one hand on Gus's knee. Giving the teacher pep talk. She'd be next, she knew. He should have talked to her first, then Gus. You always save the most important for last, and she wished he'd done it that way, for Gus's sake.

It also felt good, being saved for last.

He came to her and touched her shoulder. "Hey."

"Hi."

"You look *so* pretty. Wow."

She smiled. "Thanks."

"How do you feel?" He knelt in the aisle next to her seat.

"*Mm*, not awesome. But okay." She looked at him; she needed to see herself in his eyes. "Do you really think I should be here?"

He didn't answer. Instead, he put his hand on the back of her head and kissed her cheek. She closed her eyes.

"Everyone's so excited to hear you play."

He stood and walked up the aisle, and Lucy was feeling the imprint of his lips on her face and feeling it and feeling it, and then she thought, *Wait, who is "everyone"?*

The audience, Lucy, who else? Calm down.

She couldn't keep herself from turning to watch Will take his seat. Aruna didn't seem to be there; that was a relief. He was with someone else, though. He talked to the woman in the seat next to his and pointed to the program, leaning in close. Not like a date; the woman wasn't young. But they were definitely there together.

Lucy recognized her.

The director of the Academy. Lucy had been to enough

symphony events to know who she was. Will had invited the director of the Academy? Who now saw Lucy staring at her and lifted her program in a wave. Lucy turned back around toward the stage.

That was a little odd. Lucy hadn't talked to anyone at the Academy yet, and neither had her mom. Maybe it was coincidence; Will was friendly with a lot of people from when he had his local TV show.

When she looked again to see if she'd been imagining it, she saw, seated on Will's other side, a gray-bearded man, familiar somehow. He was somebody important, but she couldn't think who.

And next to him: a younger guy Lucy recognized right away. He had produced the recording Lucy had made with the Cleveland Orchestra, the one Will had played in the car the night of the party.

Next to the Academy director: Lib Thomas in her signature dyed-red hair. She wrote for the *New York Times*.

Four important people in their world, sitting with Will. Talking to him.

And she knew they were there because he'd told them to be there. It couldn't be for Gus; Will wouldn't dare do anything like that without discussing it with Grandpa, and if he had, Lucy would know, because Grandpa would be bragging about it every chance he got.

They were there to see her, and Will had brought them.

Why would he *do* that?

Will finally saw her looking. He grinned, sheepish. She faced the stage again.

The point of this was no pressure. No competition. Yes, performance spoke her grandfather's language, and now he'd have to listen to what *she* wanted to say in that language. But mostly, mostly, this was hers.

Will knew how much she needed that.

Her face burned, and not from the kiss anymore. She clenched her fingers around the hem of her dress, and she wasn't there, not there in San Francisco, no. But back in Prague, her grandfather acting like everything was A-OK while Lucy found out her grandmother was dying and she wouldn't get to say good-bye. Acting like he'd had her best interests in mind while betraying her.

Will wouldn't do that. He wouldn't betray her, he wouldn't . . .

I can see my future . . . never having my own success again.

He'd said that, in the car that night. After confessing why he'd told Diane Krasner that Lucy had returned to the piano and that he'd had a part in it.

I guess I wanted to impress her, he'd said.

She felt sick. She tried to resist but couldn't help reframing the whole last month in a way that made it seem like, from the beginning, he'd urged her toward all this so that he could say he was the one to bring Lucy back. Make it about him.

No, she thought. *No.*

Not when they were so close. She trusted him. They were practically . . .

The program started up, and Lucy could barely follow what was happening. She wanted to walk out, and she knew she could. No one could make her do this. Not even Will.

But she'd worked so hard to get here. More than the practice.

More than the hours. What she'd given to reclaim this: hurting Gus; defying her grandfather, again; reconciling with her mother, finally; and despite the doubts and nerves, she'd looked forward to the energy she got only from performing, from sharing all of that hard work with others. The whole thing didn't feel complete until you put it out there.

Like Will had said.

He'd been right, about so many things.

Wrong about her, and what she could accept, even from him. He would try to talk his way out of it, she knew, like he'd talked his way out of how he'd told Diane in the first place. And talked her into the showcase. And talked her out of her worry that Gus would stay mad. All his talking made sense, was the thing. Even his explanation about this night, the one she'd get later, might make sense.

But, no. To bring those people here, tonight, at this time of year, the phone calls he'd have to have made and the buildup he would have had to give her. And never mention it, when they'd been talking every day? There was no explanation.

He knew this wasn't what she wanted.

Yes, she needed an audience. But she didn't need it to be the *New York Times* or the Cleveland Orchestra or the people in the seats behind her now.

She'd only needed it to be Will.

But apparently she wasn't enough of an audience for him.

The first musician went up—an adorable little girl in a puffy green dress, maybe six years old. Lucy remembered being that age, having to use an extender to reach the pedals. The girl launched into Aaron Copland's *The Cat and the Mouse*, the kind of piece that made you work the whole keyboard, racing up and down. For a minute Lucy got lost in watching her. She was good. But six. Six.

Lucy imagined being six again. Getting to do it all over, knowing what she knew now. And realized she wouldn't do it over. She had tread that water and gotten to the other side. She wouldn't go back, and she wouldn't change anything. Except one thing: She would give herself the chance to see her grandmother one more time.

The picture of her grandmother's face, the face that had always loved and approved of her, came to Lucy's mind. What would her grandmother *really* have thought about Lucy walking out at Prague? Lucy closed her eyes and imagined her grandmother with her now, speaking into this moment. *You didn't do that for me, Lucy,* she would say. Lovingly, gently. But honestly. *You did it for you.*

And she'd be right.

Lucy had needed, for a long time before Prague, to step back. To breathe. She just hadn't known how.

Her grandmother dying gave her the excuse she'd needed.

I don't mind, the memory of her grandmother said.

But Lucy did mind.

And from now on, she could only play or not play for her own reasons. She had to stand on her choices. Stop blaming. Not let Will give her an excuse not to, not let Gus, not let anyone.

She opened her eyes. Applause filled the hall, and the little girl bowed.

Tonight Lucy had come to play.

The second musician was halfway through his piece before she even started paying attention to him.

She was thinking. She turned to take one last look at Will and noticed, a few rows behind him, Carson and Reyna. Carson waved, so big that several people around them were appalled and Reyna yanked his arm down. Lucy stifled a laugh and faced the stage again.

The sight of them let a little air into her soul. This night, whatever was going wrong, wasn't like not getting to say good-bye to Grandma. It wasn't anything *like* that.

The third performer was an elderly man whose name sounded familiar to Lucy, like he'd once been a big deal. From the way he fumbled, she could tell that putting him on the program had been one of those things done out of respect for his legacy and not because he was great anymore.

He looked happy, though, and not embarrassed by that, his wrinkly, spotted hands stiff on the keys but still making music.

On his face: love. Even as his fingers missed a few notes. And even as Lucy could sense discomfort around her, people wishing he'd hurry up and finish so they could relax.

Love.

That was the piece that had been missing, way before Prague. That was the piece that had been missing in her life until Will came and made her feel it, for their work together and for beauty and also for him, though it was hard sometimes to separate those things. Maybe she didn't love Will like she thought. Or couldn't, in this moment.

But what they'd done together, what had been opened by becoming so close, she could still love that. She could love their conversations and their hours at the piano and the results of their work. She could even love the way it hurt right now, because when was the last time she gave her whole heart to something?

That, all of it, belonged to her. She didn't have to let Will take it away, the way she'd let her grandfather, the business, herself, take her love for music.

She would hold on to what was hers. Let go of what wasn't.

The old man finished. The applause was polite and relieved.

Lucy stood up for him. She couldn't tell if he saw her before he shuffled into the wings, apparently forgetting he was supposed to come back down the stage stairs. And if anyone had followed her lead in giving a standing ovation, she didn't know, and she didn't care. She kept her eyes straight ahead.

It was her turn now.

♪

She made her decision at the keys. The Brahms had been a safe choice all along, the kind of work people expected at a concert like this, impressive enough but not a piece she'd be likely to screw up. She realized that had been Will's plan—for her to play something she'd nail for his guests. So he could say, *Look, I resurrected Lucy Beck-Moreau from her quitting grave.*

When she started playing the Philip Glass—*Metamorphosis I*—a wave of rustling washed through the audience. People checking their programs. Murmuring.

Philip Glass? she heard them thinking. Twentieth-century composers were rarely performed at these things. The piece was not technically challenging in the show-offy way the audience had paid for. *This* was the big Lucy Beck-Moreau comeback?

The theme was repetitive. But every time it came back around, Lucy tried to find something new to discover in it.

When she finished Part I, she was tempted, momentarily, to move into II. The series of pieces were meant to be heard together. But she couldn't take up that much time, and anyway, she'd made her point.

She stood to bow and received uncertain applause. When she straightened up, she scanned the crowd, not for Will, or Carson and Reyna, but for her mother. There she was, stage right and down front, sitting with Lucy's dad on one side and Grandpa Beck on the other, Martin next to him. Lucy smiled at her and held out a hand, the way you do when you're acknowledging a pit orchestra. Her mother stretched out her arm in reply.

Like the old man before her, Lucy exited into the wings. She found him sitting on a metal folding chair in front of the curtain rigging. He looked up at her with watery eyes. "That was nice," he said.

"I want to be like you," she replied.

He laughed. "No. Keep being like you."

She found another folding chair and sat next to him, so she could watch Gus from the wings.

35.

The reception after the showcase was a crush of people. Lucy stayed near her family. Usually, Grandpa Beck would be working the crowd, taking Gus around, making him talk to people. Tonight Lucy's dad was Gus's chaperone, and her grandfather seemed abnormally subdued.

"Interesting choice, Lucy," he said.

"Did you like it?" she asked.

"No," he said. "But I didn't hate it."

It was the best she could expect from him, most likely. "What *do* you like, Grandpa? What do you love?"

He gave her a quizzical look. "I'm sorry?"

"What do you love?" she repeated.

"All of it. I love it all."

Lucy laughed.

"You think I'm joking. I've given my life to this, Lucy. My money. My time. I could be sipping mai tais on the coast of New Zealand." He gazed out on the room. She thought of him eight years before, weeping to see Leon Fleisher recover his second hand. "I know I'm an old crank. I can't explain myself, especially with your grandmother gone. Don't expect me to."

"I...won't." Already she was thinking how she'd tell this

story to Will before realizing she probably wouldn't. It would take a while to break that habit, him being her audience.

Lucy's mother came over with a glass of champagne. "This is the most people I've ever seen at this thing," her mother said. They were clustered in a safe corner of the lobby, watching Gus and her dad circulate. "Diane Krasner will be happy. Lots of big donors."

Grandpa Beck narrowed his eyes. "Who is Gustav talking to *now*? Good God. Will brought the entire establishment. Does he think we don't know how to market Gus?"

Lucy held her tongue. Let him think what he wanted, that Will's entourage of influencers were for Gus. Hopefully Gus thought that, too.

She'd been deciding whether or not to talk to Will; then she saw him near the bar with the record-company producer, and it was the producer who waved her over. "Be right back," she said to her mom.

She wove through bodies, her heart in her throat, stopped a couple of times by people saying, "Great to see you up there, Lucy" or "I never would have recognized you!" When she reached Will, he introduced her to the producer, John Tommassini. She shook his hand. "I remember. How are you?"

"Very well, thanks. You've grown up." He smiled at Will. "Of course, I would have loved to have heard the Brahms!"

Will laughed, uncomfortable.

Tommassini sipped his drink and said, "I'm loving the ideas Will's been pitching us for collaborations with you two."

Lucy looked at Will, but he avoided her eyes. John continued: "It's such a great hook. Student and teacher, both former

294

child stars, together. It doesn't hurt that you're both good-looking. Maybe a little airbrushing for you, Will!" He grinned. "Sad to say, but that's the reality of marketing now."

"Will isn't..." Lucy started to say that he wasn't her teacher. It wouldn't exactly be true, though. "You can call my dad about it," she told Tommassini. "I have to find my brother."

Will followed her. "Hang on, Lucy." She turned around. "I didn't know you were into Glass." He tried for the Will chuckle, but it fell flat. "Seriously, though. You...it was great. Kind of weird. But good-weird." He took her arm gently. "I can't hear in this crowd. But I want to talk. Here." He pointed to the bottom of the sweeping staircase that went up to the next level's lobby.

"I was going to do the Brahms," Lucy said, when they got to the stairs, voice unsteady. "Until I saw you with all those people."

"You pulled that out of your hat on the spot? Wow."

She thought about the day before, at the coffee shop. How important it had been to her that he not be mad at her. Now it felt just as important to her to not be mad at him. She didn't want that. She was tired of anger.

"Why'd you invite them?" she asked, finally meeting his eyes. And she saw in them that he was working out his explanation, switching gears, maybe to something rehearsed. "Be yourself with me," she said. "Remember? Just tell me."

He looked at her then and was real, not the charmer or the convincer. "This is myself." He lowered his gaze. "I guess I saw an opportunity for my own...I don't know. It didn't start that way, though. That day, my first day at your house—not the party, but my first day with Gus—when I asked you if you ever wanted to play again, and you said you didn't know. The look on your face." He put his hand over his heart and lifted his head. "I could tell you did know, and you wanted to, but you were in a bind about it, inside yourself. When you came to me for help, it was like a dream."

"I trusted you," Lucy said. "I shouldn't have. I mean...you tried to get me to play within just a couple of hours of meeting me when I said I didn't anymore. From that second, I shouldn't have trusted you."

He looked crushed, and even as she said it, she knew it had been sincere, him inviting her to the piano that night.

"I promise you it wasn't until Diane came to my party that I got, you know, preoccupied. With this other idea. Ideas."

She remembered Gus asking, *Why?* when she'd told him about Diane approaching Will. "Why was she even at your party? Does she always come? Did you invite her before or after I said I'd be there?"

He rubbed the back of his head. "You can probably guess."

She nodded, going over all the moments since then that had meant so much. "What about everything else?" she asked, quiet. And for an anxious second, it seemed as if he didn't know what she meant.

In an instant he figured it out. "Everything else. Everything else was...a surprise. And so lovely. And as real as you up on that stage tonight." He glanced over his shoulder and lowered his voice. "And I swear to *God*, Lucy, I never had anything but the best intentions. Maybe with the career stuff, recently, I went off track. Okay, not maybe. But with the 'everything else,' I really was, I tried to be, my best self with you."

She couldn't speak but thought, *Me too.*

He sighed. "Even that's a rationalization, right? I'll stop."

"Okay," she said softly.

"Is there anything...do you want to say anything to me? Ask me anything? I'll be honest."

Was it what I thought it was? He'd be honest. She wasn't sure she was ready to know. Then it struck her that they'd been talking in the past tense. And now they were exchanging final words. She snapped out of her hurt and confusion.

"No. We're not saying good-bye. You know why?"

"Because you want to record a four-hands album with me for Tommassini?" he joked without a smile. "No? Okay. Why?"

"Because you're going to keep teaching Gus," she said, resolute. It would mean she couldn't totally avoid him. He'd be part of their family's life. She couldn't just exit stage right and never look back. Or, she was choosing not to.

"Wait," Will said, baffled, holding up his hands. "You're not going to tell your mom what a...jackass I've been?"

"It's for Gus. He still loves you. He still needs you."

He dropped his arms.

"But," Lucy said, "if I see you doing anything with his career that he's not sure he wants, you're going to have to deal with me."

"Okay. And thank you. For giving me another chance. With Gus."

They *were* saying good-bye, even if they were going to see each other again and again. Good-bye was happening. "Thank you, too," she said, even though she wasn't feeling it, in case she never got a chance to say it later.

"You're strong, you know. A very strong person." He smiled his crooked smile. "It's one of the things I love you for."

She shook her head, and now, after holding it together through the evening's ordeal, *now* the tears threatened to spill. "Don't...talk to me like that. I'm strong but not that strong."

His smile disappeared. "I'm sorry, Lucy," he said. And when she started to walk away, he touched her elbow gently. "Hey, the director of the Academy loved what you did. I don't think you'll have a problem, even with the whole mortal-enemies-with-your-grandpa thing."

She let herself look at him one more time. "I'll see you around."

♪

It was hard to get Gus away from his admirers. Lucy watched Will go to him and stay by his side the rest of the night. She found Martin and waited with him. "I don't know if you saw me," he said. "But I cried my eyes out to see you on stage. And you did so well." Lucy huddled against him, and he put his arm around her. They stayed that way until the crowd thinned and eventually dispersed.

She watched Will say good-bye to her parents and grand-father.

Gus saw her waiting, and turned away.

"Gustav!" Martin called. "Get over here and talk to your sis-ter." He gave Lucy a last pat. "I'll see you tomorrow, doll."

Gus, obedient, approached Lucy. She desperately wanted to hug him, but she also respected his right to not want to be hugged. "You blew them away," she said. "It was perfect. I'm super proud of you."

"Thanks."

"I have something for you."

"I don't want the bow tie."

"I know." She opened her palm, where she'd been warming Will's nail clippers. "Here."

He took them out of her hand. "Um. Okay."

"They're a good-luck charm. Trust me."

Gus put the clippers in his pocket. And she could see it was hard for him to say it, but he straightened up his back and said, "I'm proud of you, too."

She fought not to cry, which she knew would mortify him. "Gus," she said, stooping a little to be closer to his face, "Will is all yours, okay? You can have him."

"Are you guys still going to be friends?"

"Not like we were."

On the car ride home, she felt the CD she'd made for Will in her coat pocket. She hadn't given it to him, and never would.

♪

Reyna had left her a voice mail earlier that day that she'd somehow missed.

"Hey. Carson told me about your thing, and I also saw it in the paper. I'm coming. You can't stop me. And I wanted to say it was really cool to see your name like that, and I thought, *Hey, I know her, she's my best friend.* And I wanted to say break a leg or whatever. I love you."

IV.

Da Capo

(FROM THE BEGINNING)

The mid-January cold, for San Francisco, was brutal.
Lucy walked the couple of miles, anyway, and let the wind slice
through her, swearing under her breath with a kind of deranged
glee. She wore a scarf that Felicia Pettis had given her when
they'd met for coffee after Christmas. "It's not a gift," she'd said,
when Lucy expressed chagrin that she didn't have anything for
Felicia. "Just something I saw that made me think of you." She
wound the purply fabric around Lucy's neck and snapped a picture with her phone.

Lucy's mom had offered and expected to give her a ride this
morning, standing in the foyer, ready. She'd looked a little hurt
when Lucy had said no.

"It's the first day," Lucy had said. "I want to kind of . . . keep it
personal. Make it mine."

It wouldn't be like before, when she'd go to cities but not see
them, when she'd perform but be too stressed to think about
the beauty of the music, when she'd trudge to the piano like it
was a punishment.

This time, the second she felt herself not caring, she'd pay
attention, she'd ask herself: *What do you love, Lucy?*

And she'd remember. Ryan Adams and the first sip of coffee
in the morning. Her mom singing along with the B-52s. Vivaldi,

and Beethoven's French horns. And people, even though they were complicated.

Not that she'd always know what she loved, or even what she wanted. She needed, actually, to feel uncertain. She held on to her doubt the way she used to hold on to the security of a good grade from Mr. Charles, or the assurance of best friendship forever from Reyna, or Will's adoration and attention.

Now, she didn't want to know her future.

All she wanted was to be there, for every little minute.

She opened the wide double doors of the Academy, and made her entrance.

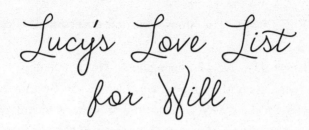

Lucy's Love List for Will

Legal Tender, The B-52s—My mom used to play this in the car all the time when I was little, and it always worked to keep me entertained. I guess she was really into the B-52s when she was young. (I try to picture her at a show—can't do it.)

More, Usher—I know, but Reyna has brainwashed me. Good workout song.

Changing gears:

Everybody Knows, Ryan Adams—It's those two little drumbeats in the intro that kill me. Every time.

Fold, José Gonzáles—Look up the lyrics. Exactly where I am right now.

Lodestar, Sarah Harmer—Starts like no big deal and turns into this epic masterpiece. Inspired by a D. H. Lawrence poem. It's basically perfect.

Sugar on the Floor, Elton John—Another one of my mom's, from a collection of rare masters and B sides. There's an Etta James version, too, which is just okay IMHO. Elton makes it sound sadder. Too sad. So:

Happier, Guster—I discovered Guster one night when I went down some Internet wormhole. I have this song in my head, like, all the time.

The Rifle's Spiral, The Shins—**Current obsession. Play count over 100.**

Challengers, The New Pornographers—**No comment.**

Symphony No. 5, third movement, Ludwig van Beethoven, as performed by the New York Philharmonic, Leonard Bernstein conducting—**Some performances of this are too slow, or the horns aren't loud enough. This is my favorite version, and I wish everyone knew the third movement the way they know the first.**

Four Seasons, Op. 8, Winter: Allegro con molto, Antonio Vivaldi, as performed by the London Philharmonic Orchestra, Itzhak Perlman conducting and on violin—**And some performances of THIS are too fast. Or you don't really hear it because it's so familiar. Somehow this recording makes it sound new every time.**

Cello Suite No. 2 in D Minor, Johann Sebastian Bach, as performed by Matt Haimovitz—**Sort of in love with Matt Haimovitz. And I wish I could play cello. Maybe I will someday.**

Metamorphosis I, Philip Glass—**I've been learning this one. Weirdly satisfying to play. The repetition means something, though I haven't yet figured out what.**

Acknowledgments

A host of people helped see me through the writing of this book by being present in various important ways:

Mike Martin, thank you for that talk on the couch in Winston-Salem and for showing me beauty and possibility when I most needed to believe. You know the ways in which this story is yours. Thank you, Sarah Martin, for your support.

Ann Cannon, thank you from the absolute depths of my heart for your understanding and wisdom.

Thank you, Matt Kirby, Stephanie Perkins, Mark Pett, Liz Zarr, the Glen Workshop community, my church family, Bob, and everyone who took the time to offer advice and hospitality, send notes of encouragement, say prayers, and offer company during a difficult year.

E. Lockhart, Adele Griffin, Robby Auld, Susan Houg, and Tom Conroy each gave particular help with the story, and I am grateful.

The entire team at Little, Brown Books for Young Readers has been so good to me. Thank you!

Julie Scheina, you are amazing. Thank you for holding the lantern high.

Michael Bourret, you are truly one of the best gifts in my life. Let's keep doing this.

And thank you to my readers, young and less young, for letting me continue to have this life.

Reading Group Guide

1. The first time Lucy meets Will, he toasts to "the wonder of beauty in all its forms," and this idea strikes a chord with her. Identify the moments in the novel where Lucy feels joy in and an awareness of the beauty in everything. What do these moments teach her? How do they ultimately help her reconcile her feelings toward music and playing?

2. Describe the contentious relationships Lucy has with her grandfather and her mother. Why does Lucy see them as obstacles to her happiness and love of the piano? How does her perception of each of them change over the course of the novel?

3. "Music, her grandfather always told her, was language. A special language, a gift from the Muses, something all people are born understanding but few people can thoroughly translate." People in Lucy's life feel that she is obligated to use the great gifts she's been given. Does Lucy agree? Does her thinking change over time? Do you agree that people with great talent like Lucy's owe the world their translation? Why or why not?

4. Reyna, Lucy's best friend, wonders whether Lucy simply misses music for the attention she received, and Lucy questions this herself. Considering Lucy's crush on her English teacher, Mr. Charles, do you think Lucy is simply someone

who seeks the spotlight? Why or why not? How much is Lucy's craving an audience due to her being a musician versus simply being human?

5. An intermezzo is a short movement between the larger segments of a musical piece. Why, do you think, does the author choose to call the brief flashback chapters intermezzos? Consider how this nonlinear structure shapes the narrative. What insights into Lucy's character do these chapters provide?

6. Lucy feels betrayed by her family for not telling her when Grandma Beck is gravely ill. Consider the role of betrayal in Lucy's other relationships, particularly those with Will and her brother, Gustav. What does Lucy learn about violating trust?

7. The Beck-Moreaus are a privileged family. How do the family's wealth and status shape the story? What aspects of their privilege does Lucy wrestle with? How would the story be different if Lucy's family came from a more modest background?

8. Throughout the novel, Lucy comes to terms with the idea of acting for herself rather than seeking permission or gratification from others. How are Lucy's decisions to cut her hair and to purge her closet a part of this process? Identify other moments in the story where Lucy acts independently, influenced solely by her own desires. How do these moments help her on her path to self-discovery?

9. "Brain, heart, and means. 'Without heart, you're a machine.'" Describe the role of love in the book. Consider not only romantic love but also familial love and a passion for one's craft. What lessons about love must Lucy learn in order to move on from quitting music?

10. Will is a key supportive figure in Lucy's rediscovery of her passion for music. But Will is a complex character who battles his own insecurities. How do Will's complicated feelings involving music and success affect his relationship with Lucy? Do you believe that Will's explanation of his motives at the end of the story is genuine? Why or why not?

11. A musical variation is a theme of music that is repeated but altered in some elemental way, such as melody, rhythm, or pitch. Interpret the title *The Lucy Variations* in light of this definition. In what ways does it speak to Lucy's return to the piano? What foundational aspect of music does she return to, and what elements will she change?

12. Listen to the songs on "Lucy's Love List for Will." How does each song speak to the themes or tone of the novel? Is music a big part of your life? Take a moment to consider what you would include on your own love list and why.

Turn the page for a peek at
Sara Zarr's newest novel,
cowritten with Tara Altebrando

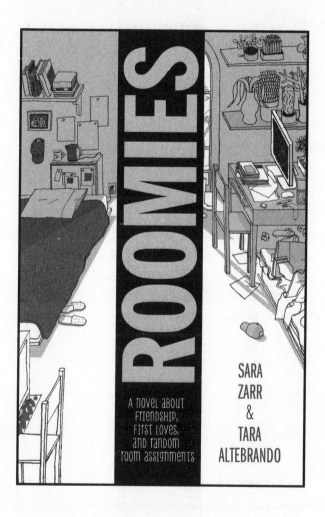

A novel about
friendship,
first loves,
and random
room assignments

SARA
ZARR
&
TARA
ALTEBRANDO

Available Now!

MONDAY, JUNE 24
NEW JERSEY

Sometimes there are signs. Or things I can't help but interpret as signs. Maybe from fate or the universe or God, if there is one. Or maybe from the grandmother I barely knew but who I've always been told is in heaven.

Watching and judging.

Like Santa.

There are just times when it really feels like some*one* or some-*thing* is paying attention. Even to little old me. And right now he or she or it is looking down on me lying on my bed, where I am seething because of a five-minutes-ago fight with my mother about how I am going to spend this, my last summer at home before college. I have plans to meet my friends at the beach tomorrow and she thinks I should be…well, she doesn't even know *what* she wants me to be doing instead. Here's a hint: It is probably the exact opposite of whatever I want to be doing at any given moment.

I seriously only graduated last week. The cap and gown are still hanging right there on the back of my bedroom door.

Someone, some power, must see me gripping the bedspread beneath my fingers and he (or she or it) must feel some kind of pity for me because he (or she or it) takes it upon himself (or herself or itself) to trigger someone on the opposite coast, someone named Helen Blake, who works in Student Housing at UC Berkeley, to sit down at her computer and type in my e-mail address and send me a message that makes my phone buzz on the bed next to me and that helps me to calm down, and to release the bedspread, and to remember that nothing, not even living with your mother, is forever, though it mostly feels that way.

Dear Elizabeth Logan, it says. **I am pleased to provide you with your dorm room assignment and contact information for your roommate this coming school year. While it is by no means mandatory for you to get in touch, some students find that there are practical issues they would like to discuss before orientation week.**

Below the dorm info is a name—Lauren Cole—a snail mail address in San Francisco, an e-mail address, and a phone number. It is enough to make me spring up off the bed and rush to my desk. There is a light, gritty layer of dust on my open laptop's keyboard; I haven't used it since school ended but something about sending e-mail from it— instead of from my phone—feels more official, more serious.

I am nothing if not officially serious about going away to school.

So I type in this Lauren's address—calling seems crazy—and I put **Hi Roomie!** as the subject; then I think for a second that I have no idea what to say, but it turns out I do.

Dear Lauren,
You don't know me but I got an e-mail from Berkeley
telling me that we're going to be roommates. I am so

excited to "meet" you! I've been waiting and waiting. Since I'm moving to California from New Jersey, I'm not bringing that much stuff at all—only what I can fit in two suitcases. Maybe I'll ship stuff? I'll probably pack a hundred times in the next 65 days (not like I'm counting, ha ha), so I can be sure everything I want to bring will fit. My mother says she'll give me money for a mini-fridge or microwave. Are you already planning on bringing either of those?

I think about wrapping it up but I am really just getting going so I don't stop. Not yet. I rub my fingers together to get rid of some dust, then dig in again.

I'm so jealous that you live in San Francisco. You must really like it if you're staying close for college. It's cool that you're going to live in the dorms. I swear I've been wanting to go away to college ever since I found out it was possible to do that. It's all I think about lately. Getting out of this place.

I should stop now. No one sends e-mails this long. But as it turns out I am not quite done with the stuff that needs to come off my chest so that I can maybe breathe again, so that I can maybe survive the summer and the move to the land of the Man Who Left, otherwise known as Dad.

This may sound crazy but I've never been to California—even though my father moved to San Francisco a bunch of years ago. I haven't seen him since I was pretty little, and I never talk to him, so it's not like that's the reason I picked Berkeley. Anyway, I promise not to be too annoyingly touristy or anything.

I'm babbling. So yeah. Let me know about the microwave/fridge situation.

Elizabeth (but everyone calls me EB) Logan

I send it before the feeling of release turns sour. Then I head over to Facebook and search for Lauren Cole. Turns out there are a couple of fan pages for famous Lauren Coles I've never heard of. And one at the University of Florida, but none that looks like she might be my roommate, a fact I find depressing. Who *isn't* on Facebook?

MONDAY, JUNE 24
SAN FRANCISCO

It's a rare quiet moment in the house. When I say *rare*, I'm using it in the real sense of the word: rare like a meteor shower, rare like a white tiger, like a double yolk or a red diamond. Rare as in I use up about a third of this precious silence trying to remember when it last was. Silent. For another fifteen minutes I try to decide how not to waste it. I have the day off from both my jobs. Should I take a nap? Hook my iPod up to the living room stereo and blast it? Make a deluxe quesadilla, which, for a change, I wouldn't have to share?

I opt for a combination of stereo takeover and nap, putting on a mellow playlist at a soothing volume and stretching out on the floor—with a blanket under me so as to avoid Cheerio dust. Finally and blissfully, I'm alone. It isn't long before I make the muscle-twitching, gape-mouthed descent into sleep. After what seems like about ninety seconds, I become aware of the sound of the van idling outside.

Already? No. No.

Sometimes in the moments surrounding REM sleep, you hear

things that aren't really there. I forbid my eyes to open. But there's the sound of the van door sliding on its track. (Note that I did not say *minivan*.) My mother's voice. The babbling of P.J.; the cry of Francis; Jack and Marcus fighting. For some reason I don't hear Gertie out there. Soon enough that reason becomes apparent.

"Why are you on the floor?"

Gertie plops onto my stomach. Oof. "Because I like the floor," I say.

"Why?"

"Because I said so."

"Why are your eyes closed?"

"Because it makes the room nice and dark."

She touches each of my eyelids gently, and I feel her weight shift as she leans over my face, expelling her soft grape-juice-and-baby-carrot breath. She pets my hair and I hope to God she hasn't been picking her nose. "Are you *dead*?" she asks in a dramatic whisper.

"Yes."

Gertie is absolutely still for a count of three; then she bounces on my stomach and I'm forced to open my eyes and roll over to get her off me. "No you're not! No you're not!" She laughs like a maniac. "Mama says come help."

❀

The next chance I have to think is five hours later, after Dad's come home, after we've gotten through the ordeal that is dinner, after baths and toothbrushing and all the bargaining and coercion and threat-making that help those things happen, and after Francis is down but the rest of them are living up the twenty minutes before story time and, at last, lights-out.

It's the first opportunity I've had to look at my e-mail in three days. There are two screens of new messages, mostly spam. As I sort through it, I find some stuff from my best friend, Zoe—links to videos and sites I'll probably never have time to look at—and a message from my dad. He sends these one- or two-sentence notes from work when he's bored or thinking of me. This says, **Garfield has been violated. Investigating.** There's a picture attached of the mug I gave him when I was in first grade. It's got a big lipstick print on the rim. I write back: **That is a bold red. Inquire among VIPs.**

On the third screen, the page of oldest messages, there are a few from Berkeley. One of them has to be about my housing request. I'll save those to open last; I'm too nervous now. I go back to the first screen to start clicking off the spam and find a message I didn't notice the first time. The subject line is **Hi Roomie!** and I almost junk it for porn, but when I see the preview of the first line, a chill comes over me.

I open and read it through.

Then I frantically click over to the Berkeley messages and find the one telling me about my roommate.

So it's true. My request has been denied. "Crap," I mutter.

"Can I play Dora?" It's Gertie.

I minimize the window—I'm not sure why; it's not like Gertie cares about my e-mail or can understand what she's seeing. She breathes down my neck, her sticky hand already leaving a mark on my desk, which I've just cleaned for what feels like the tenth time today, making use of the industrial-size tub of Clorox Wipes I pay for with my own money. "No," I say. "Can you go... occupy yourself or something?"

I try not to sound mean. I'm already in trouble for being "mean" to Jack, even though he's the one who completely spilled cranberry juice all over my favorite sweater, at some point between the inter-ruption of my nap and dinner. I'd saved up for like a month to buy that sweater. I yelled at Jack and called him a moron, and when Mom found me and said, "He's six, Lauren. He didn't do it out of malice," what came out of my mouth was "I wish I were an only child." And Mom gave me that look she has and walked out, reminding me to apologize to Jack before dinner. At which point he didn't care anymore, having moved on to the crucial task of making sure his various food groups didn't touch.

So even though I want to physically toss Gertie out of my room, I don't. Because actually it's not my room. It's *our* room—I share it with Gertie and P.J., my sisters. Jack and Marcus are down the hall. Francis still sleeps in my parents' room in the bassinet.

"Here," I say to Gertie, getting up and pulling my old Mr. Potato Head down from the high shelf in the closet. Her brown eyes widen. I rarely let her touch Mr. Potato Head. Grandpa Cole gave him to me, and all the pieces are there and the box is still in good shape. Mr. Potato Head has sentimental value, so he's one of the few things I'm not forced to share. "You have to play with this in here. Sit on the bed and be quiet, okay? It's almost lights-out."

She nods, probably afraid that if she says anything else I'll change my mind.

I get back to the e-mail.

This is what I want to write:

Dear EB,

(Already I'm calling her Ebb in my head, even though I'm sure that what she means by EB is Eee Bee.)

I requested a single. All I've wanted for the last decade is a
room of my own. Some privacy. A place to be alone with
my thoughts where they are not constantly interrupted by
someone else making some kind of racket, or even someone
else just quietly trying to exist in the same space as me.
When I got the full scholarship I knew it would probably
be pressing my luck to ask for a single, but the box
was there to check so I checked it. A "roomie" is really
not what I had in mind. Really not what I had in mind
at all.

Of course, I don't write any of that. It's not Ebb's fault my parents
wanted a big family.

Dear EB,
Hey. I hadn't really thought about appliances.

(Where am I supposed to get the money for this stuff? My
magic money tree? I can probably find a decent microwave at
Goodwill if I look every couple of days. Mini-fridges are harder to
come by.)

Why don't you do the fridge part and I'll take care of the
microwave.

San Francisco is okay. We live in a foggy neighborhood on
the south side of the park so it's not like we have a view of
the Golden Gate Bridge and cable cars going by or
anything. Only the smelly old Muni trains.

I reread her e-mail. I feel as though it would be polite to acknowledge what she said about her dad, or about New Jersey, or ask a question, or something, but P.J. runs in and lunges for Mr. Potato Head so I wrap it up.

Nice to meet you.

Lauren Cole

"*Tato head!*" P.J. shrieks. I scan the e-mail one more time and I know it looks kind of rudely abrupt, but I have to save Mr. Potato Head. And anyway, I wanted a single.

I click Send, close my laptop, and put it up on the high shelf. Gertie lets out a dolphin-pitched death scream and when I turn around, P.J. has got one of Mr. P.'s ears and is about to run away with it. I grab her by the waist. She screams. Gertie screams.

If Mr. P.'s mouth were attached, he would probably scream, too.

TUESDAY, JUNE 25
NEW JERSEY

That's it? was what I thought when I first read Lauren's e-mail late last night. And now that I'm reading it aloud to my friends, Justine twists her face into a grimace and says, "That's it?" Even though the end of the school year was a little bit strained, Justine and I have been friends for so long that it sometimes feels like we can read each other's minds.

I toss my phone down onto the beach blanket in front of me. "That's all she wrote, as they say."

Justine and Morgan—a newer friend of ours, mostly from senior year—are trying to get me on a strict early-morning beachgoing schedule between now and when I leave for Berkeley, so as to maximize surfing and time together. We're coated in sunscreen and sitting in chairs under umbrellas, reading articles in shiny teen magazines about things like dorm decor and tips for living on your own for the first time, while Alex, Danny, and Mitch surf. Justine tosses her magazine onto our blanket before saying, "Maybe she was busy. You know. Dashed it off without thinking."

I shoot her a look that says, *Come on*.

"Well, I tried." She turns to face the water and I see a smile form at the corners of her mouth. "What's her e-mail address, Ice Queen at condescending-mail-dot-com?"

Morgan lets out a chuckle but doesn't look up from her mag.

I say, "*That's* more like it," and look back at the article I've been reading about the Top Ten Things to Pack for College. A pillow. Headphones. Flip-flops for the shower...

I wish I could pack a few friends.

"I wouldn't worry about it." Morgan holds her magazine out to me but I'm not ready to trade so she tosses hers onto the blanket, too. "You'll find some super-dorky shrubbery major like yourself and you'll barely be in your room anyway. You'll be too busy planting bushes."

"It's not called shrubbery," I say for the gazillionth time.

"You know she's just messing with you." Justine flashes a smile at Morgan, who returns it.

I let it go. But there's a part of me that's still annoyed that my friends don't get it. That no one in the whole of Point Pleasant gets it, except for Tim at Beech Design—and even he looked at me like I had two heads when I walked up to him while he was working on the Schroeders' backyard last summer and told him, with six-month-old Vivian Schroeder on my hip, that I wanted a job. He said he couldn't pay me and I said I didn't care—that I'd keep my babysitting job to make the money I needed. So he told me to come in the next morning to talk about hours. I'd been watching him and his small staff for weeks—carving up that yard and putting it back together again so that it felt like there were rooms outside, places worth being. I knew

I'd found my calling. I'll be a paid full-time employee this summer starting Friday, and I still babysit for Vivian occasionally at night.

"I've never understood why you have to go all the way to California when there's a great program at Rutgers," Justine says. "Plus, *I'll* be there."

"We've been through this," I say, thinking, *Yes, you'll be there,* and Danny and Alex and everyone else we know, except for Morgan, who'll be a short drive away at NJIT, and Mitch, who's going to Seton Hall. "Too close to the mother ship."

"So you say." Justine gets up and grabs her board.

Morgan gets up, too. "Coming in?"

I haven't surfed much so far this season—there's no surfing during peak beach hours, which end up generally being when I'm free. And I'm not even sure I'm going to try to surf out in California, though my friends are all convinced that that is secretly part of the whole point of my going west. Bigger waves.

"In a minute," I say, and they both turn and walk off toward the boys—their boyfriends and mine; Justine, much to my chagrin, likes to call us "the six-pack." Then I pick up my phone and read the e-mail again, trying to decide if it really is sort of rude (like I actually thought there were cable cars on her street?) or just straightforward. I'm not sure. But I feel dumb for having told her that stuff about my dad. Justine always says she loves that I wear my heart on my sleeve, but I've been thinking it wouldn't be a bad idea to put on a few layers when I leave for school. I guess I thought it'd be easier to get some of the weird stuff out over e-mail. That way, when this Lauren person and I settle in for our first night sharing a room and I say, "Oh, my dad's gay"—when I'm forced to tell the whole story, like I inevitably will be—maybe she'll be a little bit prepared. I could do without the "no ways" and weirdly sympathetic "really?s" followed by those "not that there's anything wrong with its."

I honestly *don't* think there's anything wrong with it.

The wrong thing, let's face it, was abandoning me.

I hit Reply and think for a minute about how to respond—whether to even bother—while watching Alex ride a pretty big wave for a good long while. I'm going to miss him and his wild salty hair and goofy laugh, but things have been tense lately so I'm not sure how much.

Lauren, I type. And then I go back to the subject heading and delete the **Roomie!** bit—leaving only the **re:** and the **Hi**—because it seems dumb now. We're clearly not going to be e-mail buds.

Mini-fridge it is, I type, but what else is there to say? **Forgive me for blabbing about my dad? Would it kill you to ask a question, maybe get a little e-mail volley going? Do you eat Rice-A-Roni, "The San Francisco Treat," like, every night?**

I take a deep breath and write, **I'll see you in August!,** then delete the exclamation mark and then put it back and delete it again a few times. I sign it **Elizabeth**.

"EB!" Alex is standing at the water's edge. He cups a hand to his mouth when he yells, "Come on in!" and for a second, I close my eyes against the sun and see my mother in a black bandeau suit and me as a young girl in a polka-dot bikini—right here on the same beach—and we are happy and playing in the surf and then busy making sand castles and forts and then, later, knocking down those castles and forts and flying kites in the shapes of mermaids and bats and dragons.

That was all when she was happy.

That was all before.

I get up and grab my board and set out in Alex's direction, suddenly very much hoping I didn't send the exclamation mark but feeling pretty sure I did. A wave crashes behind Alex, right at his ankles, and he gets thrown off-balance and has to recover. I think, *I feel like that most of the time*, and when I reach him, I decide I'll kiss him— right there on the beach with anyone watching who wants to—and see if it steadies me.

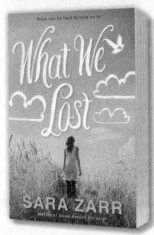